Coffee, Murder, and a Scone: A Mystic Brew Cafe Novel

Mystic Brew Cafe

Brandi A. Mendenhall

Published by Brandi A. Mendenhall, 2025.

COFFEE, MURDER, AND A SCONE: A MYSTIC BREW CAFE NOVEL

First edition. September 4, 2025.

Copyright © 2025 Brandi A. Mendenhall.

ISBN: 979-8986835730

Written by Brandi A. Mendenhall.

This book is dedicated to my KiKi. I would never have finished it without your push. Thank you, Paul, for all that you do.

A large thank you to Kelley James for your beta reading insights. Without you, this book would still have some major plot holes.

Prologue

Paranormal investigations. Yeah, the first thing that probably popped into your mind was the image of nerdy people using all sorts of digital equipment to try and catch images, video or sounds of ghosts. The type of person to run around in an abandoned house in the middle of the night and saying they are so scarred on night vision cameras.

Psychic readings. I'm guessing you picture an old woman with a gauzy veil over her face. She is wearing the most gauche clothing one could buy, gazing into a crystal ball or flipping tarot cards. She is telling you how the next woman or man you meet will be your true love.

Chakra alignment. Now you visualize some skinny twiggy woman in a pair of skintight yoga pants. She is probably striking a yoga pose, holding a crystal in one hand as she preaches about breathing. She gets you to buy a bunch of rocks and tells you that all your troubles will be solved as soon as everything is aligned.

Welcome to the world of misconceptions.

The images that came to mind would never have given you an accurate description of what I am like. I wear tennis shoes, t-shirts, and sneakers. I love my blue jeans and t-shirts more than coffee and I LOVE coffee. I wear my mousy brown hair in a ponytail ninety percent of the time. I never plaster my face with cosmetics because I just don't care what other people think. To top off that description, I love food and hate exercise...so I am not skinny. My poor six-foot frame can handle the extra fifty pounds. I know I am not beautiful as many have told me so, but I like to think that I have generous curves in the right places. Granted those curves sometimes resemble scoops of ice cream more than some hot super model, but it is who I am.

My name is Violet Blueblade. I have spent most of my adult life fighting back against these notions. None of them sum up what I do for a living, but then again, they also don't define me as a person. I am a mystic. I can see and speak with post-living people. I can discern future possibilities by looking at cards with pictures on them. I can see a living beings' glowing energy. I have even been known to get sudden neurological images.

I run a little shop called Mystic Brew Café. Let me clarify a little more. I don't exactly run the café. My nieces take care of all the hard work on it. I am just the proprietor. My part of the business is in the mystic part of the title as well as the name on the bottom of the checks. Those who know me and my abilities come to the café to get their fortunes read, their chakra's aligned, their auras cleansed. They come to me when they hear a bump in the night. I even assisted a police officer once in locating a missing child. That of course, was purely by my discerning ability to pick up on the clues that he missed and not on my mystic abilities.

I am a perfect reclusive introvert. I spend most of my time reading books, writing my own failed novels, crafting, or assisting my nieces with the shop. I refuse to attend any events where there are more than ten people. I rarely talk to anyone unless I am working with a client. I hate the thought of being in the public eye. It is worse having to come up with some inane way of breaking the ice with someone that walks into the shop just to get a coffee. Most of the time I just stare at them until they either leave the shop or order something. My nieces have relegated me to working in the back most of the time which is fine by me.

I know I am not the easiest person to get to know, and I love it like that. To me, if you have found out what a decent person I am, you put in the work to get to know me instead of just judging me by what I appear to be. I have a VERY limited circle of friends. I think my circle is only four people, with two being my nieces. It was my nieces who were encouraging me to expand my circle. Let me explain how it all happened.

Chapter One

"Aw...for fuck's sake Auntie!" Serene yelled. "How could you do this to us?"

"Fuck off Serene..." Tessa groused. "It isn't your place to make the decision. The café belongs to Aunt Vi. If she wants to sell it or close it down that is her choice."

"You two..." I said with a sigh. I rubbed my temples and closed my eyes, trying to keep my calm inner balance. It was hard considering I have spent the better part of a week without much sleep. "I didn't make this decision lightly. I wanted to talk with you girls about just taking over completely."

"Why didn't you lead with that first Auntie?" Serene demanded grumpily. "I would be more than happy to take over."

"Together Serene..." I remarked with a raised brow. The café wouldn't last long with just one or the other running the shop. Tessa was a remarkable person when it came to making pastries and sweets, but she lacked slightly on the customer side of things. Serene was perfect in the customer relations side, but she lacked the ability to pull off those sweets that helped keep the shop afloat.

"Can we table this discussion for a moment." Tessa settled two cups of coffee on the table in front of her aunt and then sat down with her energy drink. "What is the real reason you want to do this Aunt Vi? There is more that you are not telling us. I can see you haven't been sleeping well. Does it have to do with this?" she mumbled as she motioned to the shop and her aunt.

"Oh Tessa." I groused gratefully as I took a sip of the coffee and sighed. Tessa was more like me than I wanted to admit. She seemed to know what I was thinking all the time almost as if she could read my mind. I paused as that thought crossed my mind and then I shook my head with a sigh. "My reasons for getting rid of the shop are my own. It isn't a decision I rushed into. In fact, I really don't want to get rid of it. But if you girls want to co-own the café, I will write it over to you right now. If you don't want to do it together, then I will find someone else to take over."

"I don't see why I can't run it..." Serene groused. She tossed her long brown hair over her shoulder and harumphed. "I mean, I already watch the place while you do your thing anyways."

"Serene, I know you think I," I stumble as my vision clouded slightly, and the image of a very handsome man walked into the shop. The sudden flashes of our bodies entwined together in the most erotic poses caused me to gasp as my coffee drops from my hand. The scene flashes to a woman's body that is visibly dead and mangled. This scene is over dramatized several times with multiple women in different ways until it finally comes to rest on me tied, gagged, and very dead.

"Talk it out Auntie..." Serene says as she wipes up the spilled coffee. Her eyes narrow at her sister for a moment as she noticed the coffee was in a to-go cup instead of a china cup, like normal. She then glanced at the second cup on the table in a to-go cup as well. "It helps if you talk it out."

"No..." I whimper as the vision finally clears. I close my eyes and shudder. "I'm sorry baby girl. I'll clean it up. It was my fault."

The chime above the door goes off and the hairs on the back of my neck stand on end. I can't bring myself to look at the person who just entered. My psychic intuition tells me that the thing I have been trying to avoid this whole time has been set in motion. I am unable to stop the chain of events now.

The scent of pure man, leather and spices assault my senses as I focus on dramatically and slowly picking up the second to-go coffee. I turn my back to the person at the door, knowing I was too late to stop it. These images would come true, and I swallowed hard at that thought. My breathing became erratic. While I was ready to experience all this man had to show me in the bedroom, I was far from ready to be dragged into a murder saga. I especially wasn't ready to be part of that saga.

I had been seated with the girls to the left of the front door in the cozy little window. We had a couple of worn leather couches and leather recliners set up with a fatigued wooden coffee table that I had picked up in a secondhand shop. The tabletop was worn and scuffed but showed the love that it had endured. I had decorated it with a large mandala crocheted lace doily. With my coffee cup in hand, I walked from the conversation area into the more modern and classic table area.

This area had wrought iron tables big enough for two people. The chairs were wrought iron with padded purple seats. The tabletops had been made of mosaic tiles to look like flowers and woodland scenes. This area was situated in front of the glass display case that we put the pastries that Tessa makes. The coffee station was set up behind this along with the register and in the wall behind this was the door to the kitchen. I threaded through the tables to the small alcove on the right side of the door, hoping to disappear before the man could stop me.

The girls had created a small corner with a table that could hold four. It was where they put me during the day to draw clients in. The window outside the alcove was painted to frame my back as I sat at the table with the words 'famous mystic' at the top and bottom. There were purple drapes that hung down to give the space some privacy as needed.

Inside, the area was sectioned off with purple bead curtains. Serena had painted a sign that looked professional and had hung it above the space to proclaim this the mystic area. I pushed into the alcove, looking for a retreat, when a hand caught my bare arm. I dropped the cup once again, spilling my coffee all over the floor as erotic images filled my mind. I mentally took note of all those that were interesting, almost gagging as they switched over to dead lifeless eyes.

"DON'T. TOUCH. ME!" I ground out between clenched teeth. The uninvited man pulled his hand back and apologized in a smooth masculine voice. "Tessa, Serene, please help this customer."

I rushed to my chair as if my life depended on it. Dropping my head into my arms, I sat there like a child playing heads up seven-up. I couldn't look. I couldn't see that handsome Italian man. I couldn't see one more image of his body. Ok, maybe I could see his body once more, but I couldn't see one more dead woman. I just couldn't. I guess the most important part was I couldn't see my repeated death.

Everyone knows they will die one day, but no one wants to be reminded of it over and over again. What was driving me insane was how the neurological flashes would progress. I would see a hot man, I would do things with this man that I had never done before, then I would see strange dead women, and then I would see myself dead. If that wasn't enough to turn a person's libido off, I wasn't sure what was.

Was this devilishly handsome man I kept seeing the killer? If he was, I was sure he could have found a much better-looking woman to seduce than I. A smarter man wouldn't pick a mystic. That had to be a recipe for disaster on his end, knowing that at some point I would see what is happening.

"He is gone Aunt Vi..." Tessa said softly as she parted the beads and sat down at the table. The beads clicked together again as Serene entered and settled onto a chair. "What is going on? You can't keep us in the dark!"

"I can..." I groaned as I sat up and looked at both girls as if I was just waking up. "And I will. What you don't know...can't hurt you."

"Can't hurt us?" Serene narrowed her gaze on her aunt. "What are you seeing that would have you saying something like that?"

"Trust me when I say, it is best if you don't know." Tessa had settled an actual china cup of coffee in front of me, and I grabbed a long pull. The sigh escaping my lips sounded morose, the caffeine like a balm to my frayed nerves. "Sorry girls, the mystic part of the café is shutting down for the day. I'll see you both tomorrow."

"TESSA..." SERENE GROWLED as they watched their aunt disappear out of the café. "Are you getting visions now?"

"No..." Tessa flipped her long hair over her shoulder and snorted, raising one lip and rolling her eyes. "What makes you think that?"

"Auntie Vi takes her coffee in a china cup, not in a to-go cup. You made her two coffees this morning."

"So, I was being practical."

"No, you knew she was going to drop them. Spill it sis!"

"Fine!" Tessa stuck her tongue out at her sister and they both watched their aunt pull out of the parking lot. "Don't tell Aunt Vi, but I am starting to get visions. They are just brief glimpses of..."

"Ah ha!" Serene smiled like the cat who caught the canary. "I knew our powers would start to manifest at some point. I can't wait to see what mine will be."

"You don't know that you will get powers. After all, dad never had any powers." Tessa stood to help the customer that was walking to the door. "Stop smiling like you just scored big and get out here, it looks like it is going to be a busy day!"

Chapter Two

I was sitting comfortably in my alcove the next morning. The sun hadn't peeked over the horizon just yet and I was currently nursing a fine cup of coffee with my eyes closed. Yesterday had been enough to give a sane person the heebie-jeebies. While I couldn't claim that I was a sane person, I could claim how creeped out I had become.

I jumped at every little noise in the shop as Tessa clanged around in the back room. I almost screamed when Serene patted my shoulder, settling a cup of coffee in front of me. If the visions were not enough to make me squeamish, I spent most of my nights tossing and turning with those images parading around in my mind.

They would start off delicious and end up making me break out in a cold sweat. I would wander around my living room for an hour or two, trying to shake those thoughts and eventually I ended up back in bed. The process would start all over, jumping out of bed with gasping breath as I finally gave up and took a shower. I was beginning to feel as if my mind would never be the same.

"Good morning," came a very soft masculine voice.

It was smooth and deep, bringing the scent of leather, musk and spice. The same scent I inhaled yesterday. I tilted my head towards his voice, raising a brow and holding up a finger. The man had some patience. He stood there, not moving, only staring a hole in my head, waiting for me to open my eyes and turn around. I wondered exactly how long I could get away with this. Taking a sip of the coffee, I leaned a little closer to the window just as my body knew instinctively that the sun had finally crested above the horizon.

I sighed, turning back to the man, my eyes still closed. Maybe if I didn't look at him, I could pretend that these murders were not going to happen. Maybe if I wished in one hand and spit in the other, I could see which one got fuller first. With a deep inhale of his scent once more and a final taste of my coffee, I peeled open one eye, then promptly shut it again.

There were absolutely no words to describe how much he affected me. Being that I was a proper lady, I didn't rip his clothes off and kiss him. Instead, I forced myself to open my eyes and motion towards the chair directly across from me. The smile that lit up that face was enough to make my toes curl in my shoes. That isn't easy with my sneakers being a little tight on a normal day.

This man was taller than me. He stood probably around six foot, four inches. I was pushing it at six feet on the nose. He had a full head of black hair that was styled in a high and tight fashion. He had large brown eyes that were framed by those thick lashes that every girl dreamed of having. My gaze focused on those strong masculine lips before trailing along to the whole package. He was fit. It was more of a runner's fit than a body builder fit. The whole package made my mouth go dry as I offered a smile in return.

"Good marrow stranger," I replied to his earlier greeting. Serene was a doll and replaced my empty coffee cup with a full one, setting a to-go cup on the table near the stranger. "You seem lost."

"I do?" he raised a brow with that smile still in place. He walked to the other side of the table and sat down in the chair right next to me. His hands instantly cupped his to-go cup as he looked at me sideways. "What makes you say that?"

"You're sitting here," I answered with a chuckle. "No one comes to me unless they need something, so what type of advice are you in need of stranger? Fortune?" I assessed his soft-looking dark blue cashmere sweater, his black Calvin Klein jeans, his high-end boots by a designer I didn't recognize. I shook my head. "Naw, you have plenty of fortune. Luck?" I looked around him at his aura, taking in the heavy tones of red and pink. "Seems you have enough luck to create that fortune. Love?" I raised my brow and tilted my head, tucking hair behind my ear as I did so.

"Haven't been doing so well in the love department." he blushed. "Can you nudge me in the right direction?"

"Stranger," I sucked in a deep breath, trying to ignore the pulsing red of his aura right now. "That isn't a strong suit of mine."

"Steven," he murmured, watching me intently with those deep fathomless brown eyes. "As opposed to stranger."

"Very well, Steven. I can tell you that your aura is full of passion, sex and love...you only need to aim it in the right direction."

"Auntie Vi," Tessa interjected anxiously as she poked her head through the beads. "Uh, oh. Hello again." Tessa winked at Steven and turned her gaze back to her aunt. "Sorry to interrupt a reading..."

"There wasn't a reading going on..." I snapped, realizing that I had been leaning closer to the addictive man. I pulled back, leaning against the back of my chair, hoping my cheeks were not as red as they felt.

"Reggie is out back again, claims there is a hex on the door."

"Oh dear." I rubbed my face tiredly with my hands and sighed. "I'll be there in a moment. Give Reggie a sandwich or two while he waits, my dear." I turned my gaze back to the man next to me. His intoxicating scent had been stirred up by Tessa's departure and I had to inhale through my mouth to keep from mauling him. "My apologies, but I need to take care of this. If you need a more guided hand to your love predicament, I might suggest stepping into Daisy's down on fourth. She has a pretty good hand where heart matters are concerned."

"Well, thank you." He rose from the chair and stuck his hand out to shake. I pointedly ignored it as I rose from my chair and moved in the opposite direction around the table. "Would you know someone who could investigate a strange noise in my house?"

"Chat with Daisy my dear...and please come again!"

I darted out of the alcove, the front end, through the back room, and into the alley behind the shop. I couldn't get away from him fast enough. Being an overweight woman, it wasn't easy to rush anywhere. It seemed even sub-consciously my body was drawn to him though. I was practically sitting in his lap when Tessa had interrupted. I turned around to view this hex that had Reggie upset and sucked in a startled breath.

The back door of our shop was indeed tampered with, but not with a hex as Reggie kept insisting. He was grasping at my arm and waving his other hand at the door shouting the word hex. I squared my shoulders, pulling together all my calming thoughts, grasped Reggie's arms, looked deep into his eyes, and proclaimed over his shouts that everything was fine.

Reggie caught the undertones of my calm voice, and his aura settled. Reggie was our town homeless man. He was homeless because he chose to be and not because of circumstances. He was currently wearing a pair of worn combat boots, a dirty and ripped pair of black jeans, and a stained long-sleeved heavy metal t-shirt. He had pulled on a green plaid flannel and a lightweight jacket. Both had seen better days. My heart ached at seeing him in this state. He could use a shower and a good night's rest, but those are things he wouldn't accept from me.

Tessa had a bag of yesterday's sandwiches, and she thrust them into his hands with two cups of coffee. He shook his head, mumbling about hexes and crazy witches as he shuffled off with his goodies. My gaze turned back to the door. I had long since given up on understanding the living. The dead were so much easier to understand. Why a living being found it necessary to spray things on buildings was beyond my grasp of rationale. Some miscreants had decided to paint a pentagram upside down on our back door with some foul words.

"I'll grab the camera..." Tessa spat in anger as she stepped back into the shop. This wasn't the first time someone had graffitied our building. It certainly wouldn't be the last. I could only hope that eventually someone would catch them and talk some sense into them. Tessa returned, snapping pictures for the officers when we called it in. She handed me the bucket of paint and brush. "That was one fine specimen this morning Auntie Vi."

"You," I gaped, wagging my paint brush at her. "Zip that trap. I'll have you kindly know that I hadn't noticed."

"Right, which was why you were practically drooling in his lap." Tessa held her hands up in defense as I slapped her thigh with the brush. "Okay, okay...I just think you two would make a cute couple, is all." Tessa caught the fear that flashed across my face as she pried open the paint can and stirred the paint. "Or not...I mean..."

"Tessa..." I gripped the wooden handle of the paintbrush as a lifeline. "There are things that you don't know."

"You mean like the dead women?" she snapped, seeming to pull into herself as she tucked her arms into the pocket of her hoodie.

"The dead..." I glanced up, my eyes widening. A smile split my face for a split second, then I nodded. "You have the sight. I always thought your pa had it as well, but he would never tell me."

"Yeah..." Tessa kicked a rock and shrugged her shoulders. "It isn't as powerful as yours Auntie Vi, but I saw you smash your coffee cup yesterday. This morning, I saw two dead women. One was a stranger but the other..."

"Was me?" I reckoned with a nod. When my niece remained silent, I sighed, dipping the paint brush into the bucket and then covering the words and symbol on the door. "I know what you saw. I see it too."

"In connection with that man then?"

"Yes." I let the air out of my lungs as I furiously scrubbed out the black paint with the white. I would need to put another two or three coats on before the image was totally hidden, but this made me feel a little better.

"That's why you were trying to get rid of the shop. If you didn't meet him, you wouldn't be murdered. Smart move Aunt Vi."

"The only problem is, I didn't move fast enough."

"Aunt Vi..." Tessa tilted her head and tucked deeper into her hoodie. "Is that man responsible for the women?"

"I don't know baby girl." I wrapped my arm around her shoulders and sighed as I watched the paint dry for a moment. "His aura is clear, and I don't get bad vibes from him. I would say no, but the images I see," I shuddered and shivered. "It is probably best to steer well away just in case."

"It's a shame." I walked inside and began cleaning the paint brush in the sink in the bathroom. "You two would have been perfect for each other." Tessa tossed this out as she pulled her apron off the hook by the back door.

"Bite that tongue darling. I am happy being single."

"Aunt Vi. Serene and I are tired of it just being you and Pa. We need fresh blood in this family." Tessa flushed when she realized what she had said. "Sorry, I didn't mean..."

"It's okay. I understand." I swiped the hair from my face and groaned. Tessa was right. After their ma had passed a few years ago, it was down to just me and my brother to care for the girls. While they were not strictly girls anymore, they did still need guidance. I sighed, closed my eyes, and shrugged. "I doubt he was interested that way. He just seems lost."

"You have always been good about scooping up lost souls. Maybe it is time you scooped one up for yourself." Tessa kissed my cheek and disappeared back into the shop to make the police report. I turned to the mirror of the bathroom, looking at the dark circles under my eyes, my tangled nest of hair, and my fat cheeks. If that man was truly interested in me, I'd be the luckiest woman in the world. With a hearty laugh, I stepped out of the bathroom and back into my alcove.

Chapter Three

"Good marrow," came the now familiar masculine voice. Steven didn't wait, simply settled into the chair next to me, facing the window as I was. I had my hands wrapped around my cup of coffee, my eyes closed, and my head tilted back just slightly. I wasn't about to give up my routine for anyone, so I simply raised a brow in his direction and continued to sit, unseeing out the window. I heard the chair slide across the floor but then quiet filled the alcove again.

My senses flooded open as the sun crested over the horizon, bringing with it the warmth of the day and the new. I let out a fulfilled sigh and opened my eyes, turning my head to see that Steven was sitting in the chair the same way I had been. His eyes were still closed and his hands wrapped around his to-go cup. I couldn't help but laugh at his pose and he cracked open his eyes and looked at me with a smile. "Madame, why are you laughing at me."

"You have invaded my space three mornings in a row. Either my coffee is to die for or," I hesitated slightly at that phrase. "You have something you desperately need." I twisted my chair around and settled at the table. My hands twitched towards the tarot cards that were always available. He noticed my hands and motioned towards them.

"A tarot reading today perhaps?" He adjusted his chair to face me.

"I read your aura yesterday, wasn't that enough help?" I teased, leaning a little closer. I shuffled the cards and inhaled that delightful scent.

"Problem still..." he tilted his head and tapped his fingers nervously against the table. "Unresolved."

"I see." I cleared my throat. For the best reading, I needed him to touch my cards and impart some of his energy. His energy is what would make the cards tell me his fortune. I held back. Part of me didn't want to go through the hassle of cleansing my cards after a murderer touched them. That would involve a full moon, a tub of salt, and lots of mediation. I did not have the time or inclination to want to go through that hassle.

I couldn't say one hundred percent that he was a murderer, though. I still didn't get any bad vibes from him. The only vibes I got were ones that made my toes curl, my breath catch, and my inside turn to molten liquid. I reached my hand out, setting the cards in front of him. "Cut, shuffle, touch. I need your energy."

Steven picked up the deck, shuffled a few cards, cut the deck and then put them back on the table. With a single finger, he pushed the deck back in front of me. My smile trembled slightly. He remembered that I don't like to be touched. I picked up the cards, feeling the jolt of energy from him. He was powerful. His passion, sex, and love were strained, but that wasn't the underlying cause for him to seek out my café. I tossed three cards to the side of the table and then dealt the next four. Steven watched me, not the cards.

His eyes never left my face. My hands began to shake as the picture began to solidify. Death, death, death, love, death. I reached to the three cards I had dealt off the top. My mouth worked up and down, my throat wouldn't work, I couldn't speak, couldn't swallow, I started coughing hard. Serene charged through the beaded curtain and slapped a glass of water into my hands. Tessa was hovering just outside the alcove.

"It's okay Aunt Vi. Breathe..." she said kindly, patting my back.

"Is she okay?" Steven inquired with concern.

"She's fine..." Serene glanced at the cards then up at her sister just on the other side of the beads. "It's been a very long time since she has seen a spread like this."

"That bad, huh?" Steven turned his gaze to me as I sat there gasping like a fish out of water. I gulped down half the glass and pushed myself back against the chair. Serene brought another full glass of water and then my nieces disappeared.

"I haven't seen this much death," my eyes closed, and I swallowed hard. "Well, truthfully since last night, but in my cards since my mother passed away."

"You saw death last night?"

"Long story." I pointed to each card and watched as he followed my hands. "Death, Death, Death, Love, Death." His placid face fell, giving way to sadness.

"So, even if Daisy's love spell finds the woman for me, she is going to die." He nodded, his gaze moving back up to me. "You have been very helpful. Thank you."

"Daisy worked a finder spell for you?" I squeaked in shock.

Daisy hardly ever assisted in spells. I had only sent him to her shop to get him out of mine. Contrary to what the people usually thought about witchcraft and love spells, you cannot cast a love spell. Witchcraft involves the work of intent. You can't make someone love you if they are not inclined to be in love with you. That is the way the spells work.

Daisy had cast a finder spell. While there are multiple uses and intentions for a finder spell, it boils down to locating an object or person. People of witchcraft would use a finder spell to find their lost car keys or to help remember where they stashed an item. Daisy went a step further. She had assisted him by casting a finder spell that would lead him towards the person he was destined to find. He nodded, smiling sadly.

"Daisy said the same thing you said, my passion, sex and love aura are strong, it just needs to be aimed in the right direction. Then, she said she was sorry the first three didn't work out as I had lots to give." He frowned when I guffawed. I hid my smile behind my hands and motioned for him to continue. He pointed to the first three cards, then put the last two together as he talked.

"Allison died of cervical cancer a year after we got married. Layla died in a boating accident in Morocco during a photo shoot. Zoe died three years ago after a horse tossed her. Now your clairvoyance is saying the next woman will also die. It's enough to turn a person crazy."

"Steven..." I gulped and placed my hand on his, my eyes glazing over with images I couldn't stop. "I'm sorry for your loss, but my fortune doesn't say your fourth lover will die."

"I'm confused." His hand turned, his fingers threading with mine. I could tell he wasn't aware he was doing it. Damn that daffy Daisy for putting a finder spell on him. I briefly wondered if Daisy had explained how that spell worked since he was staring at the cards. "If they don't say she will die, what does this mean?"

"Reading the cards can be murky and disorienting at times. Part of it comes down to the person you are reading for, and if you can untangle your thoughts, feelings and emotions from that person." I shivered and tried to cover by adjusting in my seat and crossing my legs. The feel of his fingers stroking mine was making liquid fire burn in the pit of my stomach and lower. "The cards can also be interpreted in multiple ways. You need an experienced reader to know the best way to interpret the images. Each card could mean something different when paired with the other cards."

"I see..." Steven scooted his chair closer, his thigh touching mine now. "Show me what this means." His eyes darted back up to mine and I clenched my teeth. "Of course, I am taking it that you are experienced. Otherwise, there wouldn't be people lined up out there to speak with you." His smile disarmed me for a moment. A line of people? I glanced up and saw four of my regular customers waiting patiently just on the other side of the beads.

"This is your fortune..." I motioned my hands over the cards. "Each card represents things that happen at some point in the past, present, or future. With my regulars," I nodded my head to the people waiting outside. "I would only pull three cards. One for past, one for present, and one for future. I don't know you, so I had to pull more. I pulled three for past, one for present and one for future. As you have pointed out, you have experienced death three times in the past. In the present, you will experience love. Somewhere in the future you will experience another death. It doesn't mean it is tied to the person you love. It only means that you will experience a death. These..." I grabbed the card for his present and felt his fingers running lightly along my neck. "This is your present. Nothing really shocking here. Love for a handsome man like you isn't a strange concept..." I flipped another card and snorted. "This represents danger in your present."

"Danger?" His low sensual voice whispered in my ear making me shiver yet again. "Could that be the ghost who is haunting me?"

"Your being haunted?" That piqued my interest. More than his fingers currently delving into my hair. I jumped out of my seat and ushered him to the curtain. "I'm sorry Steven, but I have other people waiting. Give my niece your information and she will set up a time for me to check out the haunting. Monica!" I smiled a bright smile I didn't feel and motioned for the next person to come inside.

Being away from Steven's roaming hands would help settle my nerves, but it wasn't going to do anything for my libido. Monica wasted no time sitting down at the table, grabbing the tarot deck and shuffling them like crazy. I watched for a moment as Steven talked with Tessa. I wanted to laugh as her eyes grew wide, then settled back into normal. It was when they narrowed and looked my direction that I began to worry. Whatever Tessa cooked up; I was sure I could handle it. After all, that girl was more like me every minute of every day.

Chapter Four

Tessa had cooked up something alright. She not only spun a lovely yarn about thunderstorms and dark being perfect spirit hunting weather, but she had also worked in how much I loved lasagna and garlic bread. Somehow my checking out Steven's haunting had become an impromptu date the next time it rained.

Turned out, since we were in a very dry spell, that drought ended two nights later. I found myself staring at Tessa with the most venomous glare I could produce. She was too busy laughing as Serene came rushing through the front door, make-up palette and hair implements in tow. She was holding a hair straightener and was clicking the panels together in glee. I held my hands out and began backing up.

"Oh no you two don't. I am not a rag doll for you to play dress up with."

"Of course not, Auntie Vi!" Serene snickered, her perfectly cocked eyebrow giving just a hint of her amusement. "I just want to make sure that this Steven doesn't run away in fright at the first sign of your frizzy hair." She clicked the hair straightener a few more times for emphasis.

"We can't have that poor man more frightened of you than his ghost. Look at those dreadful jeans." Tessa clicked her tongue and crossed her arms over her chest. "I mean seriously Aunt Vi...when was the last time you washed them."

"My jeans are washed every day, you know that..." I continued to back up, beginning to wonder just where I went wrong with these two. I finally tossed my hands up. The fate sisters were working strongly against me at the moment. Daisy tossing a finding spell on Steven. The girls pressing me to find someone. Their incessant need to hook me up every chance they got. I was done for. The least I could do was go with aplomb. "Fine, but nothing over the top. You know how I am."

I was a little frightened when they both readily agreed. Tessa went through my closet looking for anything remotely feminine. She dragged out a pair of black strappy sandals. I loved those sandals in the summer, but right now, it would be a little wet. She seemed to agree with my assessment and tossed them back into the closet until she found a pair of black leather ankle high boots. She tossed those by the bed and continued her search.

My perusal of what she was doing was obstructed as soon as Serene began her ministrations on my face. I hated wearing makeup as I didn't like having to scrub my face over and over to get all the crude out of my pores. It took what seemed like forever for Serene to finish her preparations.

When I was finally able to see Tessa again, she was lying on my bed, her cell phone in hand. She pointed very authoritatively at the outfit on the bed and commanded that I go and get dressed now. While I wasn't one to be ordered about, I felt that this night would progress so much faster if I just did as she commanded without complaint.

I was only in the bathroom for seven minutes tops. The sight of both girls ringed around Tessa's phone was enough to make my eyes narrow. I put both hands on my hips and coughed, waiting for them to notice I was in the room. Serene only glanced up once, grunted, and then returned to the phone.

"What in the light of the Goddess are you two staring at in such fascination?"

"Auntie Vi," Serene started. "If you don't want this man, I'll take him."

"His house is phat," Tessa chuckled, tossing her phone to her aunt. She climbed off the bed and tucked and fluffed her outfit. "I think Serene is right. One of us women need to land this fish. I would hope it would be you Auntie Vi since you are more his age. Okay, a smidgen older, but still, he is way older than we are."

"I can't believe you two!" I groused, my hands swiping through the pictures on the internet. Steven had a damn fine house for sure. I knew the man had money from reading his aura and noticing those expensive clothes he wears. What I couldn't believe was how the girls were talking about him. "I would have thought we raised you better. You respect people for who they are, not for what they own."

"With money I can respect him a little more." Tessa remarked with a giggle, smiling as she stepped back and clapped her hands. "That's as good as it gets from your wardrobe Aunt Vi. I programmed his address into your phone's GPS. It will start giving you directions when you press this button." She showed me the button on the phone, and I nodded. "Good luck hunting that ghost. And do try to enjoy yourself!"

"Agreed..." Serene said, hugging her as she moved towards the front door.

"Oh my..." Tessa said with a sniffle.

"Our little baby has grown up!" Serene added with a sniffle of her own. I politely showed them one of my most powerful fingers and they crumpled up in laughter.

"I can hear you two! Lock up when you leave!"

Grabbing my keys and a small bag of items, I ran to my car, hoping I wouldn't look like a drowned rat in five seconds. Once inside my car, I pressed the button Tessa had shown me and was pulling out of the driveway with nervous knots in my stomach. What in the world was I thinking?

At forty I was too old to be flirting with a man. I was also too old to be dealing with the stress of ejecting a spirit from someone's house. I was pretty sure that what Steven thought was a spirit was some type of rodent that had gotten into the house. Most hauntings were like that. Paranormal explanations were always rare.

As I slowly pulled into the long winding driveway, I had to wonder if getting involved in the haunting of a murderer was such a brilliant move. It could be that he was being haunted by the three dead women I kept seeing in my vision. I found myself gaping at the mansion as I pulled up the long flower-lined drive.

The flower beds were a little bare as spring had yet to arrive in full force. The house claimed my gaze now. Even though I had seen pictures on the internet, being here in person made it even more awe-inspiring. The house was two stories with a large chimney in the back that peeked over the roof. The floor to ceiling windows on the front of the house looked more like happy eyes peeking out of the brick. There was a large sweeping walkway that started at the street and moved lazily in curves down the front lawn to the massive double doors. I veered slightly to the left, opting to go to the back entrance than to the front.

To the left of the house there was a large expanse of property. There were at least two different gardens with stone benches and fountains set up. On the right of the house was another expanse but this side had a massive forest of elm trees. With a sigh, I slowly braked under a carport next to a service door. I glanced around quickly to see if there were any cameras.

Feeling confident that I was hidden, I shimmied out of the skirt that the girls had dressed me in, kicked off the ankle boots, and shimmied into a pair of jeans. I was reaching for the door handle to the car when I noticed that there was movement at the door.

"Shoot," I groaned as I caught sight of Steven grinning from ear to ear as I grabbed my bag and climbed out of the vehicle. "Guess I wasn't as hidden as I had hoped."

"Ah, no," he chuckled as he held the door open and swept his arm towards it, inviting me in. "I was alerted the moment you pulled into the drive. High end security systems are all the rage now, haven't you heard?"

"Obviously not," I laughed in genuine amusement. "My apologies for the X-rated show. My nieces thought this was a date and not a work thing."

"I wouldn't call that X-rated, more like B-grade." He stepped closer, his arm wrapping comfortably around my waist to open the kitchen swinging door. "Although I have to admit that lacy black underwear for a work thing is always appropriate in my book."

"Right," I inhaled deeply, noting the delicious aroma of dinner as well as him. "Point me in the direction of your haunting."

"Let's have dinner first while it is still warm. I pulled it out of the oven just a few minutes ago."

I settled down at the table as he instructed and tried to hide my drool as I settled my work bag next to my feet. The bag was a simple little leather case that Serena had picked up for me at a thrift shop. She had squealed in delight when I opened the gift and then proceeded to show me the small little frog that had been stamped into the leather.

I had felt such overwhelming love for my niece that I had cried and spilled my water on it. The stamped frog now looked like a small spotted cow from the water discoloration. I still loved the hell out of this little bag with the little pockets for all my ghost hunting gadgets.

I focused my attention on the man sitting next to me at a table that was large enough to seat twelve. He had settled a plate of mouthwatering lasagna with a small plate that held a slice of garlic bread with extra butter. I averted my gaze from the food and hid the drool by taking a sip of the cool water that he had poured at some point.

"Tell me, what should I expect from this ghost hunting experience," he offered casually as he took a sip of his own water.

"Well, ghosts are really just entities on a different spectral plane that intersect with ours." I murmured as I sampled the lasagna. I felt my soul shout in euphoria. It was delectable. I closed my eyes in heaven as I tore a chunk off the garlic bread. When I opened them, I noticed that he had scooted a little closer to me. "Most of the entities are not harmful. They just like to cause a little mischief here and there. It gets dreadfully boring when no one can see or communicate with you."

"I'm not sure that is what we are dealing with."

"Tell me, Steven. What has your entity been doing?"

"I have been shoved out of my bed while sound asleep."

"That could have been a matter of simply rolling over in your sleep." I offered as he grunted and took a good hard look at me.

"I have been tripped going down the stairs to the basement several times."

"A matter of misjudging the steps..." I remarked as I ate in thought.

"Right," he chewed in thoughtful silence for a moment, leaned back in his chair with a sigh, then shook his head. "All completely explainable, until I watched a heavy award launch into the air off the mantle and fly towards my head. There is no way you could explain that."

"Force of a magnetic field..."

"The award is glass." Steven chuckled as I watched him with a perplexed look on my face. "Yeah, I didn't think you would be able to explain that one. Tell me, Violet..." he leaned forward and looked me deep in the eyes. I felt as if he was peering directly into my soul. "What happened to bring an amazing woman such as yourself into this line of business. Especially, since you keep trying to convince me that my haunting is something other than the paranormal."

"It isn't a business. It is simply who I am and something to keep myself busy." I stumbled under his gaze. There was something breathtaking about his intensity. He seemed to be waiting on the razor edge of a cliff for my answer. "I happen to have a skill that is unique and valuable to others. I provide it for those who truly need assistance."

"I have to admit, I'm not exactly sure I believe in all this mysticism."

"Most adults don't."

"Children do then?" he asked in fascination.

"Children believe in more than an adult because their imaginations haven't been crushed by society telling them not to believe. When we are children, we believe in things like Santa Claus and the Easter Bunny because a fantasy world where mythical beings bring us presents is totally possible. As we get older, we realize that our parents were those magical beings and that nothing like that could possibly happen in real life. People like me, we still have a good touch of our inner imagination and open our minds eye to see those possibilities. Anything can happen if you believe it can."

"If I were to suspend reality and get in touch with my imagination, would I be able to see them?"

"Alas, if it were that easy, I am sure there would be more people like me out there." I laughed at the thought of a world of clairvoyants and mystics. "I think it helps that some of us are wired a little different than others."

"How so?" he nudged my wrist with his fingers and scooted his chair a little closer. I cleared my throat, enjoying the sizzle of electricity as he touched my skin, then scooted the chair back from the table.

"I think we should start investigating this entity. Shall we clean up?"

"Right." Steven inhaled deeply, looking disappointed as he scooted back from the table as well. "I'll clean up later. Let me show you where the incidents have been happening. Shall we start in the bedroom and end in the basement then?"

"That sounds," I swallowed hard, thinking of all the images of him and I in his bed that have flashed through my mind in the last few days. "That sounds like a plan Steven. Lead the way."

Chapter Five

Steven's bedroom was ah-maz-ing. I mean, if I was going to redecorate my bedroom and I had millions to do it the way I wanted, this room would be it. The windows had those electronic curtains that opened and closed to let in the light or shut it out. The walls were a dark but tasteful shade of blue with white trim accents. I took in the black and white mural that had been painted against one wall. It was a mountain scene with hidden details everywhere you glanced. I caught the dark outline of a moose hidden in some trees and smiled.

Turning my gaze to the bed, I noticed that he had made his bed. He was at least a fastidious murderer. Shaking off my thoughts, I glanced around the floor looking for any signs of a murder that he might have covered up. When all I saw were clean light gray carpets, I sighed and closed my eyes.

Opening my mind's eye, I listened to the soft pitter patter of the rain outside, the gentle whoosh of the heater as it kicked in, the soft sound of my breath and his. Nothing seemed out of place. I moved closer to the bed and opened my sense even more, reaching out to the poster of the bed to steady myself. The moment my hand touched the mahogany wood of that frame I was instantly transported to a hot sexy night. Thankfully this time it wasn't my night with Steven.

"Are you alright?" Steven caught me as I stumbled. "You look like you saw something."

"I did," I gasped as I tried to hide my flaming cheeks. "I don't think our entity is in here right now. Show me the mantle where the award fell off."

"Flew off..." he chuckled as he patted my arms and turned towards the door. "It's this way."

I wiped sweat off my brow, closed my eyes for a moment, then sighed and followed him down the stairs and to the ground floor. The mantle was in the living room just off the kitchen. It was decked out with a large television and a very expensive entertainment system. The mantle was set above the largest fireplace I had ever seen inside a home. I was sure he could roast a pig inside that thing if he wanted.

There was a wet bar set up on the back side of the living room near a pair of French doors. Spying something glittering on the floor near the bar I moved over to inspect it. It was a piece of shattered glass. Frowning, I picked it up. The image of the item shuddering into the air and then hurling towards the body standing right where I was now rushed into my mind. I turned to look back at the mantle and nodded. It was at least forty feet to the other side of the room.

"Sorry about that," he murmured, taking the glass from my fingers and dropping it into a trash can. "I thought I had picked up all the pieces."

"I can honestly agree with you," I wandered around the living room, randomly touching items here and there. "This is not a little mischief. This one is aiming to cause serious harm. Show me the basement."

I followed Steven into the kitchen, into a pantry, then down a pair of rickety steps into an unfinished cellar. This was a nice unfinished cellar. The walls were natural stones, the floor was a smooth concrete, and it was open and massive. There were large supports that were placed around the room at strategic locations. Each of the supports were natural stones.

I marveled at the full recording studio set up in the far corner of the room. Turning in circles for a moment, I wondered what the hell this man did for a living when he wasn't murdering women. I shook my head and leaned against one of the support columns and gasped as a vision came to me. It was the image of a pair of strong masculine hands wrapped around a pale slender throat. The face of the woman was turning blue as she slapped and pounded at the arms holding her in place.

I could smell Steven's scent of leather and spice, feel those warm hands, see his face in front of her as she lost consciousness. I came out of the vision and panicked. Steven was holding my upper arms with concern in his eyes as he kept asking me if everything was alright.

"I..." I gasped. I swallowed hard as I stepped out of his grip. "I...I don't think your entity will show tonight. I should be going." I moved to step around him, getting as far as the stairs, when I stumbled to a stop. Standing on the stairs leading up was a demon dog. "Oh crackers," I growled just as it launched that spectral body at me.

"What the holy hell?" Steven yelled as I crashed into his chest with my back. We both tumbled to the ground as the slathering hell beast pinned us both to the ground. I put my hands up and shoved to keep its gnashing teeth away from me. "What in hell is that?" he demanded as we both struggled to remain intact.

"Later, can you reach my bag?" I huffed as I tried to push my knees up and shove the rabid animal off.

"Yes."

"Perfect. Reach into the pocket on the front. Toss one of those bad boys to the other side of the room."

"I've got it. Seriously?" Steven scoffed at what he held in his hand. "How the hell is a dog bone going to help with a ghost?"

"Just toss the damn thing already! That's it. Smell that delicious treat. You want that instead of us, right? Go for it! Good dog."

Steven tossed the dog bone to the side away from the stairs and watched in amazement as the hell beast immediately sighted on the bone, then scrambled off us to gobble it down. I watched as the demon dog imitated snarfing down the treat, then turned towards us with a placid woof, sat down on his haunches, and wagged his tail before slowly disappearing. I scrambled out of Steven's grasp and back onto my feet, dusting off my behind as if there had been a speck of dirt on his concrete floor. I walked a step to my bag and picked it up. Steven continued to sit on the floor gaping like a fish with his mouth working open and closed. I watched him for a moment, then began laughing, then bent over double as I couldn't stop. Breathing was getting difficult.

"That was..." he started.

"That is what we call a barghest. The faery tales and ghost stories are pretty accurate on naming creatures. It is the ghost of a dog that had been mistreated in life. Animal entities are usually more malevolent than human ones as they don't have the higher thinking capacity that humans have. They know basic survival. When you tossed the bone, he saw food and went after it."

"How did...what caused..."

I reached down and caught Steven's hand as he kept motioning towards the spot where the beast had disappeared. I helped him up to his feet and did a quick visual check to make sure its claws hadn't ripped into him. "The bone is treated with wolfs bane."

"Wolfs bane?"

"It's a common enough herb, although poisonous to humans. Legends have it that you can kill a werewolf with it." I guffawed at his incredulous stare as I moved towards the stairwell. "Relax Steven. There are no werewolves that I am aware of. It is simply a legend."

"That's it then?" he murmured softly as we stepped up to the pantry. "No more haunting?"

"No..." I shook my head as I got out of the enclosed space with him. As much as this man made my motor run, I still couldn't shake the image of him hovering over that poor woman while she died from being choked. "I am afraid your large barghest wasn't tall enough to reach that award off your mantel to hurl it at you. That would require a pair of hands. I am afraid your entity doesn't want to show tonight. I am confident that you can sleep tonight without any interruption though."

"You say that because..."

"Because if I came into your house and took out your pet, would you show up? No, you would be too upset over losing them that you would spend a day or two stewing. I'll be back tomorrow to check on the spirit. Get some sleep."

"Tell me..." he begged as he caught my hand as I moved towards the service door off the kitchen. "Before the beast showed up, you looked as if you saw something you didn't like. What did you see?"

"Honestly?" I asked as I leaned against the wall of his kitchen.

I couldn't name the emotion that flooded across his face as he waited for an answer. Should I tell him what I saw and see how he reacted? Should I just flee from his house and be thankful that he hadn't killed me while that demon dog tried to rip my throat out? Should I just shrug it off and pretend I didn't see a single thing? As I looked into those deep brown eyes, I knew I would never be able to lie to this man. There was something honest and innocent about him that sucked me in. Maybe it was those rugged good looks, maybe it was the way he smelled, or maybe it was just how open and honest he seemed. Whatever it was, I opened my mouth and out came the truth.

"Before you even walked into my café, I have been having visions of you and me. They have been plaguing me for a few weeks to the point I was ready to give my café to the girls and leave town for a while. Wouldn't you know it that you walked through my door that morning while I am begging the girls to take over. In these visions I also see women who have been murdered in a most grotesque way. I wanted nothing to do with you."

"But you still came to check out the haunting," he prompted, leaning against the counter as he watched my reaction. "What did you see downstairs?"

"I saw you standing above a woman. Your hands were clasped around her throat, and you were squeezing the life out of her. I watched her face turn blue from lack of air and then when the last of her breath faded from her body, I snapped to, and you were grasping my arms."

"You think I am a murderer?"

"I think you are tangled up in something far deeper than just a haunting." I closed my eyes for a moment and sighed. "I came tonight because I honestly don't feel any malice from you. It takes a very trained and sensitive person to be able to fool me. I have been doing this type of work for thirty years." I looked at him with a grin. "I can be completely open when I say that I don't think you have the sensitivity to the spiritual world to fool me. Have a restful night, Steven. You might not get another one for a few nights."

I walked out into the rainy evening and climbed into my car. Letting out a deep breath, I put the car in gear and circled out of the carport and down the long winding road back to the street. I thought about the vision I had in his basement. Is there any way I could have imagined him strangling that woman? Is there a point of view that would make it seem that it was him? Visions are all about point of view. It may seem like a simple task to see something and report it out, but they are not that simple.

What looks like a man strangling a woman, taken from a different point of view could be a man trying to untie a rope or something. I shook myself as I pulled into the drive of my home. The problem with foresight is that you wouldn't know what the truth is until it actually happened. I shuddered as I walked into my house and dropped my bag next to the front door. I guess time would tell.

Chapter Six

"I am telling you Tessa, something went wrong last night. I know it. I feel it in my skin." Serena remarked as I walked through the back door to the café. I stood next to the door and listened to the conversation for a moment. It seemed both my girls were showing signs of the gift.

"That's impossible. There is no way you can feel that something is off Serena. You are just trying to manifest power by saying you have it."

"I'm serious Tessa!" Serena shuddered and glanced at the front door. "It felt like I was getting choked. I couldn't breathe. I was freezing cold. Then it was as if the sun came out and warmed me up. I could breathe again. It was terrifying. Oh, Aunty Vi..." Serena gasped as her gaze swept to the back door.

"Is that all you felt?" I asked as I stepped into the room. I poured a cup of coffee and sliced a piece of zucchini bread for my breakfast. I slapped an overly generous amount of butter on the bread and then stepped into the café to settle at one of the tables. "Did you smell or taste anything?"

"It smelled like..." Serena tilted her head, those brown curls bouncing as she thought hard. "It smelled like leather and spice."

"And you felt like you were being choked?" Tessa snorted. "I seriously..." the words came to a stop when she noticed her aunt holding her hands up and giving her sister a ponderous glance.

"Close your eyes for me, baby girl. I want you to breath deep and slow. Think about what you felt. Did it feel like hands wrapped around your throat, something pressing on your chest, or maybe just the air was getting thinner?" My stomach dropped when she told me what she had smelled. That was exactly how Steven smelled, and it wasn't making my case for him any easier.

"There was something against..." she shuddered as she tilted her head. "There was something pressing against my throat. It wasn't a hand though. I'm not sure what it was. It felt like, I don't know, maybe a rope or something."

"I see." I closed my eyes as I took a sip of my coffee.

If Serena had those feelings last night while I was having my vision, was I seeing her death, or was she just picking up on my panic? Tessa had claimed that she had seen visions of the dead women. Was she seeing them on her own or was she getting feedback? No matter how you spun those dice, the girls were manifesting their powers. I was elated to know that I wouldn't be the last of our line, but I was also dismayed.

What, in the holy light, was going on? I had just popped a heavenly bite of my zucchini bread into my mouth when the door to the café jingled. I didn't have to turn around to know who had just walked in. Steven had a presence that woke up my senses so much faster than greeting the sun first thing in the morning. With a heavy sigh, I turned and gave him a soft smile before picking up my breakfast and moving over to my little window.

"I told you I was getting my powers..." Serena whispered in a snooty voice to her sister when she thought I couldn't hear her.

"No, you're not. She didn't say you were getting your powers. She just asked you a bunch of questions," Tessa snarled.

"Why do you think you should be the only one to have the gift? You are just like me. We both have the same father and same aunt."

"Girls..." I chastised loud enough for them to hear. "The manifestation of your powers was bound to happen. You are both still special in your own ways."

"See," Serena huffed triumphantly. "I told you so."

"Do you sit in this window every morning?" Steven asked from a chair that had been quietly moved to put him right next to me.

"Every morning. It is my sun salutation. I greet the rising sun and in return, he fills me with his warmth and light. I do the same thing for the moon at night. Hush now."

I closed my eyes as I turned my face to the window and felt the moment the sun rose above the horizon. I inhaled deeply, taking in the warmth and energy of the light. When I felt complete, I turned and popped another bite of my breakfast into my mouth as I watched Steven twist his to go cup in circles on the table. He looked exhausted. The spirit shouldn't have bothered him last night. He should have been able to sleep restfully without interruption. Why then, was he looking as if he hadn't even crawled into bed?

I opened my mind's eye and scanned his aura. That vibrant red and pink aura had some brown bleeding into it. Brown was the color of insecurity and doubt. I took a long slow sip of my coffee as he turned those brown eyes in my direction. He opened his mouth and started to ask a question. He closed his mouth, ran his fingers through those wavy black strands of hair, and then averted his gaze back to his coffee.

"What's weighing on you this morning Steven? I see insecurity and doubt creeping into your aura."

"You can really see that, huh?" he gave a half-hearted chortle before looking back into my eyes.

"I can see a lot of things." I returned the mirth before reaching out a tentative hand and placing it over his.

Immediately my mind flooded with images. I shoved all the sexy things to the side. I pushed all the horrific things into a vault to study later. There. Right in the middle of all that. His doubt and insecurity were playing through on a loop. I focused on it, and it quickly took on a life of its own.

There was a beautiful woman. Her long red hair was in tangles. The sheer panic on her face made me gasp as I studied this closer. She had a cap of some sort that had fallen off and was wrapped around her neck. I tried to twist the perspective, but this was a memory and not a vision. I watched in helpless fascination.

The image of panic quickly became blue skin as her hands scrambled and pounded at something around her neck. As the image continued to zoom in, I noticed that it wasn't just the strap of her cap. Holy mother of all that is light. I was watching his wife die from suffocation after falling off her horse. It appeared that her helmet and reins had somehow gotten tangled around her neck. A pair of strong hands reached out and began wrapping around her neck, searching and tugging, but not strangling.

I yanked my hand off Steven's. My chest heaved up and down as I tried to drag air into my lungs. Steven hadn't strangled the woman in my vision last night. I had a vision of his wife dying and him valiantly attempting to save her.

Serena crashed through the beaded curtain of my alcove. Her chest was heaving up and down just as mine was. Her hands clutched at her neck as her sister forced her into the chair across from me. I watched as the feeling disappeared, and she began gulping in fresh air. We all exchanged glances as our gazes trailed over to Steven.

"There is no need to think that you strangled your wife in that accident with the horse." I mumbled softly. "I think Serena and I just proved that it truly was an accident, and you had only been trying to untangle the reins and her helmet straps."

"How did you know..." he hesitated and shook his head. "Never mind. I am guessing you had a vision just now."

I nodded at him and smiled grimly. "And Serena, my budding little empath, felt it."

"That...was...exactly...like last night," Serena confirmed, panting.

"Well," I looked at Tessa, Serena, and then at Steven. I raised my cup in his direction and took a long sip. "It seems for better or for worse, we have become a tangled web. I can't get my girls out of this unless I help you."

"You need to do this for yourself as well, Aunt Vi..." Tessa reminded me. "We can't los..."

"Hush your mouth, my darling."

"What about you?" Steven turned his attention fully to me. I was happy to see that the brown was dissipating from his aura. "What does she mean?"

"Nothing you need worry about."

"If there is something," he began.

"I promise there is nothing. Are you really that enamored with our coffee?" I teased as I pushed his cup into his hand.

"You do have the best service in the area," he cracked a smile, his mood lightening as I distracted him from all things murder and death.

"Well then, what brings you to my café this morning?"

"I don't think Daisy's spell is working and you still need to help me with my spirit. I thought we could maybe work on both today?"

I suppressed the need to pump my fist in the air. The man wanted to spend the day with me. Wait, no. He wanted me to solve his problems. That was all. I gulped down a still scalding hot mouthful of my coffee and winced. There wasn't much I could do to help him with his spirit until I was able to see or contact it. I wouldn't be able to help him with a finder spell because I knew exactly where that finder spell would take him. There was also that small pesky voice of reason in my mind that kept telling me he might be a killer.

Do I take the whole day and spend it in his company and just hope that he isn't in the mood to murder me? Do I shut up the pesky voice and pretend for once that someone might be interested in an old used up mystic? I fanned myself for a moment as I pondered the thought of being his center of attention and focus. I had never experienced a relationship and had never wanted to until this moment. The thought of being the sole focus of a man was enough to make me consider it.

"Aunty Vi!" Serena hollered as she pushed through the beaded curtain. She tossed a folded newspaper onto the table. "You have to read that."

The picture on the front of the paper was of a raven-haired woman who was ravishing. She could have been a super model. I pulled the paper closer and skimmed through all the details until

I began to find it difficult to breath as the visions in the vault of my mind began to leak out.

A raven-haired beauty was stabbed thirty times. Blood covered the sheets and walls. I could see her cold body contorted into a paradox of life. It looked as if she was trying to shove someone away while she was running. Her body would forever be frozen in that position in my mind. Naked as the day she was born with white sheets beneath her that had turned scarlet from the blood of her body.

It said that the body was found just a few blocks from Steven's home. She had attended a party at his house three nights prior to her being found. Investigators were looking into possible suspects.

"Steven..." I growled as I flipped the paper in his direction. "Want to explain this?" I watched as he scanned the article. His olive toned skin drained making him look a sickly green.

"Victoria was at my party a few nights ago. I had no idea..."

"Were you involved with her?" I inquired with a raised brow.

"We had...a fling. We were both drunk." He turned his tortured gaze to me and then back to the paper. "I don't usually drink that much but when she made a pass at me, I couldn't...it was like I had no power to control myself."

"You slept with her that night?"

"Yes, but then..." he shuddered and gulped down some of his coffee. "I don't remember much of anything. I remember her making a pass. We made it up to my room, and then nothing after that."

"Was it just a fling or did you have feelings for her?"

"I had no feelings for Victoria. If I hadn't been out of it, I wouldn't have even..."

"Excuse me miss..." a male voice said after the tinkling of the front doorbells. "We are looking for a Mr. Steven Smalls. Does he happen to patronize your shop?"

I watched as Tessa pointed a trembling finger towards the alcove. The cop turned and nodded his thanks before heading in our direction. He frowned at the hanging beads but ducked into the alcove. His gaze settled first on Serena with a soft smile, then turned to me. He nodded his head and turned to look dead on at Steven. I cleared my throat, bringing his attention back to me.

"Why Detective Johns..." I remarked with a warm smile. "It has been ages since I have last seen you. How is little Marla doing?"

"She is doing well ma'am. Thank you for remembering her. Pardon me, but Mr. Smalls, I am here to ask you to come to the station for some questions."

"Of course, Detective Johns. Mr. Smalls will oblige you in your request, but if you would be so kind as to give me a moment. I am in the middle of finishing a reading on Mr. Smalls."

"Oh, my apologies Ms. Blueblade, but I have to take him in now."

I hesitated but finally nodded my head. Steven stood shakily from his chair and moved to step out of the alcove when he turned to me. I gave a slight shake of my head and nodded towards the door. He moved in that direction without another thought. I caught Detective Johns arm as he moved to follow.

"Detective..." I closed my eyes and then opened them. "If you don't mind a piece of advice."

"Of course, ma'am."

"I know he looks good for this case, but I advise you to look at ALL possibilities. I can promise you that I have been in contact with him for several days and there is no way he did this." I motioned to the paper and inhaled deeply. "I feel it deep in my bones. He isn't the one who committed this heinous act."

"I'll make sure to take that into consideration Ms. Blueblade. Again, my apologies for the interruption. You have a wonderful day ma'am."

Chapter Seven

Steven was questioned for several hours by Detective Johns. I had spent most of that time pacing back and forth in my alcove at the café. I wasn't sure what my next step should be. I had no leads on where to even start looking. It would be best for everyone if I just allow the police to do their job. I stopped pacing and glanced across the street to the lone blue newspaper stand.

It had been there for years and was fading quickly into a dull gray. The people of the town were taking papers from the machine so fast I thought they would start a small fire. The news of what happened to that poor woman was spreading quickly and fingers were all pressed against their lips as they read who the suspect is.

Steven may not have committed the crime, at least I didn't think he had, but he would forever have to face the scorn from the people of this town. They would always link him to the crime even if he was found innocent. That could be harder than being an actual murderer.

"Aunt Vi..." Tessa stepped into the alcove. She was wiping flour off her hands with a damp hand towel that was tucked into the strings of her apron.

"Yes, baby girl?" I sighed as I leaned against the window and turned to look at her.

"Serena was wondering if you wanted us to close up early?" She nodded to the window and the crowd of townspeople who were ringed around the faded blue newspaper machine. "Business has been pretty non-existent."

"Go ahead baby girl. We can try again tomorrow."

"A little advice Aunt Vi," she replied as she turned to close up. "Go spend some time at his place. See if you can get anything from a vision or even physical evidence. It will go a long way to help us find the real culprit behind the murders."

"Is this you trying to get me to spend more time with Steven?"

"Not at all." Tessa grinned lightly and flipped her hair over her shoulder in one of her sister's innocent moves. "I am just suggesting that you might be able to get a vision of him stabbing that woman if you happen to be in the room she was murdered in. If you do, then you can help point Detective Johns in the right direction. That will clear up this whole mess before the murderer turns his gaze to you."

"Maybe..." I murmured as she raised her shoulder and winked.

"And if you can't find evidence of him being the murderer, it doesn't hurt to spend time with a hunk of a man like that!"

"Tessa." I growled and rolled my eyes.

It was too late, she had already disappeared back into the café, leaving me to glare back out the window for another few heartbeats. Skipping heartbeats, that was. The mere thought of spending time with him inside his home, alone, was enough to make me almost rush to the front door of the café. Tessa was right. I needed to find evidence that he had either murdered Victoria or that he had nothing to do with it. If I was going to be the next victim in a line of murders, I needed to do something to protect myself.

I drove to the police station just as Steven was released. It was perfect timing on my part, or the Fate Sisters were playing with me. I pulled up to the curb and honked. Steven turned, caught sight of me behind the steering wheel, let out a heavy sigh, then climbed into my passenger seat. I waited for him to tug his seatbelt into place before pulling onto the road.

"Are you stalking me now, Violet?"

"You can call me Vi." I said with a blush at my full name on his lips. "And if anyone is stalking, it would be you. I figured you could use a ride back from the police station to the café to pick up your vehicle. I trust Detective Johns was at least decent in his questioning?"

"He didn't beat the answers out of me, if that is what you are asking." Steven sighed heavily and let out a humph. "Thank you."

"For what?"

"For everything you have done. I spent last night having dreams of my wife suffocating and that I might have made it worse. I appreciate you helping me see that I didn't choke her to death. I also appreciate whatever sort of pull you have with Detective Johns. I am sure that interview could have gone in a different direction if you hadn't spoken with him." Steven fidgeted with the side hem of his jeans as he kept his face turned toward the side window. "I wish I knew why I am being targeted."

"Sometimes we are just in the wrong place at the wrong time. As cliche as that sounds, it is true." I turned into the parking lot of the café and tapped my fingers lightly against the steering wheel. "For what it is worth, I plan to help in any way I can. As I tried to explain this morning, my girls and I are somehow tied into this whole mess, and I won't have anything happen to them."

"I understand." He frowned and nodded, reaching out to pat my hand on the gear shift before thinking twice and pulling it back. "Thank you for the ride."

"I had an ulterior motive for that." I winked with a grin. "I planned on heading over to your place to check on your entity. It has been almost twenty-four hours. I was going to see if it was active. Do you mind?"

I held my breath as he thought about it. I watched as hope, fear, confusion, and something else crossed his features. It was the something else that seemed to win out. He nodded, climbed out of my vehicle, and into his own. Once he was back on the street, I followed. I had only been to his place once, but I could almost bet, even with my horrible sense of direction, I could find his place blind. I pulled into the carport where I had parked the other night and grabbed my bag off the side seat before waiting at the side door.

He was there a moment later, pushing open the door for me to enter. It appeared that Daisy's finder spell was wearing off. Steven wasn't finding every excuse he could to touch me and that was a win in my book. Okay, maybe it wasn't. Maybe I was truly looking for his hand to brush mine. With a heavy sigh, I settled my bag on the side counter and closed my eyes.

"Shall we start...oh...I guess you are already." He snorted as he leaned against the counter next to me and watched.

I dropped my chin to my chest and tried hard not to scream in pain. Fear, anger, and hatred filled my being to the core. An entity that felt like this was out for murder. Steven wouldn't be safe until I figured out what this spirit wanted. I took a step into the room and then another. I felt Steven raise his hand to catch me and I held my hand out and back to stop him. I closed my eyes and continued to walk through his house as if I knew the exact layout by heart.

I walked slowly from one room to another. Through the kitchen, to the living room, then into the small hallway. The feel of the malevolent spirit increased, making it harder to breathe. The putrid smell of decaying flesh invaded my nose and mouth making every breath harder to take. I stopped at the end of the hall and turned to the right.

The feeling of hatred lessened. Turning to the left, the vibration of anger filled my being until I pulsed with rage. Reaching out one hand, I lightly ran my fingertips along the door. A strong wave of hatred pushed me back, slamming me towards the opposite wall. Instead, I was slammed into a warm masculine body.

Steven wrapped his arms around me. I was panting, frozen to the core, and sweating heavily. His presence helped push the cold fear of dread from my body as we both stood gasping in front of the closed door. I turned my head, not wanting to leave the warm embrace of his arms. He was looking from me to the door, his face going pale under the olive tone of his skin, his body keeping me from collapsing against the floor in sheer exhaustion.

"What the hell was that?"

"Did you see it?"

"See what?" He gasped as he unwrapped one arm from my body and reached out and touched the door. "One moment you were standing here and the next you were flying backwards."

"What is behind this door Steven?"

"Absolutely nothing."

I didn't believe him. A spirit didn't haunt an empty room, but as he grasped the handle of the door and pushed it open, he proved his point. The room was empty. The walls were wallpapered in a feminine floral pattern that was busy enough to make one dizzy. Aside from the small hanging ceiling light, there was nothing but the hardwood floors and the walls. I gaped in shock as I stared into the space. The evil I had felt in this room had disappeared, leaving behind a stuffy empty room.

Unwrapping myself from his warm and comforting embrace, I stepped inside the room and closed my eyes, opening my arms out to the side and breathing slowly. The spirit had disappeared. Frowning, I dropped my arms and growled in frustration. A quick little peak into what was haunting Steven's house wasn't getting me any closer to the killer in my visions or into what was going on with Steven. I turned in frustration and bumped into Steven's chest yet again. Looking up into his brown eyes, I tried to remind myself I wasn't here to enjoy this massive wall of throbbing man flesh.

"It seems your spirit made an appearance and then decided to leave." I inhaled deeply and almost regretted it. Almost. I was now inhaling the very scent of a man that I was having a hard time not being attracted to. Snapping my attention to the door, I moved away from him. "Let me check out the rest of the house and make sure I am not getting anything."

"Do spirits come and go as they please?" He followed me from room to room. He leaned against the door frame of each room as I held myself in a vertical cross and felt for the spirit or spirits.

"It depends on the entity and what it manifests as. Malevolent spirits like the one I just pushed against are usually not tied down to a single object. It allows them the freedom to move from one space to the other, but they do have ties. If your spirit is tied to the house, then it can emerge anywhere within the walls. If it is tied to objects, it can only appear within the spaces the objects are held."

I walked into the living room and repeated my process after clearing the four bedrooms and bathroom. There was a small staircase off the living room that would take me downstairs or up to whatever was on the second floor. I knew the kitchen was clear from walking in but would make sure it was clear again as I went through the process of searching.

"I have a feeling that this spirit is tied to objects, but how it was able to materialize into an empty room has me baffled." I cleared the living room, cleared the kitchen, then stood on the stairs. "Shall we make sure it didn't walk downstairs?"

"Walk is a loose term, I assume," he murmured in his masculine voice with a smirk as he followed me down the stairs. On the last step, I stumbled, feeling as if something had darted between my feet. His strong warm hand reached out and caught me before I face planted on the floor. Looking up, I caught the quick faint outline of a dog as it ran across the empty basement. "Are you ok?"

"Fine. Did you see Fido?" I motioned in the direction that Fido had run. When I glanced back, he shook his head and gave me a look that imitated that I was insane. With a sigh, I turned and spied a chewed up looking ball near my feet. "Come here lovely." I whistled in a sing song voice. I scooped up the well chewed ball and tossed it across the empty space. "Let me get a good look at you..."

"Holy shi..." Steven started as the apparition of the ghost dog sat in front of me and dropped the ball. "Where is your bag?"

"Upstairs, but I don't need it just yet." I scooped up the ball at my feet and tossed it again. The dog clearly turned, disappeared, then reappeared and dropped the ball once again at my feet. "You are such a good girl, aren't you now? Yes, you are. You are such a good girl!"

"Why are you talking to it like it is a real dog?"

"It is a real dog." I sighed in annoyance. It never failed. No one ever believed in what I could do or in ghosts. Those that say they do, never stick around long enough to see one. I bent down on one knee and gave the dog a good scratch behind the ears before tossing the ball once more and then walking deeper into the basement. "The basement is clear."

"Not exactly." He frowned as he watched the ball appear again at his feet this time. Hesitantly, he reached down and picked it up, imitating throwing it towards the opposite side of the room. When the ball reappeared again, he repeated the process and jumped lightly when the dog fully formed in front of him. "This is awesome on one hand and yet..."

"Creepy on the other." I nodded and snorted as I took a step up on the stairs. "I know. You eventually either learn to deal with it or you..." I gasped as the phantom feeling of being strangled caught me. I reached up, gasping, the ghost dog began growling and barking, and the lights in the basement began to flicker on and off.

"What the hell?" he demanded as he tried to help me. "What is wrong?"

"Air. Choking." I gasped.

I was so caught in the web of whatever had me that I didn't notice when he scooped me up into his arms and carried me up the stairs to the kitchen. The moment my feet touched the wooden floor, my throat opened, and I inhaled a delicious lungful of air. I spied the staircase and took one last deep shuddering breath as I turned to find my go bag. It was on the floor next to the side cabinet.

"This spirit," I croaked. Swallowing hard, I picked up my bag and resettled it on the counter. "Doesn't want you here. That is definite. What is upstairs?"

"A couple more bedrooms, another bathroom, another living space, and a storage room."

"Up we go," I remarked with a trembling smile. I was beginning to wonder if I should even be here in this place at all. The spirit didn't want Steven here and it didn't seem to want me here either. I slowly hiked up the stairs, puffing slightly at the top. I really needed to start getting some workouts in. "I'm going to clear the bedrooms, bathroom and this living space," I mumbled.

I was positive that Steven was beginning to feel I was a charlatan. He had only seen two ghosts, and they were both dogs. I had to remind myself that I didn't care if he believed me or not. This was about finding the killer that was haunting my visions. I had to be able to find some clue as to why my visions kept saying it was Steven. I made it to the end of the small hallway up here when Steven gagged behind me. The smell of burnt flesh filled the space. Reaching out a hand, I turned the knob on the door at the end of the hall and pushed it open. Inside was the storage space, but that isn't what greeted my eyes.

Before me was the image of a woman tied to a wooden stake with wood piled around her in a blaze of heat. I watched as the flames engulfed her body. Her mouth opened in a silent scream as the smell intensified. I watched as that silent scream became more intense. Her body writhed as much as possible even though she was tied to the stake.

"What in holy fu..." Steven growled as he stepped into the room behind me. I held my hands up, interrupting him. This was the angry spirit that was haunting his home, and I wanted to see what she was willing to show me.

"Arthur!" came a loud scream that pierced my head and ears.

I watched as the image slowly grew dimmer as the body turned to ash. That horrific scene would forever be burned into my brain. I am not sure who Arthur was, but I was determined to find out what it had to do with Steven. I watched as the fire slowly turned into the image of a storage room full of boxes.

"She is gone for now." I told Steven. It was then that I realized that he had wrapped his arms around my waist and was holding me close to his chest. My heart skipped a beat, my cheeks turned pink, and it was getting harder to breath as his scent of leather and spices filled my senses.

"Was that her?"

"Yes." I placed my hand over his and smiled as I slowly extracted myself from his grip. "Wait, you saw her?"

"I am not exactly sure what I saw. It seemed to be a woman burned at the stake. Did they think she was a witch?"

"Maybe. We would have to find out the history behind the house, and then the history of your family. There must be a tie to this haunting. Either she is haunting the space, or she is haunting you."

"Who is Arthur?" Steven grimaced as they slowly made their way back down the stairs to his kitchen.

"You heard her as well?" I chuckled as I eased into a space at his kitchen table. I rested my head in my hands and sighed. "I do believe that you may be a convert. I have never heard of such a thing. People who don't believe and can't see the spirits don't usually come around later in life, but I do believe you are making that transition.

"What does that mean?"

"That means, that you have gone from not seeing or hearing to believing enough in the spiritual realm to actually see and hear the alternative spectrum of reality."

"Vi," Steven sat a steaming hot cup of coffee on the table in front of me before taking the chair. "I still don't believe a single thing about this whole thing, but I can't deny that there is something happening. What I don't understand is why. Tell me what my next step should be."

"Well, other than trying to pick up the entity on film or on a record, I can't say as I have much to go on. The first step is to go to the library and do as much research on the history of your house. You can go to your family and get as much history as you can. Maybe somewhere between the two we can find information on who this woman is, what happened to her, and who this man Arthur is."

"Shall we go now?"

A quick glance at the clock told me that it was late enough in the evening that the library would be closing down. I chuckled, took one last sip of my coffee, then patted him on the arm. He watched with those large brown eyes framed with thick black lashes. This man was sinfully handsome, and it caused my heart to skip a beat as I was flooded once more with images of possible futures with him. I dug around in my bag of goodies and found a piece of selenite. I placed it in his hand and wrapped his fingers around it.

"For now, I am going to head home and get some rest. You should do the same. This should protect you for a little bit. Make sure to keep it on you tonight while you sleep just in case. I will let you know as soon as I have more information."

"Your leaving?" Steven groaned as he took a sip of his coffee. "You could stay. I have a guest room."

"As appealing as that might sound, I am pretty sure it is best to head home. You will be safe, I can promise you that."

Chapter Eight

I sat in my usual space at the Mystic Café listening to the sounds of Tessa and Serena arguing, the muted sounds of the coffee perking, and a timer going off in the back kitchen. My thoughts were jumbled from the events of the last week. I was trying desperately to find a way to sort them out.

Was Steven the person who murdered that woman? He did have three previous wives that had died. One I could rule out as murder because she died of cancer. The second I could rule out as a freak horse-riding accident. The third was still a mystery.

I could understand him having a motive of killing wives, so how did this new woman tie into this. Granted he had admitted that he slept with her, but that wasn't a wife. Would a serial killer change their motive like that? Would they go from killing their wives to killing those women they had slept with? I groaned and dropped my head into my hands as Serena stepped into the alcove. She patted me on the shoulder and sighed as she sipped her own cup of coffee.

"What's eating at you Aunt Vi?"

"Not a thing."

"That is a complete lie, and we both know it." Serena laughed heartily as she kicked back into a relaxed pose in the chair. "We both know that you are tied up over this man and are thinking hard about proving his innocence."

"I am not thinking about proving his innocence. I am going to prove it. I just don't know where to start. I am not a detective."

"I think that you worry too much, Aunt Vi. What is it you are always telling Tessa and I?"

"That we should take a breath, close our eyes, and let nature work itself out."

"Exactly. You are being shown the images of dead women. You are being shown your own death. You are also being shown a smoking hot rich man that is the possible killer. I think somewhere in there, nature will take care of itself."

"Serena, stop being so annoying!" Tessa hollered. She popped her head through the beaded curtain. "What Serena is trying so hard to say is that the Goddess wouldn't have given this gift and these visions to you Aunty Vi, if she, in her divine right, didn't think you could handle it. Trust in the power of the Goddess."

"You two..." I groaned and rolled my eyes. "Will be the death of me."

"Actually, according to your visions, Steven will be the death of you." Serena grumbled as she took another sip of her coffee.

"Right." I twisted the coffee mug around in my grip. "What I need is to get as much history on his place as possible. The vengeful spirit showed me her death last night and I don't know if she is angry at something about the place or about Steven's family."

"Shouldn't we start with a search on Steven's family history?" Tessa responded as she dropped into the only other seat at the table. "It might be quicker to find a connection that way."

"Steven will have to do that research."

"Damn." Serena and Tessa both growled at the exact same time. "We were so hoping to find out more about Mr. Hottie."

"You two, seriously. I know I taught you better, if not your father."

"You know you love our witty banter. You wouldn't know what to do with yourself if we were not here to lighten the load."

"That is why I hired you two. You can provide all the witty banter for the customers while I do nothing. I get all the profit with none of the work." I laughed as the girls rolled their eyes at me and then disappeared through the curtain.

I turned in my chair and looked out at the town in front of me. I had grown up in this town. I loved everything about this town and thought I knew everything there was to know about it. For some reason I had no knowledge of the house that Steven owned. How was that even possible? I was beginning to feel like there was more at work here than I thought. I finished off the coffee that Serena had brought me earlier and rose from my seat when the beaded curtain clicked. Glancing up, I smiled at the gentleman that stepped into my alcove.

"Salutations!" I greeted.

"Yeah, whatever you say."

I studied this man's aura and appearance. He had a naturally calm aura of light blue that was bleeding into black. Goosebumps rose on my forearms, and my head began to throb. I had thought that Steven was dressed remarkably well, but this man put him to shame. He was wearing a three-piece suit, wing tip shoes that shined brightly, and a tie with a metallic sheen. I would be afraid to touch the man for fear I would wrinkle him or leave a smudge. Suppressing a shudder, I eased back down into the chair and forced a warm smile to my face as I waved him towards the chair across from me.

"What can I do for you Mister..."

"My name is of no consequence to this meeting. You need to stay away from my brother."

"I am sorry, your brother? I believe you have me at a disadvantage sir."

"Stay away from Steven. I have hired the best investigators and lawyers that money can buy."

"Ah..." I nodded and eased back in my chair, crossing my arms over my chest. "Mr. Smalls, please..."

"That would be Dr. Smalls to you," he sneered.

I nodded and sneered right back. "Dr. Smalls, please forgive me for my ignorance, but how should I stay away from your brother when it is your brother who keeps invading my café with his pleas for help?" I tilted my head to the side and raised an eyebrow. "What your brother needs is someone who knows what is happening. Not overpriced ass-kissers."

"I don't think you know one thing about what is going on." Dr. Smalls sniffed and tugged on the cuff of his right sleeve. "A man who is a suspect in a murder needs a well-paid legal team behind him. Not some fake charlatan who tells him lots of lies to bilk his money from him."

"First sir." I stood and narrowed my gaze at him as I worked to keep my temper down. "I didn't seek Steven out; he came to me. Second, I am not a charlatan. And lastly, I didn't even know he had money, let alone ask him for any. The most money Steven has given me is around four dollars for his cups of coffee."

He opened his mouth to say something, and I held my hand up.

"Please forgive me for my rudeness, Dr. Smalls." I remarked with disdain. "If you will remove yourself from my place of business, I would greatly appreciate it. Your aura is keeping my customers away."

"I can't..."

"Yes, I am sure you can't." Tessa remarked with a wicked grin as she stood holding the beaded curtain open on one side of the alcove.

"And you probably won't ever again." Serena added as she held open the beaded curtain on the other side.

"You see, we are family here in this café and we don't take well to those who stink up our place with their vile snide remarks." I answered as he turned and walked briskly out of the alcove. "And please, if you think about returning to my café, don't."

The three of us watched as he disappeared from the café. I sank back down into my chair and dropped my head onto a hand. Why would Steven's brother accuse me of bilking money from him? For another thing, who was he? I thought I knew just about everyone in this town and yet I had never met this man or heard of him before.

"Aunty Vi?" Tessa spoke softly from my side. "I didn't get a good vibe from him."

"I agree." I sighed and lifted my head from my hand. "I'll need Steven's favorite coffee and a couple of scones to go. I think I need to stop by his place before I head over to the library."

"All ready to go!" Serena called from the front counter.

I stepped out of my alcove to see two cups of coffee and a small bag. For a moment tears welled in my eyes and my throat became tight from unshed tears. My girls were really coming into their own gifts. Would they end up with the same gifts that I had? Would they each have different gifts? Time would only tell. Swallowing the lump in my throat, I thanked the girls and headed out.

I had a murder to solve and a hot man to spend time with!

Chapter Nine

I sat in my car for a moment and wondered what I was doing here. Did I just make an excuse to come over and see him or was there really a reason for me to be here? I wasn't sure I liked the answer that was floating around in my mind. Grabbing the coffees and the bag, I walked slowly to the back door and tapped softly. I waited a few moments and then decided he probably hadn't heard it and tapped harder. The door was pulled out from under my fist.

A man who looked like Steven was standing angrily in the doorway. He glared at me as if I were a menace to society. I opened and closed my mouth like a fish before I could form words. I got no feelings from this man. He didn't have an aura. Being a person who could see auras, I had learned how to tune them out. Still, it came as a shock when I didn't see anything. The whole combination threw me off my game.

"I apologize for any trouble I might be causing, but is Steven home?"

"Steven is downstairs. He is going crazy, no thanks to you."

"Uh..."

"He is pretending to throw a ball for an invisible dog. As if that makes sense."

I smiled to myself. This stranger didn't really find me displeasing. He was upset at the strange behavior that Steven was exhibiting. I watched as he stepped back and motioned me inside. I brushed past him and almost froze in place. I was so used to getting flashes of feelings or visions when I touched people. The lack of visions and feelings made me leery. Again, I was used to ignoring those visions and feeling. Suddenly I was dealing with a person who didn't have an aura, was casting no feelings, and I couldn't see anything about their past or future. Something was off here.

The fine hairs on my arms rose and I shivered as I pushed past him and closer to the basement door. I didn't even wait to see if he had anything else to say. I flew down the stairs, seeking the calm reassurance of Steven's aura. It was the last step that caught me off guard and I felt my feet flying out from under me. The coffees miraculously landed straight down, as if sat on the concrete. The bag of scones didn't fare as well and flew across the room to land open.

"I know women tend to throw themselves at me," Steven murmured softly so only I could hear. The sound of his deep masculine growl sent shivers through my spine. I found myself concentrating hard on his lips instead of what was happening. "But this is getting a little hard to believe. I mean, almost every time I see you, you end up in my arms."

"That's me. The queen of being klutzy." I whispered as he helped me stand up.

We stood a step apart, his scent filling my senses as I looked up into those gorgeous brown eyes. He smiled down at me. I felt his hands move from my arms to my waist as he took that last tiny step closer to me. There was a little voice inside my head that said he was going to kiss me. I needed to move, but I was frozen in place. All I could do was watch as those large full lips descended towards mine. The feel of his breath on my skin, the light hint of mint, the feel of his fingers as they gripped my waist all combined to make me forget that I had been running away from something.

Sparks tingled against my lips as his brushed mine with a feather touch. I am sure the kiss would have become more if the person I had been running from didn't clear their throat. Steven's grip clenched slightly tighter before he sniffed and pulled back. His eyes focused above my head. I opened my eyes, gasped in a deep breath calming breath, then stepped aside. My bag of scones was on the floor, and it appeared that our barghest-turned-calm-dog was nosing around it.

"George." Steven growled. It was the harshest word I had ever heard him utter the whole time I had known him. Granted I had only known him for a short time. "You are still here?"

"Of course I am still here. You called me last night and wanted to know about our family history and then hung up before I got any answers as to why."

"I told you why."

"Right." George stepped down onto the basement floor and crossed his arms over his chest as he glanced from me to the bag on the floor then back again. "You think you are being accused of murder to hide something sinister in our family."

The look on George's face was enough to make my stomach churn. He looked eerily like Steven if you were just glancing in his direction. I bent to scoop up the paper bag and gently used my foot to scoot the ghost dog behind me as I watched this stranger for any indication of an aura. In my thirty years of having this gift, I had never met a person I couldn't read. George was the first and it scared me more than the poltergeist that was haunting Steven's house.

"Why would someone frame you for murder? What do you think our family history has to do with it?"

"I don't know George, but since you don't know anything, you can leave."

"I should be going..." I remarked very quietly to no one in particular. I took a couple of steps and was halted by Steven's hand on my elbow.

"George was just leaving, and you brought breakfast," he replied with a strained smile as he motioned to the coffee that was sitting on the floor. "I assume it is my favorite?"

"Favorite?" George snorted and rolled his eyes as he sneered at me and then started up the stairs. "I would hardly consider coffee and scones from the Mystic Brew Café good enough to be a favorite."

The sting of his dismissal of my café hurt more than his dismissal of me. I ducked my head and felt a slight nudge at my ankle. I glanced down to see the dog looking up at me with a sad face before it placed its head on my foot. Tears began to form in my eyes, and I fought to keep them from falling as I heard the faint sound of footsteps upstairs and then the door closing.

"I apologize for the rudeness of my family member."

"No need to be sorry. I am used to it."

"You are used to it?" Steven tilted his head and looked down at her foot where the dog had curled up and was pawing lightly at her foot. "Well, at least Tiger understands that you need an apology."

"Tiger?" I looked at the small dog on my feet. "You can still see her?"

"It seems now that I have opened my eyes to the supernatural elements, I am unable to close them. George freaked out when he saw me down here pretending to play fetch with the air. I think that is why he was being so rude."

"Understandable, but Tiger?" I inquired as I followed him up the stairs with my bag of broken scones. Steven had tossed the ball once more for the little shih tzu before scooping up the coffees. We settled at his kitchen counter on bar stools. There were only the two and so I was sitting much closer to him than I felt comfortable with. That kiss had me thinking about other things.

"Do you see the size of that dog?"

"That would be a shih tzu. A very adorable white and sable from the looks of it."

"How does the hell beast that we saw that first time compute with that tiny little thing?" Steven shook his head and chuckled as he moaned at his bite of scone. I glanced down and noticed that they were the lemon cranberry. That was interesting. Tessa didn't usually make those in the fall. Lemon cranberry scones were normally a spring item.

"You don't know much about dogs I take it?"

"Not really, my family never found animals appealing. The closest to a family pet we had was a stray tabby that used to get into the trash during winter."

"A shih tzu may be a tiny little thing, but they have the heart and courage of the biggest dog you will ever see. They are likened to lions in some cultures." I took a sip of my coffee now that my nerves were slowly smoothing out. "I met your brother this morning."

He frowned as he rubbed his face in frustration. "I take it he blustered his way in, insisted you call him doctor, and then told you to stay the hell away from me?"

"That about sums it up perfectly. I believe there was also mention that I should stop bilking you for money."

"I could find no better way to introduce a woman to my family..." he snorted and nervously glanced away. "My younger brother has a drastically inflated ego. He means well though. He just doesn't understand that this whole supernatural aspect is real."

"I can see that..." I blushed at his comment.

"Randolph made it as a big shot heart surgeon and moved away from here a few years ago. He lives in the 'big' city about two hours away and thinks that the world rotates because of him. He really is fantastic at his job, but he thinks he is God."

This made sense why his aura had black. He was a healer and naturally had the affinity to help others. The bleed of black meant that he was tied up in his ego too much and made fatal mistakes. His aura notwithstanding, I didn't get a bad vibe from him. It was more of a mutual dislike upon immediately seeing him. I hid a soft smile behind my coffee cup as I took a sip.

"And George?" I prompted.

"George," he snarled. He rose from the barstool and began nervously pacing the kitchen. "George is my cousin on my father's side. He is a real piece of work."

I watched as he fidgeted with a few plates that were in the strainer next to the sink. Steven held some deep-seated resentment towards his cousin. I wondered if it was the resemblance that had him so disquieted or if it was what had happened in their history together.

"Everyone has told me how much George looks like me. He uses it to impersonate me. It is like he wants to be me."

I filed that information away for future thought. Rising from the barstool, I walked behind the counter and placed my hand lightly on his arm. He stopped fidgeting and glanced down at my hand. For a moment I thought he would stop giving me information, but he only smiled, then patted my hand.

"He pretended to be me and slept with one of my girlfriends when I was twenty. That could easily be forgiven. We obviously were not working out as a couple. Who could fault them for getting together. I received a notification of a bank withdrawal once. When I contacted that bank, they swore I walked in and did a counter withdrawal. It is just annoying things like that. He annoys the hell out of me."

"I can understand that completely." I felt the ghostly brush of fur against my calf and glanced down. His little Tiger had moved from the basement to the kitchen and was now lying on his foot with a sad face. "Tiger is also sorry and wants you to know how sad she is for you."

Steven glanced down and he laughed softly. The sound was musical as she watched him bend down and pretend to have a ball. As if by magic, the ball from downstairs materialized in his hand and he tossed it lightly across the kitchen. We both watched as the little sable and white shih tzu bounded across the tiles, slid into the wall, and grabbed the ball. She appeared in front of us with her tail wagging and her tongue hanging out.

"I was heading over to the library to get more information on this house and its history. I just wanted to check in with you to make sure you had an 'uneventful' night."

"It could have been better," he teased with a quick side eyed glance at me. "But it wasn't the worst night I have spent in this house."

"I am glad it was a decent night. I'll keep you updated if I find out anything."

"Thank you," Steven replied. "I appreciate everything."

Chapter Ten

The library was top of the line for a town this tiny. It had travertine floors that shined with the glow of the sun through the floor to ceiling windows. They had gorgeous wooden tables with desk lamps for those who needed a place to sit and study. Some of the stacks had chairs for those who wanted to sit and while away a few hours reading.

There were two wings of the library. One side housed the children's section and the other the adult section. The checkout desk was directly in front of the entry doors that were carved wood and heavier than any door I had ever used. There were famous scenes from children's stories carved into them. It was one of the things that I loved about this library.

I was more interested in the top floor. What pulled me to the top floor was the historical documents, the microfilms, the computers, and just about anything a person doing research would need. I had pulled a couple of histories of the town and had settled into my favorite nook. I pulled out a small notepad from my back pocket and a pen. It was time to find out what I needed to know.

I spent five hours in the library glancing through all the histories on the town and the newspaper articles. There wasn't a lot of history to look through. There had been no mention of the Smalls family. I removed the last microfilm from the machine and slid it back into the small cardboard box. How in the world was it possible that there was no history on Steven's property?

What was even more frustrating was that my notepad was still empty. I had no information to move me in any direction.

I glanced up at the sound of footsteps and smiled politely at the librarian as she shelved a book near me. She smiled back and glanced at one of the books I had pulled off the shelf. She moved closer to me and noticed the newspaper microfilms I had pulled. I had a moment of panic, as if I had been caught researching something I shouldn't have been. Then she picked up my books and put them on her small cart.

"Did you find everything you were looking for Ms. Blueblade?"

"No, not really. I struck out." I gave her a grin as I handed her the microfilms.

"If it is the town history you are looking for, you might want to chat with Gertie, the head librarian. She did her dissertation on the town's history. She might be able to guide you in the right direction if nothing else."

"You are a blessing in disguise Sadie!" I squealed as I clapped my hands together. "I didn't even think about talking with her. I could have saved myself five hours of research."

"I am glad I could be of service then, Ms. Blueblade." Sadie blushed and dipped her head.

"Sadie, please call me Vi. Your coffee is on me for the next month. I'll make sure my girls know. Thank you again!"

"Gertie is not here..." Sadie called as I skipped towards the stairs that would take me down to the checkout desk. I skidded to a stop and sighed. Why would any of this be easy.

"When will she be in?"

"She is out for vacation until the end of the week. I will leave a note for her on her desk. That way she can contact you when she gets back in."

"Thank you!" I hollered as I walked out of the building.

I still found it odd that there was no mention of the estate. It looked to be well kept and at least a few hundred years old. If I had to guess, it was originally built when the town was created and then renovated and updated periodically. There had to be some history, somewhere. With no new information to go on, I sat in my car for a few minutes and tapped my fingers against the steering wheel. It was nearing dinner time. The girls would have closed the shop, so I didn't need to go there.

Heading home to my quiet little house to eat a boring bacon sandwich didn't appeal to me. I am not a people person on the best of days, but I felt like being surrounded by energy. I put my car in gear and headed to my favorite restaurant. If I couldn't talk to Gertie, maybe I could talk with Sarah. Sarah had lived in our town for almost eighty years. Surely, she would know something about the history of the town.

Finding a parking spot at the Wavering Willows was always difficult, but as my luck would have it, all of them were filled tonight. I did find a parking spot across the street at the hardware store and sent a quick prayer to the Goddess that they wouldn't have my car towed. I was able to find one table at the very back of the restaurant near the kitchens. I was thankful that there was a table at all. Wavering Willows was the favorite restaurant of the town. Finding more than an hour wait was a miracle on a beautiful almost spring evening like tonight.

Wavering Willows was a homey restaurant. The tables had been hand crafted by the owners grandfather years ago. They were worn and some wobbled, but you couldn't beat the energy that came from them. The love and warmth of families eating at them over the years could be felt even if you were not psychic. The chairs were a little newer but still just as comfy. They were black wrought iron with padded blue seats. I settled in as the waitress brought me a laminated menu. She smiled when she saw me and tucked the menu back into her arms as she settled down a cloth napkin wrapped set of silverware and a glass of water.

"Vi, it is always a pleasure to see you. Will you have your usual?"

"Thank you, Ida. I would love my usual. Is Sarah in tonight, per chance?"

"She is. Did you want me to go get her?"

"If she isn't busy and has a moment to gab. I would love to pick her brain for a moment on the town history."

"I'll see if she has a moment."

I watched as Ida disappeared behind the swinging silver door next to me. I was unwrapping the cloth silverware and setting it down when I noticed the front door to the restaurant open. Glancing up made my breath catch in my throat. Steven had stepped inside. He was wearing a black t-shirt, a pair of tan dress pants, a black belt, and black dress shoes. He looked almost like a man that was going to a laid-back business meeting instead of man just looking for dinner.

The hostess told him that they were full and that it would be at least a forty-minute wait. He looked sad but nodded in understanding. He motioned toward the bench seat by the door when his eyes caught mine. I smiled at him and waved him inside to the empty seat across from me. There was no need for him to wait for an empty table when he could eat with me. Maybe that was me wanting to spend more time with him. Or maybe I was I being a polite neighbor. I wasn't sure which it was and quite frankly at this point I was too exhausted to decide.

"It appears that you are still stalking me." I remarked with a giggle as he settled at the table in front of me. Ida returned with another set of utensils and another glass of water.

"It is not very often that Vi has a guest during dinner." Ida tilted her head and gave Steven one of her most devastating smiles. "Dare I ask if this is a dinner date?"

"It is a..." Steven began.

"It most definitely is not a dinner date, Zoe." I replied embarrassed. My cheeks had turned a rosy shade of red as I placed my napkin in my lap and sighed. "I am showing a kindness to a new friend who just moved into town."

"Back into town, actually." Steven cleared his throat with a frown. He looked perplexed as he looked down at the plastic menu he had been handed. "You know," he remarked with a sigh as he handed it back. "I will have whatever Vi is having."

"Uh...but..." Ida stammered as she shuffled from one foot to the other. "You see, what Vi..."

"You heard him, Ida." I chuckled with a secretive smile. "He will have what I am having." I watched with a grin as she disappeared into the swinging door and then glanced over to find Steven looking at me with a raised brow.

"Did I just order something I am going to regret?"

"Let's just say, Mr. Stalker, that what you ordered isn't on the menu."

"Huh..." he grinned back at me as he fidgeted with the napkin in front of him. "Stalker?"

"You seem to keep appearing everywhere I am. What is it about me that has you attracted like a bee to a flower?"

"Maybe I find you attractive..." he replied behind his glass of water.

When his eyes caught mine, I felt my heart skip a beat before beating a staccato rhythm against my chest. My hands began to feel sweaty as I dropped them into my lap. The restaurant was suddenly a thousand degrees while those eyes starred into mine. I opened and closed my mouth a time or two before I was able to utter a single word.

"That is hardly possible." I managed to squeeze out through a suddenly dry throat. "No one in their right mind has ever found boring old me attractive. I have a list a mile long to prove otherwise."

"If that list came from other men, they were idiots. If that list is something you have fabricated in your mind, then I suggest you take a harder look at yourself in the mirror." He shrugged before looking down at the table. "Who said I was in my right mind anyways? I do see an invisible ghost dog that likes to play fetch," he teased before his cheeks also turned a slight shade of pink.

"Vi!"

Both of us turned our gaze to the woman who stepped out of the kitchen holding two plates. She sat them on our table, wiped her hands on a towel hanging from her waist, then proceeded to give me an awkward hug as I sat in my chair. Sarah might be eighty, but she was still a lively woman. Her gray hair was pulled back into a bun at the nape of her neck and she was wearing a pair of sensible shoes, black slacks, and a white button up. She was the perfect example of ageing gracefully. I hoped that when I was her age, I would look half as good.

"Sarah!" I responded with a large grin. "Sarah, I would like you to meet one of our town's newest members, Mr. Steven Smalls. Steven, this is Sarah Liverton. She has lived in this town for over eighty years and has run this restaurant for at least sixty of those years."

"My darling..." Sarah remarked with a hand to her chest and a gasp. "You are having dinner with the man who everyone says murdered that poor girl."

"Sarah..." I started to admonish her but then she cracked a smile and held her hand out to him for a greeting.

"I never listen to those gossip mongers. It is a pleasure to meet you Mr. Smalls. I do recommend that you stick with Vi here. She will get this all straightened out before you know it." Sarah grabbed an empty chair from table next to us and eased down and got comfortable. "Please eat while we chat. I can always use a break from the kitchen. Ida said you had some questions on the town history."

"I am looking for a bit of history on Steven's house actually. It must be at least a hundred years old if not more. I just spent five hours at the library looking for any information they had on it but found nothing. What do you know about the Ravens Estate?"

"The Ravens Estate?" Sarah tilted her head and raised a brow in her direction. "What Ravens Estate? I have never heard of such a place."

"Come on Sarah." I watched with a hidden grin as Steven moved the food around on his plate for a moment in confusion before he placed a forkful in his mouth. The pure delight on his face brought a full smile to mine as I focused back on Sarah. "How can you not know anything about the Ravens Estate? It is almost exactly in the center of our town. Everyone has driven past it at least once a day. It sits on close to ten acres of land."

"Ten acres of land?" Sarah scratched her nose and looked down at the table in thought. "I am not sure I know where you are talking about Vi. I don't know anything about this place."

"Sarah..." someone called from the kitchen. She sighed and rolled her eyes.

"I will think about this some more and if I can think of anything I will get back to you. Enjoy your meal."

"This is weird..." I remarked as I began to pick at my own meal.

"I am not sure what you are referring to." Steven motioned to the retreating Sarah and then his plate. "I can say that I never would have pictured this as a meal. Weird would be a perfect description. Although it is delicious. Or were you referring to the fact that no one seems to know about the Ravens Estate? Who even came up with this meal, though?"

"I did..." I chuckled as his eyebrows touched his hairline in shock. "I have a very odd sense of taste some days. I was referring to the fact that there is nothing in the library that touches on the estate. Sarah is saying she has never heard of it. I have lived here my whole life, and I have never heard of it either. How can your house be so old and no one around remembers anything about it?"

"I don't know." Steven took a sip of his water and looked at me with a far-off stare. "What if my family is a bunch of aliens and we wiped everyone's memories so we could live a peaceful quiet life amidst the humans."

"Right," I rolled my eyes as I sat back in frustration. "That makes total sense."

"Hey, it makes just as much sense as ghosts and witches."

"What is wrong with witches?"

"There is nothing wrong with witches. Especially when they are chocolate brown eyed beauties that have me beguiled." He joked with a wink.

There it went again. My heart skipped another beat. Steven was wrecking all sorts of havoc on my senses, and I wasn't sure how to stop it. I tapped my thumbs against the table lightly as I contemplated the amount of flirting this man had done in the last few days. Was it really flirting? Was I making more out of this than I should be? Maybe I wanted to see something in all his jokes that made me think he really was attracted to me. Ugh! Trying to figure out if he was really into me was harder than I had ever thought possible. Maybe I should take a stroll over to Daisy's shop and get a reading.

"Vi?" Steven interrupted my thoughts with a brush of his fingers over mine. Fireworks ignited at that brief contact and immediately set off visions of the murdered women in my mind. When I yanked my hand to my chest, he nodded and let out a heavy sigh. "Sorry about that. I asked if you were ready to leave?"

I must have been deep in my own world as I was thinking about him to have missed Ida bringing the check to the table or clearing the dinner dishes. I nodded to him and rose from my chair. I took a moment to dig around in my jeans pocket for the money I usually carried with me. Not finding it, I looked at Steven in embarrassment. He only smiled and told me he had already handled the bill. Totally off guard with this turn of events, I allowed him to walk with me out of the restaurant and to the street.

"You know Vi," he began as I tucked my hands into my pockets shyly. "One of these days, if I am not arrested for the murder I didn't commit, I hope you will let me take you out on a real date."

"A real...what?" I gasped as I looked up at him.

"A date. You know, where a man takes a woman out that he is interested in, they usually end up eating a meal together, maybe go to a movie or for a walk...a date."

"I...uh..." I stammered. I had never had a man ask me to go on a date before. I wasn't exactly sure how to react. I was especially not sure if we should go on a date if he was a murderer. "Honestly," I whispered. "I have never been asked out on a date. I don't even know how to respond."

It had escaped my notice that Steven had slowly moved closer to me. His hands had wrapped around my waist. His lips were hovering over mine. If I leaned forward slightly, I would be able to mash my face against his. It would be the boldest thing I have ever done in my life. It would also be the dumbest thing I have ever done. As it was, I didn't flinch out of the way as his lips descended and pressed against mine. Those sparks I had felt earlier in the day went off again. I felt like my lips were being zapped by tiny electric shocks.

My heartbeat was thrumming like a hummingbird as my hands pressed against his chest. He was so warm and inviting as he pulled me tighter against him. I had never thought this is what it would feel like to be kissed. I had also never thought I would forget everything simply because a man was showing me some sort of attention. I heard a soft noise that came from the window of the restaurant that brought my attention back into focus. Regretfully, I pulled my lips off his and struggled to work myself out of his arms. I had been so comfortable pressed up against him that I had forgotten that we were in public.

A quick glance at the restaurant windows told me that several of the town gossip mongers had gotten a front row seat. I also noticed that Ida was smiling and clapping her hands silently. Cringing inwardly, I cleared my throat and shifted my gaze in the direction of my vehicle. Tucking a strand of my hair behind my ear, I scuffed the toe of my sneakers against the sidewalk as I tried to take a step in that direction. Klutzy me, I tripped and ended up in his arms once more.

"Careful now..." he murmured softly with a grin that sent tingles through my spine. "I wouldn't want you to get seriously hurt before our first date."

"Yeah...about that." I mouthed. I wasn't sure I could even talk. It felt like that kiss stole more than my equilibrium. He helped right me as I tried to find somewhere other than his eyes to look. If I looked at him, I wouldn't be able to say no. I should say no, shouldn't I? He hooked his finger under my chin and turned my head to look deep into my eyes.

"Say yes Vi. Put me out of my misery."

Chapter Eleven

"You said yes, right?" Serena demanded with a giddy smile as she bounced up and down on her feet. Tessa was also grinning from ear to ear in the back of the café as she put the finishing touches on some cupcakes.

"I said..." I tucked a strand of hair nervously behind my ears and avoided the gazes of the girls as I fiddled with the display of croissants. "I said no."

"What?" Tessa screeched. I distinctly heard the icing bag hit the counter.

"You didn't!" Serena gasped as she missed on her bouncing and stumbled against the counter. "What would possibly make you turn him down?"

"He is currently under investigation for murder." I reminded them with a shrug.

"You know he didn't do it. Why are you being so damn stubborn, Aunt Vi?" Tessa growled as she joined us in the main café. A customer walked in and ordered a latte. I busied myself in getting that prepared and then handed it to them with a smile I didn't feel. "Stop avoiding the conversation!"

"Tessa," I sighed and leaned against the counter. "You don't understand."

"I understand perfectly, Aunt Vi. You are scared that for once in your life, someone is interested in you. Someone who is not your family. Someone who doesn't need you to take care of them. Take a chance and go out with the man."

"No, that..." I began.

"Witches!!!" Reggie screamed as he stood out in front of the café. The door was closed, but I could still hear him. He was screaming at the top of his lungs and waving his arms at the cafe. "Witches!"

"I got him, Aunt Vi." Serena responded with a sigh. She was packing a bag with goodies from the counter and then poured a cup of coffee.

It wasn't exactly a secret that we harbored some witch like abilities. After all, the Mystic Brew Café is popular because of the mystic who reads fortunes or palms. What distressed me about Reggie was that he was usually a calm person. This was the second time he had gotten worked up. The first time had been when someone had painted the upside-down pentagram on the door. I frowned as I watched Serena speaking soothingly to him. He flung his arms around as Serena attempted to calm him down. It wasn't until he noticed the bag of food in her hands that he settled enough to stop screaming. I watched as he dug into the bag and immediately ate one of the croissants that Serena had bagged up.

Things in my small town were definitely off. Calm and peaceful Reggie was going off the rails. No one seemed to have any idea that the Ravens Estate existed. There had been a murder only a few days ago. I had been asked out on a date by a handsome man. There had to be something in the water. My gut told me it was a big spell of some sort. I just had to track it down. Once again, I contemplated talking with Daisy. She might be daffy most of the time, but she could usually recognize when things were off track.

"I say, you call up Steven and tell him you were out of your mind. Tell him you would love to go on a date." Serena replied as she entered the shop. It was as if she had never stepped outside to talk with Reggie. I rolled my eyes. "Aunty Vi, you are not as young as you used to be."

"Did you just call me old?" I teased as I grabbed a cup of tea to go and a slice of zucchini bread.

"I didn't..." Serena shook her head with a grin.

"She did, Aunt Vi! I heard it. She said you were older than dirt." Tessa added.

"I did not!"

"She did too!"

I rolled my eyes and took my pilfered items to the café door.

"Best to schedule that date in person!" Tessa hollered.

"I am going to go speak with Daisy. We haven't chatted in a very long time."

I ignored the groans I heard from the girls as the door closed behind me. Daisy really was a wonderful person, but sometimes her mind took flights of fantasy to the extreme. It was hard to have a conversation with someone who immediately started talking about fairies in the middle of a conversation.

I walked down the main street of the town and watched as a few people made comments and pointed at me. I ignored them as I focused on Daisy's shop. The town could say what they wanted. It hadn't bothered me in the forty years that I have lived here, and I wouldn't let it bother me now. I opened the door to Herb Emporium and was greeted with the overwhelming scent of mint.

The Herb Emporium was situated on the corner of the building, similar in how my cafe was situated. When you walked through the door you were always hit with the scent of some herb or another. Today happened to be mint, which meant that Daisy had just received a fresh shipment. To the right of the door were four rows of racks. Each rack held prepackaged teas.

To the left of the door were bookshelves and racks of dried herbs, fresh herbs, mortal and pestles, tea pots, cups, diffusers, and anything else you could possibly imagine using to make tea. Running straight down the aisle was a shabby worn red carpet. Daisy usually chuckled that she gave the red-carpet treatment to all her customers. I walked straight down the aisles.

The counter was at the end of the red carpet on the left. This is where Daisy stood most days. She could see the whole store from here. In the wall behind the counter was the door to her storage and workroom. She would make her own concoctions back there. To the right was a small seating area. The Herb Emporium only sold teas and herbs, but the sitting area was only two tables and four chairs.

Unlike the cafe, Daisy only used this area when doing a reading for her customers. It was also a nice area for her customers to sit and chat with each other. Her tables were white wicker with glass tops. Her chairs were also white wicker with floral patterned cushions. The brighter the florals, the more likely Daisy was to purchase them. This week the cushions were vibrant orange with ruby red amaryllis designs. I focused my gaze on the counter where Daisy was hovering and staring out the window.

She was wearing an overly large peasant top that was cut from a large hibiscus flower pattern. Her long red hair was pulled up into two messy braids that she had wrapped around her head and tucked flowers into. I was pretty sure she was wearing a broomstick skirt and a pair of loafers behind that counter. Her green eyes sparkled as she caught sight of me in the doorway.

"Violet!" Daisy greeted. "It is always an experience when you come to my shop. What brings you here? Do we have a magical quest to go on?"

"No Daisy, not this time." I wanted to roll my eyes but forced myself to give her a pleasant smile instead. "I brought you a lovely tea and a piece of zucchini bread. I thought we might chat for a bit."

"I feel like there is more." Daisy walked around the counter and tilted her head to the side as if she was listening to someone else talk to her. She was, indeed, wearing a broomstick skirt in a lovely contrasting shade of florescent yellow. "Yes. I think she is here for a reading."

"I didn't..." I began. Daisy quieted me by raising her hand and turning her head once more.

"Yes." She nodded and then smiled. "Fortune favors you in the light of the full moon sister. Come, have a seat and let me toss the bones for you."

I sat her goodies on the counter and then settled into the wicker chair that was set in the corner by the back door. Daisy rummaged around in a cabinet for a moment then settled next to me. She had tugged a small folding table over and was shaking a black velvet bag vigorously. I watched as she whispered quietly to something off to her left and then smiled once more.

Daisy was having a conversation with someone I couldn't see. I closed my eyes, inhaled deeply, then sighed. Strange Daisy could make even me confused, but sometimes she could hit the truth on the head with her readings. I watched as she dumped the small bag on the table. She immediately gasped, her hands going to her mouth, her eyes wide in shock.

"Oh, my Goddess Violet!" Daisy screeched. "It is way too soon for your light to be extinguished. Mhmmm, oh what is this?" Daisy leaned closer to the rune stones that she had dropped. "I also see a very handsome man that shines brightly. Is he overpowering your light?"

"Daisy, I really need..."

"HUSH!" she snapped. "Her divine guidance cannot be interrupted. Yes, my lady. I see. There are forces at work that cannot be seen. A cloud of misfortune, another murder, and a mystery to be solved. Love and fortune come to those who can pierce the veil. Look to the one who is destitute but rich. The one who rarely speaks. He knows the truth. He will guide you. I fear your time is drawing nigh."

"Daisy." I murmured softly as she collapsed against the back of her chair. She had closed her eyes and was breathing heavily. I moved to check on her and she snapped her green eyes open with a cheerful smile.

"Violet! It is always a pleasure to have you come in. What brings you by the shop today? Shall we go on an adventure?"

"Not today, Daisy." I gave her a soft smile and patted her hand lightly. "I brought you some tea and a piece of zucchini bread. I was just hoping to chat with you."

"That sounds delightful." She clapped her hands in delight. "I think you need some sage, gingko biloba, and some cinnamon. Come, let's get those together while we chat."

I followed Daisy around her shop while she picked up the bags of the herbs. I had no idea what I would do with all of this, but if Daisy felt I needed it, I was pretty sure I might need at least one. After attempting to chat with her for thirty minutes, I paid for the herbs and disappeared quickly out the door. I had no clue what her reading was telling me. It was apparent that she had seen my death. The question that plagued me now was could I stop it? Who was the man that spoke very little? How could one be destitute but also rich? I shook my head and mumbled to myself that daffy Daisy was good at making my head spin.

The Mystic Brew Café grew closer in my sights as I wandered slowly down the sidewalk. I was within sight of the main door when I watched Steven amble into the shop. Dang it. I didn't really want to see him right now. I also didn't need to hear the girls pushing me to accept his offer of a date. I side stepped around the main street to the alley that ran behind the shop. Reggie was sitting on his sleeping bag. He was eating what appeared to be a cupcake and drinking the last of the cup of coffee that Serena had given him. He smiled at me, waved, then mumbled something about a hex as he motioned towards the backdoor. Whatever had sent him into a tailspin earlier seemed to have dissipated. He was his usual calm self.

I made a mental note to find a winter coat for him. The one he had was looking worn. I also noticed that his sleeping bag had seen better days. The back door to the Mystic Brew was propped open. That meant that Tessa was having an off day with her baking. She must have burned something and was currently airing out the shop.

I stepped closer to the back door and heard Steven's soft baritone as he chatted with Serena. Sitting down on the step, I decided to wait him out. How long could it take for a person to order coffee and a scone? Reggie glanced at me with a frown and then scratched his head before shuffling off. I could wait out here for a while. There was no need to rush inside, right?

Chapter Twelve

I had not completed my sun salutation for a couple of days. With all the things that had happened, it had not been the first thing on my mind. I was sitting in the alcove of the Mystic Brew with my face to the window. It was pouring rain, but I was still determined to greet the rising sun even if I couldn't enjoy it's warmth. I had avoided my nieces poking and prodding to call Steven. I had also been able to avoid him. It was a small victory on my part. I wasn't sure I could call it a victory though. I was having a bit of hottie withdrawal.

I could feel the moment the sun hit the horizon, and I was just beginning to relax when I heard boots clomping through the café. With each pounding step, I cringed. When those boot steps stopped just outside the alcove, I was hunched over until my ears almost touched my shoulders. So much for the relaxing energy I just received from the sun. I knew I wasn't going to like who I would see. Would it be Dr. Smalls or Cousin George? Shifting in my seat, I glanced over my shoulder.

"George." I greeted in a monotone voice. I still couldn't read him, and it set my teeth on edge. If it wasn't for the sneer on his face, I would have been blind to his intentions. "Are you here for some of my not so delicious coffee and scones? Or are you here to fling ultimatums at me like Dr. Smalls did?"

"Neither." He clomped into the space and dropped into the chair across from me like a rock in water.

"Then how may I help you?" It was disconcerting how much he looked like Steven.

"Steven is acting like a deranged psychopath. He is wandering around the house tossing a pretend ball and talking to a pretend dog. He has fed into the bullshit you have been feeding him about ghosts. You need to stop this...this..."

"This what?" I prompted with a grin. "Tell him that there is no such thing as ghosts? I am afraid I cannot do that. He is clearly being haunted by a very angry spirit."

"Then stop trying to be a cop. Stop trying to figure out who killed Victoria and let the real police do their job."

"You want me to allow Steven to be convicted of a crime he didn't commit?"

"No. I want the police to be able to do their job without a woman complicating everything." George sneered at her and rolled his eyes. He inhaled deeply, closed his eyes for a moment, then let out that breath on a quick huff. "Look, my thoughts on you aside, I think Victoria deserves her killer brought to justice."

I studied George closely as he made this statement. He was looking at his hands which were clasped on the table. He was rubbing his thumb against the back of his hand. His body was leaning towards me, and his gaze was focused on something down and to his left. This was the posture of a man who was hiding something. I took a sip of my coffee, leaned back in my chair, and thought about what Steven had shared a few weeks ago about George stealing his girlfriend.

"Were you close with Victoria, George?" I inquired softly as his eyes snapped in my direction. "Is that the reason you don't want me investigating this? You think your cousin killed Victoria because he knew you were sleeping with her and decided that you shouldn't have her?"

"You..." he snarled. "You have no idea what the hell you are talking about."

"True. I have not been able to read your aura from the moment I met you. It leaves me clueless as to what your true nature is. Steven has given me his insight into your relationship with him. That is all I know, but I feel as if you are upset with Victoria's death. Why would you be upset, George? You had to be close to her in some way for this to make you so angry."

"Do you even know..."

"Know?" I tilted my head and gave him a confused glance. "I think I already established that I don't know. I know just as much as everyone in this town. I know a woman was murdered. I know that you and Steven both look identical. I also know that the police seem to think Steven murdered her. I see no reason why he should be the one in the cross hairs for this. You also make a perfect murder suspect. You know all the same people that Steven knows, you were probably at the same party where Victoria and Steven hooked up, and..."

"They did what?" George shouted as he shot out of the chair. "Who told you that they hooked up?"

"Steven." I frowned and tilted my head as he began to pace in the small confines of the alcove. He brushed up against the beaded curtain, making them click and clack. It appeared that I was correct in assuming that George and Victoria were an item. "He explained that he had gotten uncharacteristically drunk, and she made a pass at him. When he woke in the morning, he couldn't remember anything."

"When was this?"

"I have no idea. He just said it was during a party."

"I think he is mistaken." George tried to calm himself by rubbing his hands together as he turned to her. "I was at that same party. He did get trashed. Victoria did make a pass at him, but she thought he was me. Steven didn't sleep with her. He can't remember them sleeping together because he didn't sleep with her. I slept with her. We ended up in his bed. When Steven finally passed out, he had fallen into the bed next to us. I let him sleep it off because it was his bed. I figured we would be gone in the morning before he even woke up. I had an early appointment the next day and was gone around four in the morning. Victoria must have still been asleep when Steven finally woke."

"Ah...I see." I motioned to the chair and watched as he finally settled back down. "George, are you sure I can't get you a cup of coffee or maybe a tea to help settle your nerves?"

"I don't want any of that..." he looked at her and saw the raised brow. With a hefty sigh, he shook his head and began tapping a thumb against the tabletop. "Thank you for the offer, but no. What I want is for you to promise to stay out of this investigation and allow the police to find who truly killed Victoria."

"You loved her, didn't you?" I murmured softly as I placed my hand over his. I caught no visions, no images, and no feelings from this man. I was blind in all the ways of my gift, and it was frightening. George flinched and I pulled my hand back. "I cannot promise to stay out of this George."

"WHY?" he demanded angrily.

"I am personally tangled up in this murder in some way. I have seen my own death, and it is at the hands of the same man who killed Victoria. I will not allow him to take my life."

"That is nonsense. You couldn't..." George looked her straight in the eye and hesitated. He crossed his arms over his chest and studied her just as she had studied him earlier. "Alright. Then at least get Steven out of the house. He has been stuck in there for the last few weeks and refuses to come out no matter what I say."

"I will see what I can do." I nodded at him as he stood and left the shop.

George had been in love with Victoria. Steven was innocent of sleeping with Victoria. I wasn't sure why that made my chest feel lighter. I turned and watched the gloomy day outside as I digested this new information. If George had been in love with Victoria, then he wouldn't have killed her. I was sure that Steven hadn't killed her. Who did that leave? Who would have motive to want Steven or even George in jail?

I took a sip of my cold coffee and looked at the scene outside my window. People were still buying newspapers from the faded old blue newspaper machine. It was like they needed to know the latest information on this small-town murder because their life depended on it. I wasn't sure what they thought they would get from the same information being spat out in a million different ways. I watched as Dr. Smalls paused in front of the machine and glanced at the paper. He raised a brow, looked around, then noticed me in the window. His eyes narrowed for a moment before he continued down the street.

There had to be something about the Raven Estate that tied into the murder of Victoria. Steven was being dragged into this for a reason. Was there a hidden fortune on the estate? Was there something in the house? Was it just merely a ploy to make the town look the other way? I wasn't sure what the answers were, but I had to find out.

George wanted me to get Steven out of the house. That made me suspicious that it had something to do with the Raven Estate. I narrowed my gaze as a light popped on inside my head. Steven had not been by in the last week to tell me that the angry spirit had attacked him again. Nothing I had done would have calmed that spirit. If I did indeed take Steven out of the house, would the spirit become aggravated again?

"Girls!" I shouted into the cafe as I spun around in my seat. I watched as they ducked under the beaded curtain. "We have work to do."

"What type of work?" Tessa inquired with a raised brow and a narrowed gaze. Serena studied me for a moment before her face split into a grin. She began to bounce up and down on her feet.

"We are going shopping!" Serena announced as she clapped her hands. "Steven is going to fall all over himself when he gets a look at you, Aunty Vi."

"What?" Tessa was off guard for a moment before it dawned on her. "You are going hunting?"

"Yes." I replied dryly as a plan began to form in my mind. I was going hunting for an angry spirit, but to get the girls involved, I had to have a better motive. "This time I am hunting a man and not a ghost. I need you girls to whip me into shape."

"This is so exciting!" Serena beamed as she immediately ran from the alcove for her purse. I looked at my two excited nieces and began to wonder if I had made the right sort of plan.

Chapter Thirteen

There comes a point in every old woman's life that she must make a decision. She either becomes that frumpy old witch that has thirteen cats, or she gives up on the comfort of her jeans and t-shirts for the sake of landing a man. I was now entering this stage of my life and was greatly regretting it. I had recruited my nieces to show me how to make myself look more appealing to the opposite sex.

Six layers of make-up, ten coats of hairspray, and some full body compression undergarments had me prepared for the worst torture ever. I was encased in a layer of black polyester and then propped up on some black strappy heels. I didn't really have the nerve to tell them this was all a ploy.

"You look gorgeous, Aunt Vi!" Tessa sighed as she took in the masterpiece that her and Serena had made. "If that man doesn't have a heart attack when he sees you, then he is an idiot."

"This will complete the look!" Serena smiled as she handed her a hand clutch made of red sequin.

"Baby girl, I don't carry anything other than my phone..." I began.

"It is just for looks, Aunty Vi." Serena rolled her eyes. "Besides, you look stunning. I am not sure what exactly you are planning because I am not sensing anything in the way of romance from you, but I hope it works."

"It is going to be very hard for me to get anything past you two now that your powers are growing." I swiped a curl out of my eyes and sighed. "I am going hunting tonight for the killer. I am hoping that by getting Steven out of the house, I will get a clue."

"That makes absolutely no sense Aunt Vi." Tessa grumbled and rolled her eyes. "I guess I should say good hunting then."

I hugged both the girls and then stepped out to my car. I had just stepped off the porch when I heard a strangled gasp. I glanced up quickly and felt my heart hammering in my chest. As if by some miracle, Steven had appeared at my house. He had a pizza in one hand and a bouquet in the other. My first instinct was to gape at him in stunned silence as I tried to reason out why he was here and how in the hell he knew where I lived. My second instinct kicked in and kept my charade together.

I straightened, tilted my head to the side, and gave him a soft smile as I glanced at the car and then back to him. I wanted to seem impatient instead of shocked. I wanted him to think I had somewhere I needed to be. I wanted him to see me as a highly sought after woman. Let's face it though, I was just a small-time gal who owned a coffee shop. I wasn't really anyone special, but I wanted him to think that I was.

"Violet..." Steven gasped as he fumbled the pizza box. "I am sorry, I probably should have called."

"That would have been a little difficult since you don't have my phone number." I remarked with a smirk.

"Right, yeah..." he shuffled for a moment and then did another sweep of my body. That one glance sent my body into a tailspin. I was warm everywhere. Keeping my cool, I glanced at my car again and shifted my empty clutch from one hand to the other. "Uh, George gave me your address and suggested maybe I should apologize."

"Apologize?" I scrunched my face up in thought. "What do you have to apologize for?"

"I..." Steven cleared his throat and then straightened himself up as well. He did another sweeping glance of me before looking towards the house. "I don't know that I have anything to apologize for. I just...accepted it as a reason to come and see you."

"I see." My heart jumped rope in my chest at his admission, and I gave him a soft smile. "As fantastic as that is, I am afraid I have somewhere I need to be. Can we do a raincheck on that delightful pizza?"

"Raincheck, right?" He gave me a soft smile as he half turned away. "I will..."

"I'll take that!" Serena hollered as she ran down the steps and snatched the pizza from his hand. "Aunty Vi appreciates the flowers too! I'll make sure to put them in a vase for her."

"Bye Aunty Vi. Drive safe!" Tessa hollered from the porch as she gave a girly little wave. "Knock them dead."

"Good luck..." Steven remarked with a deep swallow. "I hope you have a fantastic night."

"Steven," I replied with a quick swallow of my own. "I could use a date, if you are interested. Care to accompany me?"

"I wouldn't be dressed appropriately."

"Nonsense!" I wrapped my free hand through his arm and lead him to my car. He was wearing a pair of black loafers, black slacks, and a baby blue button down. He was dressed more appropriately for where I was heading than I was. I tried to hide my smile as he glanced at me again from the side of his eyes. "You are dressed perfectly. Trust me."

Steven climbed into the vehicle, and I walked around to get behind the wheel. I pulled out of the drive and headed into town. The quiet in the car made dread fill me for a moment. I must be out of my mind if I thought this plan was going to work. I parked in the library lot and watched as Steven looked around confused. It was six at night and the library was closed for the evening. He turned to me as I wrapped my hand through his arm once more.

"The library?" he questioned as he took in the sight of me in my little black dress.

"The library. I have an appointment with a certain head librarian."

"You meet all head librarians dressed like this?"

"No." I gave a throaty laugh that had him tugging me closer to his body. "I must make the girls happy every now and then. They think I am heading out on a date. This is their idea of playing dress up. I didn't have the heart to tell them that my dinner date was a fifty-year-old woman named Gertie."

"I see." Steven laughed heartily. I knocked on the library door and was rewarded when she popped her head out.

"Violet, my dear! Please come in. Oh, hello there."

"Gertie, this is Steven Smalls. He is new in town."

"Actually, back in town is the correct term." Steven remarked as he shook hands with Gertie. "I lived here when I was a child. I just recently moved back to town."

"It is a pleasure Mr. Smalls. Please forgive me, my memory isn't what it used to be."

"Steven, please."

Gertie nodded and then swept her hand toward the back of the library. "Please come with me. Sadie said you had some questions on the town history. I have dinner in the back already set up. We can eat and chat."

"Thank you again for taking the time to speak with me." I answered as we settled around the small table in the back room. Gertie had ordered up a platter of sandwiches from the local deli. I settled one on the plate in front of me and then eased back as much as my compression underwear would allow. "Steven just recently moved into the Raven Estate. I was trying to do some research on the place but came up empty. The house appears to be over 100 years old, right around the time the town was founded, but I still can't seem to find any information on it. Sadie had said that you might have something."

"Raven Estate?" Gertie scrunched up her forehead. She picked up a pickle, took a bite, then munched away for a moment. "I have never heard of the Raven Estate."

"That is impossible..." Steven remarked in shock. He sat his sandwich back on his plate without taking a bite. "I live in Raven Manor. How could you not know about it? Like Vi said, it has been here for almost 100 years."

"I am sorry." Gertie held her hands up. "I have never heard of it. Now, unless you want to talk about one of the old historic buildings, I am unable to help."

"It is alright Gertie." I leaned forward and patted her softly on the arm. "It was a long shot, but I thought I would try. Can you tell me anything about the Small's family? I tried to look up their history in the census, but I couldn't find anything."

"I am afraid you have me stumped on that one. I have never heard of the Small's family." Gertie scratched in frustration at her cheek and then sighed. "I fear that I am not going to be able to help as much as I thought. My memory...it just seems to be disappearing."

"That is alright. I hear that you went on vacation last week. Did you go anywhere interesting?"

I listened to Gertie as she explained how she had made a trip to Salem. I tuned out most of what she had said. This was the second time Steven had mentioned that he was returning to the town and not new to the town. If he had lived in the town when he was a child, why did no one seem to recognize him. I took a small bite of the sandwich and chewed as Steven asked Gertie a question and kept up the conversation for me.

Gertie's memory was never faulty. The woman was always sharp. She was not only the head librarian. She was also the town historian. If her memory was failing her, it was because something was interfering with it. I had a sneaky suspicion that something more sinister was happening, but I could not grasp what it was.

The Raven Estate had been around for 100 years or longer. There seemed to be no records anywhere in the library. The only two people in the town that would know about the estate both said they knew nothing about it. That left me only one option to explore. I would have to go to the city offices and see if anyone could pull records on the place.

If the city records provided me with nothing, I had no other clues to look for. We finished eating and thanked Gertie for her time before ducking out of the library and walking to my car. I climbed inside without much conversation and started the vehicle. I was halfway to Steven's house when he cleared his throat and got my attention. I glanced at him for a moment and gave him a soft smile.

"Thank you for carrying on the conversation."

"You are very welcome. You looked deep in thought. I am sure it is the same thing I have been thinking. How in the world could no one in town know about the estate or our family?"

"Exactly what I was thinking." I pulled into the drive and pulled down to the servant entrance to the manor and turned the car off.

"Well, my lady..." he whispered as he grasped my hand on the console. I felt the energy that moved between us. "What do you plan to do next?"

"I am so glad that you asked..." I giggled like a schoolgirl as I grasped his hand back. I tugged him close and gave him a soft sweet kiss on the lips. "You are going to love this part."

"I can't wait..." he murmured against my mouth as he kissed me again. His hands dipped into the fancy hairdo the girls had created. I felt a few pins as they fell out and then didn't care. I was in control of this, right? I enjoyed his kiss for a moment and then pulled away. He groaned, eased back in the seat, but then pulled me closer once more for another kiss. I was gasping hard when he released me. "Lead on my lady. I guess our mission now has to do with my house, otherwise I am sure you would have driven me to your place to get my car."

"You are right." I sighed. If I had known kissing could be so pleasurable, I wouldn't have turned down the three offers for a date I had received a long time ago. I had to wonder if kissing was like this with everyone or was it just Steven. My senses were overloaded with that leather and spice scent. Inhaling deeply, I opened the door and stepped out of the vehicle. I waited as Steven unlocked the door, and we stepped inside. "You said you have a state-of-the-art security system. Can you check for me and see if it has been turned off today? I mean, when you haven't turned it off?"

"Uh..." he frowned but glanced at the pantry. "Yeah, just a moment." He stepped into the pantry, then returned a moment later and shook his head. "No, it has only been turned off when I did it."

"Damn."

I frowned, leaned against the counter, and sighed. I tugged in annoyance at the dress where it was pressing into a very annoyed section of my side. I kicked off the torture heels and stood there lost deep in thought. My hunch was that George or Randolph was taking advantage of Steven being out of the house. That would give me a lead into which one I should focus on. I also felt that one or the other was sneaking into the house and annoying the spirit. Since the alarm had not been turned off, I had no clue what was annoying her. The only explanation I had left was Steven.

I scratched again at the annoying section of my dress and then felt electricity crawl through my veins when Steven placed his warm hand on my shoulder. I turned and he handed me a stack of clothes. His cheeks were flushed, and he darted his gaze away for a moment. Frowning, I looked up at him.

"While I find you smoking hot in that little black dress, I am sure it is not at all comfortable. You can change into these while you continue to think and plan our next steps."

"Thank you..." I murmured as I stepped around him to the vacant room on this floor. I changed quickly into the sweats and t-shirt. I padded softly back out to the kitchen and found him drinking in the sight of me again. His eyes swept from my hair to my feet and then back again. I watched as he clenched his hands and stuffed them in his pockets. "Wow…I look that horrible in your clothes?" I teased him as I dropped my dress in a heap with my torture heels.

"Violet, if I was raised differently, I would be pressing you up against that counter and kissing you senseless right now. You look even better in sweats and my t-shirt than you did in that dress. Alas, I was raised a proper gentleman." He gave her a pink cheeked smile as he handed her a bottle of water. He cleared his throat and settled onto the barstool. "Those gears have been turning in that head of yours. What are you planning?"

"I had thought that we would have a clue tonight. Since my first guess was wrong…"

"The security system?" he nodded, taking a sip of his own bottle of water.

"Let us move on to my next gut feeling." I took a swig of my water, blushed furiously, and gave him a smile. "How do you feel about a sleep over?"

Chapter Fourteen

"Asleep over?" Steven swallowed hard as he stared at me with an open mouth. I could see him swallow hard once more. "You and me? Or were you going to invite your nieces, my cousin, and my brother?"

"You and I." I cleared my throat and tapped my fingers lightly against the counter. "I have a two-fold plan tonight. I am sure it is not what you are thinking, though. I am beginning to suspect that my family is not the only family in this town with gifts."

"You think my family has gifts?"

"Well, you did make the remark about being aliens and wiping the town's memory."

"Right. Why didn't I think about the alien thing?" he frowned and gave her a look.

"Hear me out. If your family has some type of gift like mine, then it is possible someone along your history has done something to make the town forget about your family. It also makes sense that no one in the town knows anything about this house even though it sits on several acres and can't be missed. I never would have noticed this place if you hadn't invited me over and my niece hadn't programmed the address into my GPS."

I watched as he fidgeted with the bottle of water as he studied my face. He was looking deep into my eyes as if he could read my thoughts. I gazed right back and found myself lost in those hypnotic brown orbs of his. I swallowed hard as he leaned closer to me. His intoxicating scent was everywhere in this house and it intensified the closer he got. I was finding it difficult to remember what my plan had been. Clearing my throat, I stepped back, giving me a little space and watched as he shook his head slightly and nodded in understanding.

"What is this sleepover going to entail? Shall I find some extra pillows and blankets to make a fort in the living room?" he teased quietly as he too, took a step back.

"Let's play with magic." I grinned as I took a swig of water from the bottle he had given me. "I want to see if you have any abilities. First, I am going to need my bag from the car."

Steven was kind enough to grab my bag. I moved us into the living room and cleared a nice large space on the floor. I set up five white pillar candles in the space, making note of each of the cardinal direction points. The fifth I placed in front of me as I settled into the middle. I had Steven sit across from me as I pulled out a small smudge stick and a small bowl. I made sure my bag was nearby in case I needed other things.

"This is going to be fairly boring." I lit the smudge stick and allowed it to burn for a moment before blowing it out. "I am doing a small cleansing ritual to purify the space. We don't want any negative spirits or energies to interrupt us."

I waved my hands over the smoke and brushed it over Steven to cleanse him. I repeated the process several times as I chanted in my mind. I wasn't looking for any major revelations tonight, otherwise I would have done more to cleanse the space. I repeated the smoke cleansing with myself and grinned as Steven's new resident dog appeared and settled peacefully into the leg basket I had made by sitting on the floor.

With the space and ourselves cleansed, I stubbed out the smudge stick and closed my eyes. I put my intentions out to the general ether. We wanted to find out what type of powers or abilities Steven had and if they were hidden, we wanted to bring them forth. Putting things out into the ether was risky if you didn't give exact specifications of what you want. I was slowly opening my eyes when Steven cleared his throat.

"Am I supposed to be doing something?" He whispered so softly that I almost missed it.

"No." I spoke in my normal voice and found that it sounded almost inhumanly loud. "I was cleansing the negative and speaking our intentions. We can start."

"Great. What do we do first?"

"Normally, at this age, you would already know if you had abilities. I have a sneaky suspicion that someone bound your powers. The cleansing will help loosen that binding. With no idea how to begin, we are going to cycle through everything." I grabbed a small purple velvet bag from my case, much like the bag that Daisy had used with me and handed it to him. He shook the bag, opened it, and dropped the small violet stones onto the floor. The rune stones flickered from the light of the candles. I watched him closely and sighed. "Ok, next one."

"That's it?" he frowned. "Shouldn't you tell me how to read these?"

"No." I winked. "You'd already know how to read them. It is instinctive." I pulled out a deck of cards as he swept the stones back into the back. "Shuffle, cut, and pull out a few cards."

"But we..."

"Trust me..."

Steven shrugged, shuffled the deck, then settle a few cards on the floor. He studied each card intently and then looked at me with a half shrug. He picked the cards back up as I pulled another item from my bag. This was a small cone shaped stone on a three-inch chain of silver. I placed a small map of the town on the floor and handed him the stone.

He looked at it for a moment before holding it above the map by the chain. No vibrations from the chain or stone so I sighed and pulled out another item. It was a small flat disk of black obsidian. He admired the beauty of the item as I placed it on the floor in front of him. He stared deeply into it and began making silly faces.

This was getting us nowhere. I tried to hide my annoyance at the fact that nothing was happening. I pulled out a small white plastic bowl and filled it with water. Tiger jumped from my lap and ran to the bowl, acting as if she was getting a drink, then settled onto Steven's lap. Steven looked at the bowl and sighed once more when nothing happened.

He reached down to pick up the bowl. The moment his finger touched the water inside, his body locked up and he froze. For a moment those brown eyes glazed over, and he disappeared into his mind. When he returned, he looked at me in shock.

Steven slowly lowered the bowl to the floor. Tiger ran to the bowl, barked silently at it a couple of times while wagging her tail, then ran in circles before disappearing. She reappeared with her ball in her mouth and looked up at Steven with a hopeful look. He patted her head as best he could since she wasn't corporeal and then closed his gaping mouth. He grabbed his water bottle and gulped down the contents. Afterwards, he rose from the floor, stepped over to the fireplace and lit the firewood that was stacked inside. Once the flames were stoked and licking around nicely, he turned back to me with firm resolve.

"I have abilities then."

"Seems you do. What did you see?" I hoped with everything in my being that he had seen the killer or even some clue to who that killer may be. I hoped he was seeing the murders like me. That way we could pool our visions and come away with a bigger picture. I watched his cheeks turn a dark shade of scarlet under his olive tone and knew instantly he wasn't seeing the murders.

"Let me just say that I understand why you have been avoiding me like the plague."

Great. Steven was having the same erotic visions I had been having of him. I glanced down at my lumpy out of shape body and sighed. He was embarrassed to see those images. He probably couldn't imagine himself with someone of my size. I stood from the floor in the most graceful way possible. Ok, honestly, not graceful. I rolled onto my knees and pushed up from the floor. I wasn't sure what I was doing, other than getting out of his sight. The man may have kissed me a couple of times, but there was no way he was attracted to me now that he had seen me in my full naked glory. I had stooped to grab my bag from the floor when his hands caught my forearms and turned me to face him.

Those damn wide chocolate brown eyes of his starred deep into my soul as he gently cupped my cheek and brushed his thumb over my jaw. Before I could utter a word or even move, his lips claimed mine. The soft feel of his lips pressed gently against mine stole my breath. Emotions swept through my body, warming my chilled skin, flooding my senses. His arms wrapped around my waist as he deepened the kiss, pressing more firmly, his tongue sweeping against the seam of my mouth. When I thought I couldn't take it anymore, my arms had wrapped around his shoulders, and my mouth opened to his probing. Wow!

To say that a simple pressing of lips to lips had been enough to rock my world a few days ago, now paled in comparison to the feel of his tongue as it swept against my open bottom lip and then deeper into my mouth. I stood there like a frozen doll as I hesitantly thrust my tongue into his mouth. Our tongues collided and I felt as if a volcano had erupted in my lower extremities. This man could definitely kiss. I felt a phantom pawing at my leg and regretfully pulled out of Steven's embrace. Tiger was cowering behind my leg and pawing at the fabric of the sweats. If she had been solid and alive, I am sure I would hear her whining.

"Right..." Steven cleared his throat and took a step back with a deep breath. "We have work to do. I apologize for that."

"No apology needed." I tipped my gaze to the floor knowing I had wanted to react in a similar fashion when I first met him after my visions. With as hot as I felt as this moment, I was sure my cheeks were flaming red. "Uh, Tiger...what is wrong sweetie pie?"

We both looked at Tiger as she took a cowering step back from my leg. She was looking at the fireplace and opening and closing her snout. Frowning, I glanced at the crackling fire in confusion. The wooden surround and mantle were hand carved and gorgeous. The stacked stones of the chimney were expertly laid. The hearth was made from some expensive type of stone I didn't recognize. There didn't seem to be anything wrong with the spot. Closing my eyes for a second, I glanced over at the fireplace once more. Nothing. Tiger silently whined once more and then disappeared.

"That was weird." Steven wrinkled his forehead and raised one of those perfect shaped brows in my direction. I nodded and wrapped my arms across my stomach.

"Yes, but now that we have found your ability, I say it is on to step two."

"I am still not sure what my abilities are." Steven pushed his two old fashioned Victorian wingback chairs away from the walls and nearer to the fireplace. He settled into one and motioned for me to join him. "Does this mean I have the sight, like you?"

"Yes, and your abilities will manifest as you need them now that your block is gone." I watched as he reacted to that. "Someone had inhibited your powers. That is another reason I did the cleansing spell. It helped break up the block and allow your abilities through. The more you use your abilities the more your abilities will surface." I closed my eyes and leaned my head back against the chair. I listened to the soothing sounds of the pop and crack of the fire as I inhaled the smell of wood smoke, leather, and musk. I wasn't going to get any sleep tonight. "I am exhausted and in order to get step two into motion, we should probably head off to bed."

"Bed..." he murmured. His voice dropped into a sexy smoldering sound that vibrated in my bones. Steeling myself, I cracked open one eye and nodded.

"You head off to bed. I'll watch over you tonight."

"I thought you said you were exhausted," he teased as he rose from the chair. "There is a guest room."

"I probably sho..."

"Come on, you said you were exhausted." Steven tugged me out of the chair and led us up the small staircase in the kitchen. His bedroom was on the left side of the hall. He opened the door on the right, and I glanced inside with a loud hearty laugh. The guest room was empty. Grasping my sides, I looked up at him and laughed. I had been here earlier in the month and hadn't seen any furniture except for in his room. I wasn't sure why I didn't remember that. "What?" he teased.

"You have a guest bedroom with no bed. That doesn't exactly scream comforting to me."

Steven gave me a seductive smile as he opened his bedroom door and motioned with his head. "I said I have a guest bedroom. I didn't say it was furnished. I have this huge bed. Your exhausted and tired. Climb in. I promise to be a proper gentleman. Otherwise, it is the lumpy sofa downstairs in the living room. Being that I am a gentleman, if you insist on sleeping down there, I will have to sacrifice a good night's sleep and sleep there myself."

I swallowed hard as he tugged me closer. His mouth brushed against my ear as he spoke, and I felt tiny explosions of shivers along my nerves. "I am very cranky if I must sleep on that uncomfortable couch. Help a man out and at least enjoy the comfort of the bed tonight."

"With you..." I stammered. My hand where he gripped it was sweating and clammy. I could feel my heart beating out a passionate rhythm against my chest.

"With me...on the other side. I'll even build a fortress of pillows between us if that makes you more comfortable."

"The fire..." I attempted one last time in a feeble attempt to keep my distance. I knew that if I gave in to the temptation of even just lying next to this man, I would never recover. I would begin to finally believe that someone would want this lumpy-boring-plain-me. "Someone should watch it...you should never leave a fire unattended."

"I'll take care of the fire." His lips brushed against my cheek as his hands lightly stroked my arms. "Sleep in a comfortable bed tonight Violet."

My heart clenched hard in my chest at the sound of my name on his lips. I quickly forgot all the reasons I shouldn't agree to this and nodded my head slightly. He sighed. It sounded like it was a sigh of pleasure, but I couldn't know that for sure. I had never heard such a sound. My whole body tingled as he pushed me gently into the room. When I turned around, he had disappeared.

I assumed he was banking the fire for the night. I would be wrong. He reappeared in front of me holding eight pillows. I was amazed at how quickly this man could make my body respond to a heated passionate kiss and then turn around and make me laugh. Laughter was all I could do as I helped him build a fortress of pillows down the middle of the bed. This time, he disappeared and was gone for several minutes. When he returned, he clapped his hands, smiled, and motioned towards the bed.

"Pick a side, my Goddess."

"That's a little personal, don't you think..." I teased him with a grin. "I mean we have barely known each other for a month and already you want to know what side I prefer to sleep on?"

"You like to sleep on the right side, facing the left..." he rumbled deeply.

Bang. Just like that. The damn man had taken me from passionate, to teasing, back to passionate. I felt the temperature in the room rise a hundred degrees. "I...how do you..."

"I don't know..." he tilted his head and crinkled his forehead again. "Take the right-side Violet. I can sleep on either side."

I crawled into the bed on the right and snuggled under the massive blanket. I was still slightly chilled from wearing that stupid tight black dress that I had the girls dress me in. My eyes grew heavy quickly with the scent of Steven filling my senses. I was just slipping off to dreamland when I felt the bed jiggle and shift.

The pillow that was between our heads disappeared and a I heard a soft wump as it hit the floor. I could see Steven, and he was lying on his side looking at me. Giving him a soft smile, I closed my eyes and dropped down into blissful comfortable sleep with visions of Steven wrapping his arms around me and pulling me close. It was the first time I had felt safe in a very long time.

Chapter Fifteen

Putrid decaying flesh. Grimy touch and feelings of malice filled my senses. Slowly I dragged myself out of sleep. I was lying on my back staring at a white ceiling that was unfamiliar. Inhaling deep, I coughed as the smell of decay filled my lungs. I struggled to pull my arms up and rub my eyes. I couldn't move. I was frozen to the spot. I darted my gaze around the room, looking for a reason I was paralyzed. From the corner of my eyes, I saw Steven sleeping soundly.

Damn, was I dreaming or was I awake? I sucked in another fetid breath. Another brief glance showed me Tiger. She was sitting on Steven's chest and barking furiously, albeit silently. I was able to tweak my head ever so slightly and look down a little further. Steven had moved a few more pillows last night and one arm was snaked around my waist. That was when I noticed the temperature difference. I was warm across the stomach where his arm was holding me. The rest of my body was frozen like a block of ice, even under the warm covers. I tried to open my mouth and holler, but I couldn't.

A portly man, with thinning black hair, a large handlebar mustache, and black eyes floated in front of me. He gave me a smile that showed his gleaming white teeth. That smile quickly sank deep into my stomach and made my body temp drop even more. Pressure against my arms and legs made my heart begin to race. My arms were flung out to the side and my legs were splayed wide open. My arm had been moved so forcefully that it smacked

Steven in the face. He woke up sputtering as he stared at me in shock.

I tried to move my arms, my fingers, my feet. Anything. I needed to break the grip this spirit had on me. I watched as the floating man moved closer to me. His mouth opened and pressed against mine. The smell of decay became so strong I wanted to gag. I successfully made a sound somewhere between a cough and a moan. The blankets that had been covering me were flung off. The comfortable t-shirt that I had borrowed last night was shoved up my body, exposing my bare flesh. I felt the grimy touch against my chest and breasts.

My cheeks flamed red as I realized what was happening. I was being felt up by a ghost. This couldn't possibly be happening. I had never heard of a ghost that could do something like this. His grimy touch began to slither down my ribs to my stomach and lower. Goddess help me if he tugged those sweats off me, I would die on the spot. I caught movement from the side of my eye once more. I tried again to move any part of my body. I thought I moved my hand as Steven returned to my side vision.

I had no clue what he had just done, but that disgusting ghost disappeared in a flash. I heard a soft crack sound, a feminine scream, then felt my body hit the bed. My body twitched. Glancing to the side, I noticed the clock on Steven's bedside table. It was three in the morning. My gaze darted back to Steven who was standing next to my side of the bed. He was clutching the selenite I had given him a week or so ago. It was now broken into two pieces. I watched as he panted in fear, glanced down at me, then averted his gaze.

Realizing I was half naked, I yanked the t-shirt down to cover my body, pulled the covers up to my chest, and closed my eyes as I panted as well. I was so out of my league on this. I had never in my entire life heard of a ghost that could physically touch a living person. I knew they could interact with non-living items, but never a living being.

I rolled onto my side, curled into a fetal position, and shuddered. A moment later and I felt a large warm presence wrap around me as Steven hugged me in his arms. He was still gripping the selenite, and I wrapped my hand around his. I would be lying if I said I didn't enjoy his warm body wrapped around mine. I would also be lying if I said I noticed, cause at that moment, all I could think of was that grimy touch against my body and that weird open-mouthed kiss.

Neither of us spoke. Tiger reappeared in the bed and nudged me with her ethereal little nose before curling up and falling asleep next to my head. The shock slowly wore off and I slid back off to sleep somewhere around five in the morning. When I woke again, it was around eight. I was still curled up against Steven and we were clutching that selenite in our hands. I knew Steven was awake. How, I am not sure, but when I rolled in his arms, he was looking down at me. I could see regret, fear, and something else. Swallowing, I dipped my gaze to his chest and inhaled deeply.

"I think..." I cleared my throat as my voice warbled. "I think I need to get up and head into the cafe. The girls..."

"I am sure the girls are fine..." he murmured softly. His voice was gruff and oh so damn sexy this morning. "I am more worried about you. Tiger woke me around six this morning. Then again at seven."

I nodded in understanding as he tugged me closer. I moved to pull out of his grip and then decided I didn't care anymore. After last night, I was going to take every ounce of comfort

I could get. I shuddered once more as I thought about those touches. I didn't think it was possible, but he tucked me even tighter against his chest.

We laid in bed like that for at least another hour before we relaxed enough to slowly crawl out. I noticed a blush slowly creeping up his face as my thoughts slowly turned to other things we could do in this large bed. With his new abilities, Steven might just be a little bit empathic. Now my cheeks were beet red as I thought about him picking up on my thoughts. Clearing my throat, I moved towards the door.

"I can get you another set of sweats and a t-shirt if you would like..." he murmured softly. "Then you don't have to put that dress back on...unless you just want to. I can help zip it up if you need me too."

"It took three of us to shove my flabby body into that thing." I tilted my head back in laughter. My frozen body slowly began to warm back to normal temperature. "I would appreciate a loan if you don't mind."

"Of course..." he nodded as he moved to the dresser by the door. He grabbed a shirt and a pair of sweats and handed them over. He cleared his throat, leaned against the wall, crossed his arms and smiled. "The bathroom is down the hall. You get cleaned up and I will get us something for breakfast. Sound good?"

"It sounds perfect, yes. Thank you."

I scampered as quickly into the bathroom as I could. It was embarrassing enough that he had seen me half naked. Ok, he had seen my bare body twice now. Three if you count his vision last night. I cringed as I ran the hottest shower I could stand. I scrubbed my body down with Steven's body wash and groaned inwardly. I was going to smell like his leather and spice scent all day. I might just have to pop over to my place and shower again before going to the cafe. I paused halfway through shampooing my hair.

The girls had dressed me up in the hot black dress last night under my pretense that I was going to go get my man. It had been a slight lie on my part. The man I had hoped to get was a killer. If I showed up wearing his sweats and t-shirt and smelling like his body wash and shampoo, the girls would lay off on the extreme urges to get me hitched to a man. At least I hoped this would work in my favor.

Clean, or at least as clean as a shower could make me, I dressed in the sweats and shirt and ambled downstairs to the kitchen. The delectable smell of scrambled eggs, bacon, and coffee assaulted my senses. I settled down at the kitchen table as Steven brought me a plate of food and a cup of coffee. Sighing with pleasure, I devoured the food and drank down the coffee.

"I am going to grab a shower myself. I'll be right back..." he offered as he placed his empty dishes in the sink. He placed the broken pieces of selenite on the table next to me. "Just in case."

While I knew Steven worked out, since he had the most impressive set of biceps I had seen, I was sure he wasn't strong enough to snap this piece of selenite in two with his bare hands. That meant the selenite had done the job and protected us from negative energies. I shuddered to think of how far that spirit would have gone if Steven hadn't temporarily banished it. Now that it had worked magic, the rock was useless for protection. I tossed the pieces in the trash can and retrieved my bag from the living room.

Down in the very bottom was another smaller piece of selenite. I fished it out and clutched it to my chest for a moment. This was my last piece. I didn't usually stock up on these items. Let's face it. In a small town like mine, I didn't usually need protection from a negative spirit or energy. When Steven reappeared in the kitchen, dressed, I handed him the new piece. He tucked it into the pocket of his jeans and picked up my bag. I needed to drop him off at my place and then head over to the cafe. Remembering my phone, I fished it out of the bag and checked the messages.

[Way to go Aunty Vi! Enjoy that man and don't worry about coming in. We've got this!]

I rolled my eyes as we climbed into my car. Leave it to Tessa to send a text like that. Serena's text was a little more frightful.

[What the hell happened last night? I feel violated. This can't be right.]

I dropped Steven off at my place so he could get his vehicle, then I went directly to the cafe. The girls immediately rushed to me and hugged me tight. My heart warmed to know they cared about me. Once they were assured that I was in one piece, they stepped back and took in the sight. I felt myself blushing again and sighed as Tessa smirked and went to fetch me a cup of coffee.

I glanced around the cafe and felt my heart sink. The place had been dead for the last few days, and I wasn't sure why. I opened my mouth to ask a question when Steven entered behind me. The girls looked at him, their mouths dropped open, then Serena rushed to get him a cup of coffee as well.

"Spill it, Aunty Vi!" Serena shouted over the coffee maker. "What really happened last night? Tessa said it was all good, but the feelings I was getting..."

"Grab a drink and come sit with us girls." I moved towards my alcove and settled into my chair. "This is going to be something you want to hear sitting down."

Between Steven and I we told the girls all about what happened. Serena's face showed the way I felt as I thought about what happened. Tessa looked horrified as she looked at me. The shop was eerily quiet as they processed this new information. It wasn't an easy task to take in all this new information.

Now that I was removed from that situation, I thought about the spirit. While the man was paunchy and going bald, he had an uncanny resemblance to Steven. My gut instinct told me that the female spirit, the male spirit, and the memory loss around his house and family were all tied together. Add in that Steven's abilities had been bound, and I had another lovely mystery on my hands. I reached for my tarot cards sitting on a small cabinet to my left when the doorbell rang. Serena and Tessa both jumped to assist the customer.

"Pardon me ma'am..." Detective Johns grunted as he stepped into my alcove.

"Detective Johns..." Steven nodded in greeting as he took a sip of his coffee and pushed back from the table. "I assume you are here for me?"

"Yes. Ma'am..." Detective Johns tipped his head in deference.

"Wait one moment," I raised my hand and shook my head. "Why do you need Steven?"

"There has been another murder ma'am."

"When?"

"Last night."

"Perfect. Steven, please have a seat. Detective Johns, I am afraid that you will need to take us both in then. Steven and I were together at six last night until now. We had dinner with my good friend Gertie over at the library and then went to his place for the rest of the night."

"Uh…" Detective Johns stuttered as he glanced between us.

"We can confirm that they left together last night at six to head to the library!" Serena agreed. "Steven brought a pizza for them to have a dinner date at the house but then they ended up going to have dinner with Gertie."

"That pizza was delicious, by the way." Tessa interrupted. "We should have pizza again tonight. Maybe have a game night."

"That may be, but…"

"Detective Johns, I will be happy to come to the station with Steven and give you all the information you require. I would request that we do that in an hour. You see, I didn't get much sleep last night. I would appreciate it if you allowed me to at least finish my coffee. Will that work for you?"

"Yes ma'am." Detective Johns ducked out of the alcove, the beads clacking loudly. His face had turned beet red at the innuendo I had offered. "I will see you both in an hour."

"Another murder," Steven shuddered. "Since they are pulling me in, I am afraid to find out who was murdered."

I gave Steven a sympathetic look as I reached over and patted his hand. Mercifully, I had no visions of us entwined in pleasure. Instead, I got a vivid glimpse of my body cold and still, blood pooled beneath me. Shuddering, I pulled my hand back and sighed. My earlier visions of my death had shown me strangled. Was this a good thing or a bad thing? If the killer is changing up how they plan to kill me, did that mean that I am a murder of convenience? Was I getting closer to the truth? Making the killer panic? With a heavy sigh, I downed the last of my coffee and looked up at Steven as he rotated his cup in nervousness.

"Look at it this way..." Serena offered as she stood from the table. "At least you both have each other as an alibi. The conversation with Detective Johns should be quick."

"And..." Tessa also stood from the table as she wrapped her arms around her waist. "When you get done, we can all get together and decide what to do from there. I have an awful feeling that things are going to escalate quickly."

"HEX!" shouted a voice from the front of the cafe. I shifted in my seat and glanced out the window. Reggie was standing outside the cafe door and pointing at the sidewalk.

"I've got him girls..." I murmured as I rose from my seat. As if today wasn't throwing enough curveballs already.

Chapter Sixteen

"**W**ait!" Steven murmured softly in my ear with that deep voice of his. I halted with my hand on the cafe door. I had not heard him rise from his chair or move behind me. He placed a gentle hand on my waist as we stood there watching Reggie scream the word hex to anyone passing by. "Is he always this excited?"

"No." I frowned as I leaned back against that solid wall of a man. I should be focusing on everything but him. Unfortunately, my body had different ideas. Allowing the warmth of his body to encompass me, I tilted my head to the side slightly. "Reggie is normally calm and quiet. He rarely speaks to anyone unless it is to say please or thank you. A year ago, he became upset like this when someone vandalized the empty storefront down the alley, but other than that, he is normally peaceful."

"This is the second time he has done this?"

"Third, actually."

"Why now?" Steven swallowed hard as he placed his other hand on my other hip and squeezed me tighter against his body. "Could the murderer be using him to get to us?"

I shivered involuntarily. The word 'us' reverberated down my spine and back up again. This wasn't an admission of love. It was because we were both tangled up in this mess. Inhaling deeply, I shook my head. "Not likely. Reggie has his own story to tell, when he is ready, but being homeless is his choice. There is no way that he would allow harm to come to others."

"Very well then." Steven removed his hands from my waist, wrapped one arm around me to open the cafe door, and sighed. "Let us face him together."

I heard soft sighs from behind me that I was sure would lead to extreme teasing later. Suppressing a smile, I stepped out of the cafe with Steven directly behind me. It took me a good twenty minutes to soothe Reggie down. While I handled that, Steven took pictures of what had set Reggie off in the first place.

Someone had spray painted runes on the front walk of the cafe. Runes are an ancient form of the Germanic alphabet. Each rune could mean a letter but each also had a meaning and spiritual significance to them. Today, runes are used more for their spiritual meanings than to spell out words. These runes had no ill intent that I could decipher. If I had to guess, some teenager thought they looked cool and wanted to spray them in front of the witchy cafe.

I watched as Reggie shuffled off to the back of the cafe with a frank appraisal of Steven on his way. He nodded and then turned his back on us. I rubbed my eyes as I made my way to the other side of the lot. Steven ushered me to his car, and I gratefully climbed inside.

Detective Johns made us wait at least an hour before he pulled Steven into an interrogation room. I was taken to another room by another detective. I was prepared to explain everything to this person, but they only asked if I wanted something to drink, then closed the door and disappeared. I was left in the room waiting for at least another hour. I am a very impatient woman. I have never claimed I was otherwise. Having to sit for two hours waiting for someone to do something was enough to make me want to scream. My feet bounced against the floor, my fingers tapped out a nervous rhythm against the table, and my eyes bounced back and forth from the old-fashioned rotation fan against the ceiling to the worn metal and vinyl chairs that were at the table.

My fingernail found a nice little groove on the metal table and began tracing the line back and forth as I glanced at the two-way mirror in front of me. Brief images flashed in my mind as I looked in that mirror. There were way too many to count, but I could see all the people who had been brought to this exact same room. I could feel their anger, fear, indifference, and glee as they too, waited for the detective. My stomach churned that someone or multiple someone's had been gleeful to be in this room.

Swallowing down the bile that rose in my throat, I glanced at my image again and was relieved to see myself. Removing my hands from the table, I gripped the edge of the vinyl chair and forced myself to calm down. If the detective walked in and saw me in this agitated state, they would surely expect me to be the murderer. The moment my hands gripped the chair seat I caught another flash of feelings and images.

Serena and Tessa were bound, gagged, and tossed into what appeared to be an underground cavern with water. They were so still and not moving. My stomach roiled at the image. Glancing to my right, I saw Steven sprawled on the ground. There was a bruise forming on his cheek and a gash above one eye. I was filled with a sense of pride.

I had accomplished this. I had succeeded. My gaze rotated and behind me was what appeared to be a concrete dock of some sort. Lying there on the ground, bound and gagged, but still very alive was the source of all my problems. I sneered at the woman called Violet and advanced. Glee filled me as I raised a pistol and pointed it at her.

"Ms. Blueblade."

I was helplessly caught up in the horrid vision as the trigger was pulled.

"Ms. Blueblade." Detective Johns cleared his throat and placed his hand on my shoulder.

"Holy Goddess above!" I shouted, panting as he interrupted the vision.

"Ms. Blueblade."

I ungripped the chair and looked up into his eyes before gripping the chair once more. Cold. Quiet. No more visions flooded me. "D-Detective Johns."

I kept my vision focused on him. Detective Johns was a good-looking guy. He had short curly dishwater blonde hair. He had large green eyes, a dimple in his chin, and a toned body. He was strong in the way of a man who worked hard every day and not like a body builder. I took a moment to enjoy the fit of his blue jeans and t-shirt. The sight of this confident man was enough to help me steady my nerves. He stepped to the door, waited, then stepped back inside to hand me a bottle of water. I thankfully chugged down that cool liquid in the hopes that it would help my stomach stop churning.

"Ms. Blueblade, I apologize for any inconvenience this has caused you. Can you please state for the record where you were last night around ten."

"Uh...as I said earlier at the cafe, I was with Steven all night into this morning. At ten, we were at his house."

"And where is this house?"

"The Ravens Estate."

"I'm sorry. Where were you?"

"The Ravens Estate."

I watched as he jotted a note on his notepad and then studied me again. If he investigated the Ravens Estate, he would find nothing, same as me. I didn't like the look of nervousness that crossed his face as he tried to determine if I knew something he didn't. He tapped his pen against the table for a moment then shifted in his seat.

"Can you tell me what you two were doing?"

"Detective Johns." I gave him a weak smile as I was still trying to get myself together. "Do you tell everyone what you do on your date?"

"I," he hesitated and grimaced. "No, I don't."

"Then I am sure you will understand why I refuse to answer that question. If I might ask, who have you interrogated in this room recently, say in the last four weeks?"

"That is..."

"Classified. I understand." Damn. I had hoped that I could figure out who that hand belonged to.

"Do you know something?" Detective Johns leaned closer and dropped his voice. "I don't know much about this..." he said motioning to all of me. "But it seemed like I had interrupted something when I stepped in here."

"Who was murdered detective?"

He leaned back in his chair again and sighed softly. His face had gone completely blank as he thought. I would know tomorrow who was murdered if I wanted to purchase the newspaper, but I was hoping for an answer now. He must have come to the same conclusion as he tapped his pen against the notepad. "Miranda June."

I nodded, not knowing who this person was. It was another woman though. No shock there. "Was she blonde, blue eyes, around my height?"

"How did you..."

"I've seen her." I tapped my mind and frowned. "I know you don't know much about all of this..." I murmured softly as I, too, motioned to all of me. "But I can promise that I wasn't the killer. Steven wasn't either. I do know that the next woman killed will be a red head with brown eyes. If we don't catch this murderer soon..."

"We are doing all we can."

"If you don't catch the murderer soon, Detective Johns." I inhaled deeply and placed both my hands on the worn table. "I will be murdered after the red head."

He nodded with that same calculating look. I stood as he collected his notepad, then motioned to the door. "I believe I have all the information I need, Ms. Blueblade. Thank you for taking the time to come down to the station."

I took the dismissal and quickly rushed out of that room. Steven was standing at the front door to the police station leaning against the doorframe. Trying to force an image of calm, I walked slowly to him, then placed my hand in his as he turned to walk us out of the station. When we were finally enclosed in his car, I let out the breath I had held in. I had seen through the eyes of the murderer, and I didn't like it.

Steven was quiet as we drove back to the cafe. It was one in the afternoon, and the girls had already closed the shop. I fished my keys out of my pocket and stopped when Steven wrapped his hand around mine. I looked up at him and saw the same turmoil on his face that I was feeling. He leaned forward and caught my lips in a sweet kiss before letting go and pressing his forehead against mine.

"I am sorry you have gotten caught up in all of this." He squeezed my hand softly and inhaled deeply. "I am happy that I have gotten a chance to know you, Violet. This is getting too serious and too violent though. You need to distance yourself from me."

"Are you..." I gasped as I reeled back and stared at him with wide eyes. "Are you breaking up with me?"

"Breaking up?" Steven furrowed his brow. It took only moments for the thoughts to roll through his head before he chuckled. "Breaking up would imply that at some point you had agreed to become my girlfriend or to even go on a date with me."

"Can't blame a girl for liking the chase," I smirked with a grin. I slid out of the vehicle and turned before closing the door. "My house in a few hours?"

"Is that a date, Vi?"

I shrugged as the door closed before I worked my way to my vehicle. No matter what Steven suggested, I wasn't going to distance myself from this. My life, and possibly my niece's lives, were at stake. I don't think I could even spend a day without thinking of Steven or catching a glimpse of him. In this short time, I had grown attached to him. As crazy as that sounded, I was waffling on the idea of remaining single the rest of my life.

Climbing into my vehicle, I headed home to find the girls already there. They were whipping up a storm in the kitchen and singing along to the music. I booted up my computer and settled in the dining room. I did an internet search on the Ravens Estate and got very little information. This was the same page the girls had looked up when they had searched his address. The estate had been built at the turn of the industrial age. The house was indeed several hundred years old.

I tried to find history on the original owners of the property but the only thing that popped up was a Chatter page. Chatter was a website where anyone in the world could add or edit information. The Chatter page only gave the dimensions, some random pictures of what the interior looked like, and that the estate had been handed down to the oldest male member of the same family since it had been built. Tapping my finger against the keyboard, I scrolled to the history page. Only two people had edited the history in the last few years. Randolph and George.

I cleared my search and typed in George's name. George had one social media account which I shamelessly scrolled through. There was very little information on that account. It held mainly pictures of him at parties, with women, playing a sport, or lounging around doing nothing. I found the people search page that listed his career as a bartender. He lived in the next town over. Finding nothing interesting that gave me insight was frustrating. I cleared my search history and did a search for Randolph.

This was a little more insightful. I found his professional pages that held testimonials from all his patients that found him to be warm and friendly. That was not the Dr. Smalls I had met. I skimmed through these pages and then found he had a few social media accounts. Most of them were of him and his ex-wife and his two children. They made an adorable family.

It was a shame that his marriage had ended last year. I couldn't tell from any of the social media sites where their relationship had broken down. All the pictures showed a happy and exuberant family. I clicked on the local people page and saw that he lived two hours away in another city. Not much information to find there.

I cleared my search one last time and made a last-ditch effort to track the family tree for the Smalls family. I was unable to find any information on them. Groaning, I buried my face in my hands. The images of my murder from a few hours earlier swam through my mind and I shuddered as I sat there. I didn't want to see those images again. I didn't want to feel his sense of accomplishment or his sense of pride. I wanted to be free of this, to see what a relationship would be like, to continue to live my life. I jumped at the sound of the doorbell. Wiping tears from my cheeks, I started to rise and get the door, but I heard Serena greeting my visitor.

Dropping back into the chair, I watched as Steven rounded the corner with another bouquet of flowers and a bottle of wine. I have never been one to drink liquor. I never like the way it made me feel. After the last twenty-four hours though, I was teetering. Serena attempted to scoop that bottle out of his hands and I cleared my throat. Her eyes darted to me, widened, then darted away as she disappeared. Today was going to be a day of firsts for me.

Chapter Seventeen

"Tessa...Aunty Vi is going to drink." Serena loudly whispered.

"Aunt Vi never drinks. She hasn't since G-Ma and G-Pa passed." Tessa rolled her eyes and pulled a loaf of fresh baked rye bread out of the oven.

"I went to take the bottle of wine that Steven brought over to go with dinner, and I just got..."

"Got what?"

"It felt like she mentally shoved me away from it."

"Naw..." Tessa moved over to the kitchen doorway and peeked around the corner. Her jaw dropped open as she watched her aunt uncork the bottle of wine, pour a few fingers into a wine glass, then settled back into her chair as she took a sip. "Hollyhocks! She truly is. What else happened last night?"

"I don't know, but I think we need to forget about leaving. I say we crash dinner and get all the details."

"You're right. Better get in there and get the conversation started. I'll plate up dinner and bring it in."

"I THINK WE NEED..." I started as I took a second sip of wine. I had only had two sips, but I was already beginning to feel the liquor as it streamed through my blood.

"Aunty Vi, I hope you don't mind, but Tessa and I are starving. We are going to join you two for dinner." Serena announced loudly as she clambered into the dining room. She captured the bottle of wine and poured herself a large glass before sitting down across from Steven.

"It will be a pleasure to have dinner with all of you," Steven grinned with a wink. "Violet and I were going to go over all the information we have and decide our next move."

"Steven!" I hollered a little louder than I had anticipated. "Are you able to remote link into your house security system?"

"I think so..." He shot me a confused look as he pulled out his cell phone. "I am new to all this. I used to live in a studio apartment above a restaurant in New York. My security alarm was a cat that would hiss if you got too close to it."

I filed that information away for later discussion when the girls were not around. "I have a theory, and I am trying to find out if it is true. Can you attempt to check your security system to see if it has been turned off today...like while we were at the police station."

Steven nodded and tapped away on his phone. Tessa brought in two plates of food and sat them down in front of me and Steven before returning to the kitchen. I reached for my wineglass and came up empty handed. Eyeing Serena, she shrugged and motioned to the kitchen door. When Tessa came back in, I raised my brow at her and motioned to the empty spot where my wine glass had been. She shook her head, but I doubled-down on my glare until she retrieved it and placed it back on the table.

"How did you..." Steven started in shock. "How did you know someone was at the house?"

"It seems that the spirit only gets angry when you are away from the house. She takes it out on you when you are there at night. My guess is, someone is sneaking into your house while you are out. She doesn't like this person."

"Then why attack me?"

"I'm not sure. Still working on that part." I gave Steven a grin as I took a bite of the dinner the girls had made.

"Aunty Vi, what happened last night that you are not telling us?" Tessa tossed out in the silence that had fallen.

"Nothing. We told you everything."

"What happened at the station?" This was Serena. Her face was scrunched up and she took a long sip of her wine. "It didn't feel...nice."

Suddenly I wasn't as hungry as I had been. I rested back against the dining room chair and crossed my arms over my chest as I told them all about the vision I had. Steven went pale under his tan. The girls both shrank back into their chairs. The room became silent once more. I toyed with my fork for a moment and then glanced up at Steven.

"Who is Miranda June to you, Steven?"

"No one. I don't know her. They showed me pictures." He went paler if that was even possible. "I can honestly say I have never met her before."

"We have one murdered woman that you know and one that you don't. Is this all really centered on you or is there something else that we are missing?"

"What's the plan and how can we help?" Tessa offered.

"There is nothing online about the Small's family or about the Ravens Estate." I swallowed down the rest of the wine and sighed. "I have no idea if we are even on the right track at this point."

"What about this underground water room?" Steven looked hopeful. "How many places around here could match that?"

"This was a rich mining town back in the old days." Serena tossed her hair over her shoulder as she poured herself some more wine. "There could be a lot of places in the mine that look like it. There are also some natural caverns that could have water in them. I could do some research and see if I can get some images that match."

I nodded in agreement. I had seen the hand of the killer, but it was non-descript. It was a man's hand. It had fingernails and fingers. Aside from that, I couldn't say any more. The girls seemed at a loss for anything else to do. Steven was angrily bunching up his napkin and releasing it. He glanced at me a time or two and then at the girls. Something was bugging him. After another thirty minutes of listening to each other breath, the girls excused themselves and left. I was stuck in my house watching an angry Steven. The wine was working miracles for me because I wasn't scared one bit at his anger. He glanced up at me and grabbed his napkin tightly.

"You saw your death before today. The girls were going to tell me that a while ago, but you stopped them. Why?"

"The easy answer..." I looked straight into those eyes I loved so much. I leaned forward and propped my head on my hands. "I didn't know you. For all I knew, you were the killer. You don't just tell the killer that you saw them murder you."

"The difficult answer?" he demanded.

"Ah...the difficult answer." I sighed as I began clearing the table. Steven rose to help. We made it to the kitchen and placed the dishes in the sink. I turned and found myself pressed against the sink with him looking down into my eyes. "Does there have to be a difficult answer?"

"Violet?" he growled.

"I like you, Steven. I like you more than I should. That is the difficult answer. Even when I thought you might be the murderer, I was head over heels infatuated with you. I didn't want you to know that I had been seeing my murder for the last two months because you might have been the murderer. It wouldn't have been a smart move. If you were not the murderer, I didn't want you to know that I had been seeing my death because then you would try to be the hero and rescue me. I am not a damsel that needs to be rescued. That makes this all so complicated."

"No," he grinned and tucked a strand of hair behind my ear. My brain flooded with images that made my toes curl. "This isn't that complicated. You will never be a damsel that needs rescuing, and I will never be the hero that races to save you. You know why?"

"Wh-why?" I stammered, ignoring the fact that he didn't protest his innocence yet again.

"Because you are an awesomely independent and brilliant woman who can handle herself. If I do anything, it is to aide you. I will ride by your side and help you slay the demon or murderer. I will cheer you on because Violet..." Steven dipped his head, his lips brushing mine lightly. "You are worth more than any woman I have ever known."

"Pretty words," I whispered as I wrapped my arms around his neck. "Actions speak louder than words."

"Then let me show you."

When he claimed my lips, I swear I felt as if I was floating. The scruff from his beard rasped against my chin and cheek as he deepened the kiss. The wine I had drank during dinner was loosening my desire to keep him at bay. His hands gripped my waist and tugged me closer. I could feel his hard chest as it pressed against me. My body began a slow simmering burn as he brushed those hands against my belly, then my ribs. I found myself running my hands along his shoulders, and down his chest. I wanted to press them against his back and pull him even closer. Steven pulled his lips off mine, panting heavily as he pressed his forehead against mine.

"You don't drink, do you?" he remarked unsteadily as he gently kissed my cheeks, my nose, my forehead.

"No." I threaded my fingers into that mass of thick black curls and tugged him back for another kiss. I felt like I was drowning. I needed his kiss like I needed air.

"Then I am going to practice extreme restraint, kiss you goodnight, and say goodbye." Steven cupped my cheeks and gave me another kiss before pulling away and giving us space. "You are worth savoring but only when you are one hundred percent committed. I don't want there to be any doubt in that mind of yours that I want you."

"But I..."

"No Vi. I want to wake up wrapped around you. I want to feel your heart beat next to mine as you sleep. I want to feel the soft flutter of your breath against my chest as you dream. I want all of this, but I don't want you to wake up in the morning and say it was just because you had a glass of wine." He reached out and tugged gently on my limp brown hair that refused to stay in the ponytail. "I know you can't see it right now." He inhaled a shaky breath.

"I see..." I nodded and wrapped my arms around my waist. He was telling me the truth now. I felt it deep in my gut. What was burning hot from desire was now cold as ice. He wanted to have sex. He just didn't want to have sex with me. I have been a convenient outlet for his desires. I dropped my gaze to the floor and dropped back against the sink.

"No, you don't." Steven was suddenly there in front of me. "You have an amazing gift. You can see things. You can see snippets of the future. You can see ghosts. You can read fortunes and other people's auras. I haven't seen you charge once for giving readings to those people in your cafe because you are doing it to help them. You jumped into a murder investigation to help a total stranger. You care for the homeless man behind your business. You are an amazing woman, and I can see that. I saw it the moment I glimpsed you sitting at the couch in your cafe. A woman like that..." he growled and grabbed my hips, tugging me closer. "A woman like you. You. Are. Worth. The. Wait."

"Right..." I nodded, trying to hide the rejection I was feeling. I suddenly remembered that someone had been in his house, and I jumped, waving my hands in the air. It was the perfect timing because I not only slapped him, but then I jerked my head up and head butted him. All passionate feelings fled leaving me as clear headed as if I hadn't had a glass of wine. He cringed, grabbing his forehead, catching me in the eye with his elbow. "Hollyhocks!" I hollered.

"What the hell..." he groaned as he stepped back and caught my flailing arm. "I know you are angry, but really?"

"No." I shouted. I inhaled deeply and pulled my calm arm out of his grip. "I mean, yes I am slightly upset, but no, I just remembered something."

"Yes?"

"You can't go home."

"Why?" Steven accepted a frozen bag of corn that I had pulled from the freezer and placed it against his forehead. I grabbed myself a frozen bag of carrots for my eye.

"Someone went into the house. That lady spirit is going to be really ticked. You'll have to spend the night here."

Chapter Eighteen

I woke up to a throbbing skull. My stomach churned around like it was in a stormy sea. I rolled to my side and felt like I was hit with a truck. This was why I never drank. I was such a lightweight when it came to liquor. It wasn't even funny. First order of business was to take a steaming hot shower. Second order of business was to get some coffee and painkiller. Third order of business was to...oh holy Goddess. I threw myself at Steven last night and he turned me down. I moaned in agony and tugged the covers over my head. Oh Goddess. I even made him sleep here last night because the spirit was going to be highly agitated.

OK. I could do this. I was an adult. First order of business was to take a steaming hot shower. Second order of business was to get some coffee and painkillers. Third order of business was to sneak out of my house and to the cafe as quickly as I could to avoid Steven. Piece of cake. I could do this. I stumbled miserably out of the bed, grabbed my clothes, and disappeared into the bathroom.

The door to the guest bedroom was still closed. I showered as quickly as I could, dressed, peeked out into the hall, saw the door still closed, then disappeared quietly down the stairs to the main level. My still wet feet slipped on the kitchen tiles making me run into Steven's bare chest. He was holding a cup of coffee in one hand. He caught me around the waist and kept me from falling on my ample backside all without spilling a drop of that magic brew. This man was a miracle worker in so many ways. I watched with a dropped jaw as he spun me around, carefully settled the cup of coffee in my hand, then with his other, dropped two pain killers into my free hand.

No words were spoken as he shuffle-walked me to the kitchen table. He motioned for me to take the meds and drink the coffee as he walked over to the stove. He was making eggs and bacon. My stomach rumbled and I groaned. My body wanted something to eat but I wasn't sure I would keep it down. I gulped down the painkiller with a steaming hot sip of magic brew and then dropped my head into my hands. He was barefoot, wearing only his jeans, showing me his muscular chest. How did I compete with this? Half a glass of wine and I was a wasted idiot the next morning. He looked as fresh as a daisy, and he had finished off the other half the bottle.

"Eat the crackers first," he commanded as he settled down next to me at the table with a plate.

I munched on the soda crackers. Once my stomach settled, I became adventurous and ate the food he had given me. Now that I was feeling more like a human being, I had to find a way to extract myself from the awkward situation I had put myself in. I need to stop over at Crystal Cove and pick up some more selenite. A few high-powered magnets might also help. If I could find a way to banish the angry ghost, then at least he wouldn't have to sleep here. I would be able to avoid him for a little while. I opened my mouth to tell him I had errands to run when he intervened.

"We have errands to run today, I assume." Steven's brow rose as he glanced my way. "I'll grab my shirt, slip on my shoes, and we can go."

"I think..." I swallowed a large gulp of my coffee. "I think we should give each other a little space today."

"Why?" Steven yanked my chair next to his. He cupped my chin with one hand and kissed the tip of my nose. "Let's run over to my place and I will grab some spare clothes. Then we will run whatever errands you have."

"Steven..." I shook my head and scrambled out of the chair. "I still barely know you. I don't even know what you do for a living. It must be a pretty good paying job if you haven't been to work for a few weeks."

"I'm self-employed."

"Meaning?" I asked, tossing my hands in the air. "I am also self-employed, but you know I run a cafe."

"I tell you what." He moved the plates to the sink. "I am going to grab my shirt and shoes and be right back. I will let that brilliant mind of yours work out why it is best if we stick together for now."

Steven was right. Of course he was. If we separated, he would be picked up for another murder. Or worse. He would go back home and the spirit would do some nasty things. I tilted my head in thought at that. While I had experienced the seething anger the woman manifested with, I had yet to see her do anything to Steven. On the other hand, I had experienced the male spirit. He had violated me on a physical and astral plane.

Maybe I was looking at this spirit problem wrong. Maybe it was the male ghost that was attacking Steven and not the female. As the wheels spun in my head on this situation, he returned. He was wearing the same clothes he had on yesterday. Gritting my teeth, I tried not to stare at how good he still looked in rumpled clothing. It was really getting to be annoying how amazing he could look in any situation.

I picked my phone up off the table and headed towards the front door, grabbing my keys on the way out. Steven climbed into my vehicle without another word. On the drive over to his place, I thought about where we were with this whole situation. I had to look at the facts and try to separate out my feelings.

I had sultry sexy Steven sitting in the seat next to me. He owned the Ravens Estate. He was currently being haunted by three ghosts, one of which was a tiny barghest that manifested from a shih tzu. Steven was also featured in all the passionate visions I had been having. Those visions also included a lot of murder. All information I had at this point said he wasn't a killer, and I was finding myself attracted to the man. Sighing, I pulled up into his driveway. I waited as he went to grab his stuff.

Randolph was Steven's younger brother. He was a sought-after heart surgeon. He was divorced, had two children, and was not the polite person that everyone on social media said he was. I had seen the anger and bitter hatred the man was holding in. Whether the man hated Steven or hated the situation, I wasn't sure.

Steven climbed into my car, and I pulled out and headed back into town. Next up we had George, Steven's cousin. There was no love lost between Steven and George. It appeared that trouble either found George, or he went looking for it. The first murdered woman in town was George's girlfriend, and he was upset about it. Since I still couldn't read him, it was hard to tell. I pulled into my parking space at Mystic Brew and sat there for a moment. I had forgotten that Steven was with me. It wasn't until he placed his hand over mine on the gearshift that I flicked my eyes to his.

"We take this one step at a time. One breath at a time. Always together. We can get through this." he murmured softly.

I felt my frayed nerves calming under that smooth steady voice and I nodded. Once I had exited the vehicle, he caught my hand, led me across the street, and down the end of the walk. I frowned as I knew we had things to do. Why would he lead me in a direction we didn't need to go? We stood in front of an empty storefront.

I had heard rumors that a business would open soon. I had yet to see any changes to the place. The only change had been large drop clothes covering the storefront windows. I felt my jaw drop open as Steven inserted a key and opened the door.

"You?" I gasped. "You bought this storefront?"

"Yes." He guided me gently into the shop with a soft warm hand on my lower back. I stood dumbfounded in the doorway. His front to my back. "Welcome to Belle Vue."

"Beautiful View?" I chuckled as I gazed from one gorgeous photo to another. The drop clothes over the windows now made sense. "You sell artwork?"

"No. I sell photo shoots, pictures to papers, and occasionally I get requests for portraits. Being able to sell my photos would be a dream. I thought since I had a chance to start over. I would give it a shot. I am a photojournalist, Violet. I take pictures for anyone who will pay. It isn't glamorous and it doesn't make me millions. I used to moonlight with a band in New York as a drummer. Between both jobs I was able to barely make rent."

"But..." I frowned and looked at his clothes. He leaned against a counter with his arms crossed over his chest. He waited patiently for me to get my words together. "The Ravens Estate, your clothing, your car, it all screams..."

"Money?" he gave a soft nod. He didn't smile or frown. He just watched me for a moment, then sighed as he tucked his hands into his pockets. "The Ravens Estate came with a nice tidy little sum. I purchased the new car because my old vehicle was a run-down Vespa that had seen better days. I bought myself new clothes because..." he averted his gaze and crossed his arms over his chest again. "Well, wearing ripped and dirty jeans and t-shirts is great, but at some point, I want people to take me seriously. The remaining funds are being used to fix up the estate."

"The glass award?" I gulped.

"I took first place in a photo contest. The prize was a glass award and five hundred dollars." He sighed and tucked his hands into his pockets once more. He tipped his gaze towards the wooden floors and scrunched up his face. "I understand if this changes things between..."

I slid my arms through his and rested my head on his chest. The thought that he had been someone famous or someone rich had never appealed to me. I was attracted to the man, not the money or prestige. The idea that I was completely wrong about what he was had my heart beating double time. I didn't have to compete with money. I wouldn't have to compete for his attention. He had pulled his hands out of his pockets and was hugging me back when I remembered that he wasn't truly interested in me. I cleared my throat and stepped out of his arms. I took one more look around the shop, mentally marking the pictures I was going to buy for the cafe.

"We have errands to run and a murderer to catch." I reminded him.

"Errands...right."

He locked up his shop and together we strode down the walk to Crystal Cove. Crystal Cove was the epitome of what a metaphysical shop would look like. The moment you walked into the store, there was soft gentle rhythmic drums playing on the speakers. You could smell the sandalwood incense the second the door opened.

The inside was dimly lit. The shop itself was only a tiny room. There were racks on one side that held tie-dyed t-shirts, handbags, scarfs and altar cloths. There were bookcases along the perimeter of the room that held everything from boxes of incense sticks, cones, metaphysical books, tarot decks, and small statuettes of various gods and goddesses.

The checkout counter was situated in the middle of the wall to the right and was surrounded by two glass cases filled with crystals and jewelry. There were two large curio cabinets on either side that were filled with large crystals, crystal balls, and all the other more expensive items.

There was an open doorway in the back of the shop that was where Kristofer held his aura readings, circles, and other Wiccan related meetings. I loved this shop because everywhere you turned it was a kaleidoscope of color. I greeted Kristofer who was busy restocking the shelves with some tarot decks.

Kristofer was shorter than us by about a foot. He had bright red hair that he kept short, large brown eyes, and a full beard. He pushed up thick framed black glasses as he turned with a smile to give me a hug. Kristofer was a stocky man who reminded me of a certain jovial holiday figure. His cheeks and nose were almost always pink to match his bright pink t-shirt. Today he was wearing a pair of black cargo shorts and flip flops. I introduced Steven to Kristofer while I picked up two more large pieces of selenite, a few strong magnets, a leather cord, and a pendant of snowflake obsidian.

Snowflake obsidian was like selenite but protected the user from physical harm. I was confident this would keep Steven safe from any physical attacks from the spirits. I exchanged a few words with Kristofer before I thanked him for his help and stepped out of the shop. Outside of his shop, I threaded the snowflake obsidian pendant onto the leather cord and then slipped it over Steven's head. He looked at me with a weird face.

"What?" I snapped.

"Sweetheart, the man is supposed to gift jewelry to the woman, not the other way around. The gift is usually given after a few dates."

He wiggled his eyebrows at me before wrapping his arm through mine and resting his head against my shoulder. I couldn't stop the full belly laugh that escaped me as I slapped playfully at his chest. We walked down the walk hand in hand to the cafe. Reggie was standing outside of the front door. He looked as if he had forgotten something important until he saw me. A broad grin split his face as he spied us holding hands. Steven unwrapped his hand from mine and held it out to Reggie with a smile.

"Good morning, sir!" he waited a moment for Reggie to shake his hand.

"Morning!" Reggie replied and shook hands with him. I found myself without words. Reggie was a quiet soul. He rarely spoke and when he did, it was only to those few residents that he knew.

"Would you care for a cup of coffee and a muffin?" Steven prompted as he held open the cafe door.

"I wouldn't object."

Shaking my head, I watched as Reggie walked proudly into my cafe as if he wasn't scorned by everyone in this town. It took me a second to notice that Steven was still holding the door and waiting for me. Closing my mouth to keep the flies from getting in, I scrambled in behind them and nodded to the girls. I settled into my space in the alcove as I listened to Reggie and Steven hold a conversation. I watched the exchange for a few minutes as I sipped my coffee, a feeling of comfort filled me. If I needed solid proof that Steven wasn't a killer, this would have been it. Reggie would never have openly chatted with a murderer. Reggie was the best judge of a person's character I had ever seen.

"Excuse me..." a tall red head whispered at the beaded curtain.

"How may I help you?" I inquired as I motioned to the chair across from me.

"I thought..." she started. She settled into the chair across from me. The cup of tea was forgotten as she picked at her cuticle for a moment. "I have been..."

"Take your time, my dear."

I patted her gently on the hand and then yanked my hand back. I saw an image of her lying naked in the middle of the park. Her red hair was fanned out behind her head. The moon shine made her pale skin translucent as she starred unseeingly up at the sky. Her lips were blue, her brown eyes were glazed over, and there was a faint purple mark around her neck. I sucked in a quick deep breath and steadied my nerves. She was the next victim.

Chapter Nineteen

The small alcove was bursting with bodies. The young woman was talking at a fast clip now. I heard nothing as I studied the images in my head. What time of night? Were there clues that I was missing? Why was she naked in the middle of a public place? Who was this woman? More important, did she have any ties to Steven? I shook the sight out of my mind. I needed to focus on the woman now. I might be able to get a clue out of my cards.

"Come with me ma'am." Tessa remarked as she caught her arm and tried to lead her from the alcove.

"We will get you a fresh hot cup of tea now..." Serena answered with a nod.

"Violet will just need a moment before she can read your fortune. It will only be a moment." Steven promised as the girls expertly worked to move her out of the alcove.

"Wait." I held my hand up and smiled up at her with confidence I didn't feel. I motioned to the chair next to me. "I apologize, but I had a small vision just now. If you sit, I will read your fortune."

"Violet..." Steven murmured softly into my ear as he pulled a chair to sit closer to me. "You look like you have seen a ghost. Are you sure you can do this right now?"

"I need to." I choked.

I couldn't bring myself to tell him in front of a customer that I saw her death, or that mine was next. I picked up my stack of cards and shuffled them. I then sat them in front of her and asked her to shuffle. Her hands shook as she looked back and forth between Steven and me. Her lower lip trembled slightly when she sat them on the table in front of me.

Inhaling deeply, I reached out and pulled the first card. Turning it over, I felt my stomach heave. My body was threatening to introduce itself to my customer. I pulled another card and another. One after another lifted from the pile and laid face up to show me her grisly murder in sharp detail. Her fate was sealed. There was nothing I would be able to do to save her.

The young woman looked up at me with puppy dog eyes. She was begging for good news. I could see it in the way she huddled in on herself. She was holding her cup of tea but close to her chest in a gesture of comfort. Her brown eyes were wide as she looked up at me. Her red hair was swept back in a messy bun, and it was threatening to fall apart any moment.

I was gripped with the choice of telling her and making her last days miserable or not telling her and giving her piece of mind. It was not a situation I was faced with on a daily basis. How do you tell someone they are going to die and there was no rescue?

At the same time, she had to know something was off. There was no other reason she would be sitting across from me at this moment. She was hoping I could do something, but why? What or who made her think that I could give her the answer she sought? I was a precog who could see ghosts. I had never told the town that I was anything else.

I was not some paranormal knight that could slay all troubles. Maybe she had clues she could give me now. Maybe I could rescue her. I needed something to go on. A sense of calm and warmth flooded my senses, and I glanced down at my lap to find Steven's hand on my knee. I had been jiggling my leg up and down without realizing it.

Twining my fingers with his, I sat back and tried to project a sense of outward calm. I studied the cards closer, hoping for that gap in the fortune that I could exploit. There really wasn't any wiggle room on this. She was destined to die. I looked up at the woman and gave her a small frown. Her eyes closed for a moment. That is when I noticed the dark circles under her eyes. I should have noticed that sooner.

"May I know your name dear?" I started.

"Elizabeth."

"Elizabeth, why did you come to me?"

"I..." she hesitated as she glanced over at Steven once more before returning her gaze to the cards and then back to me. "I just don't know where else to go. I have tried everything else. I figured it couldn't hurt."

"What is happening?" I leaned forward and used my free hand to cover hers once more. There was no image of her death. Instead, I felt Steven's calm flow from me to her. Visibly she relaxed and sat back in her chair. "Tell me everything."

"What does this mean?" she asked, motioning to the cards on the table.

"Tell me what is going on first." I prompted. "This," I motioned to the cards. "Can change based on your energy. You are much more relaxed now. Explain what is going on that brought you to the Mystic Brew Cafe this morning."

"What does it matter?" she scoffed and took a sip of her tea.

"It matters." Steven murmured softly as he gave her a soft smile and a tilted head. "Trust me when I say I was a skeptic at first, myself. The things she has told me and shown me have been spot on. The more she knows, the more specific Violet can be."

"Is that how you are still free?" Elizabeth snarled. Steven studied her for a moment and then a look of recognition crossed his face. "Yes, I am Victoria's cousin. I can't believe you are still free, you murderer."

"I had..." Steven began.

"Elizabeth..." I interrupted. I squeezed Steven's hand under the table and felt him sigh. "While I am sure you wanted a chance to verbally tell Steven off, I feel like you came here for a different reason. Why did you come to the Mystic Brew?"

"Trixie said I should talk to you." Her eyes darted to the left as she said this. "She said that you were able to use your gift to get him off. Thought you might be able to help since the police haven't been able to."

"What do the police need to help you with?"

"I am being followed. This person keeps waking me up in the middle of the night by banging on the house. I tried filing a police report, but they can't find any evidence that it is happening."

"Elizabeth, I can't catch a stalker. Are you sure it is a person?"

"Yes. I saw a shape one night. I am pretty sure it is a man."

"Could you describe him?"

"If I could describe him, I am sure the cops could arrest him," she snapped.

"Right. My apologies."

"I need answers. What does this say?"

"This says that you are experiencing troubles." I tapped a card and looked her dead in the eyes. "It also says that everything will end soon." I hated the look of relief in her eyes since I knew that end was her death. I also hated that she seemed happy with that response. If Steven had not still be holding my hand, I would have probably been vibrating out of my seat.

"Well, that is a relief." Elizabeth knocked her knuckles against the table, grabbed her tea, and stood. "I would thank you, but..." she glanced at Steven and then disappeared through the beaded curtain. I waited until she walked out the front door before I slumped in my chair.

"It's okay, liebchen." Reggie spoke from the other side of the beaded curtain. "You didn't have another choice. Nasty business these murders have been. It will all resolve soon. Don't drink the water."

I watched Reggie leave the cafe behind Elizabeth. Steven looked at me and I looked at him. That was the most I had ever heard Reggie say in one conversation. He had called me beloved. I felt a tear slip down my cheek at the endearment. I had never expected him to ever care about me. I cared for him because I couldn't stand to think of anyone being homeless. I knew that he chose to be homeless, but even then, it hurt to think of what he had to endure. Steven used the pad of his thumb to wipe the tear off my cheek, and I turned to him. I wrapped my arms around him and buried my head against his chest. How did I get myself into this mess?

I felt as if I was walking a tightrope. I was balancing the fate of my nieces, myself, Steven, and now Elizabeth in my arms as I walked across this imaginary chasm of negative energy. It all centered on Steven and his estate. There had to be some clue that I was missing. My gut instincts told me that it was either Randolph or George, but I had no proof. I also had no idea why they would do this. I pulled out of Steven's arms and hitched in a deep breath as Serena and Tessa each stepped into the alcove to give me a hug and kiss on the forehead.

"Steven..." I tugged his hand that was clasping mine again. "Was Randolph upset when you inherited the Ravens Estate?"

"He was and wasn't." Steven shrugged lightly and snorted. "He wanted the house, but he didn't want to live in a podunk little town. He is too important for something like that. He had hinted that he should get the money that was part of the estate. I would have given it to him, but it was part of the inheritance that the money was used mainly for fixing the place up."

I tapped my fingers against the table and sighed. "Did Randolph get a divorce last year?"

"Yes." He tilted his head and looked at me. "You think Randolph is behind all of this? He is a heart surgeon. He saves lives. He doesn't take them."

"I was just wondering." I bit my lip and took a sip of my cold coffee. "Where does George fall into the inheritance of the estate?"

"I guess he would be next after me and Randolph. I am not sure how all this works." He watched the gears turn once more in my head. "You think it might be because of the estate?"

"I have no clue. It seems odd that we have murders in town and that you are being haunted by two angry spirits. The few repairs you have done on your place don't seem like enough to anger a spirit. You are fixing things, not ripping them apart and changing them."

We were both quiet while thinking about this. I slugged back my coffee and grimaced as the cold liquid sloshed around in my gut. Tiger had been barking like mad the other night at the fireplace. Either she didn't like fire, or she didn't like the fireplace.

Might that be a clue? I needed to search around in that fireplace and see if there were any clues.

I also needed to make plans to stake out Elizabeth's place tonight. I know the cards told me she would die, but I still had to try and prevent it. Steven seemed to read my mind and grabbed my empty cup and took it to the counter. He took one last swig of his coffee before dropping it in the trash bin. I watched as he held his hand out to me and my heart skipped a beat.

No matter what I thought of his brother and cousin. No matter that I had just straight out lied to a woman about her fate. No matter that I was the dumpiest looking woman on the planet, he was still looking at me as if I was a diamond that he wanted to keep. I slipped my hand into his as we walked out of the cafe and to my car.

I drove us back to his place repeating a mantra. I will open myself to fate. I will open myself to fate. I will open myself to fate. No one could master fate. It was the first thing my mother had taught me. You could try all you wanted to, but the Fate Sisters were in control whether you liked it or not. Sometimes you had to just allow fate to happen.

I took a moment to center myself. I had been through the estate several times with my third eye open and still haven't found anything significant. This time, I was going to focus on the fireplace. Once inside the kitchen, Tiger appeared with a wagging tail and a cute silent yip yap. We both showed affection for the little beastie as it disappeared into the house.

Moving purposefully into the living room, I studied the fireplace and the wooden surround closer. There was an intricate carving on the wooden surround. It was images of trees and leaves. The carving was gorgeous, and I ran my fingers over it lovingly. I pressed lightly here and there, thinking there might have been a hidden panel. When nothing clicked or popped, I turned my gaze to the stones.

Each stone was hand quarried and stacked. None of them seemed loose or looked as if they were hiding anything. I frowned as I turned my gaze to the hearth. Steven had been watching me quietly across the room. When he noticed I was looking at the hearth, he disappeared and reappeared with a metal bucket and small hand broom.

I bent down to help him clear out the ashes from the fire he lit the other day. Together we moved the andiron out of the firebox. The hearth, while covered in soot, didn't reveal any hidden catches or loose stones either. I glanced behind me and caught sight of Tiger. Steven turned to look as well.

Tiger was sitting on the floor as far from us as she could get. She appeared to be shaking or barking. I wasn't sure. Her image flickered in and out. I stood and moved away from the fireplace and Steven followed, reaching down and patting the dog on the head. She turned in a circle, glanced back at the fireplace, barked once more, then headed toward the kitchen. That cinched it. There was something in that fireplace.

I moved back and was thankful that his fireplace was huge. Getting down on my knees, I inched myself into the chimney. The flue was a few inches above my head, allowing me the space to turn around a bit without bumping into anything. After blindly sweeping my hands along the stones against the back, I felt a tap on my thigh.

Glancing down, I grasped the flashlight Steven was holding out toward me. Flicking it on, I examined every inch of the inside and gasped when I found a missing stone. I reached out to put my hand into the hole. Thoughts of creepy crawly spiders and every other icky bug swam through my head as I felt around.

Thankfully, there were no spiders or bugs but there was something metal. I dropped the flashlight onto the hearth and reached in with both hands. I tugged and pried until the item came free and fell against my chest. It bounced off my chest and hit the hearth, popping open, spilling its contents to glitter in the light of the flashlight.

Chapter Twenty

Steven and I both gasped in awe. Lying on the stones was an old tobacco tin. Inside that tin was a veritable fortune. Rare gems of every shape, size, and color glittered back at us. I spied a piece of shiny gold at the bottom of the stash and pushed some of the jewels out of the way. At the bottom was a simple gold chain with a tiny sapphire set into a gold cage. Dropping the pendant back into the pile, I looked up at Steven. He had picked up the round tin and was pulling out folded up papers. We both began to unfold the papers. When I realized what I was seeing, I scampered out of the fireplace, dusted off my knees, and headed to the kitchen.

"What is this?" he demanded as he slid onto a barstool next to me. "I mean, why would Tiger be upset by this? Animals don't care about money."

I coughed as I leaned back against his counter casually. "It appears that the person who turned off your security system has been looking for this. That means, it is either George or Randolph. Unless there are others that might know your security password."

"No one knows my security password. I didn't even give it to George or Randolph." He glanced back at the living room where he had left the jewels and the papers. "Let me see if I have this straight." He closed his eyes, rotated on the stool and copied my position by leaning back on the counter as he stared up at the ceiling.

"I moved in a few months ago and suddenly I am haunted by an angry spirit. That spirit is angry because someone keeps coming into the house looking for that stash. George appears after the first murder to check in on me. We haven't talked for at least five years. Randolph takes a two-hour drive to get mixed up in this as well. On top of that, we have two murdered women who are somehow involved and a town that has forgotten that my family and this estate exist. Do I have this all straight?"

"That sums it up pretty nice. You are forgetting that someone is also trying to pin the murders on you so they can take off with that small fortune in there."

"Right," he play-slapped his forehead and rolled his eyes. "How could I have forgotten that lovely tidbit?" He snapped his finger and gave her a smile. "There is a bright spot in all of this though."

"Hmmm..." I hummed without really listening. I was trying to shove the pieces of this puzzle together to make it all fit before Elizabeth died.

"In the middle of all this chaos, I found a beautiful psychic whom I think might fancy me. I mean, if the pink in her cheeks after I kiss her is any indication."

"Mmhmmm..." I mumbled again. Something was slowly clicking in my brain, and I still wasn't listening. I should have noticed the soft nudge at my ankle. I should have noticed the very masculine body that was now standing in front of me instead of sitting beside me.

"She is brilliant, has the softest pair of lips, the most earth-shattering chocolate brown eyes I have ever seen, and is kind and caring. She makes a fantastic cup of coffee, and I am guessing her niece learned baking from her. I also know she is not listening to a single word I am saying right now. So how about it?" He raised a brow at me and watched as my glazed eyes snapped up to him. His hands had pinned me against the counter, and he was now standing between my thighs.

"Huh, what?" I gasped. My cheeks heated immediately when I realized how intimately he was standing with me. "How about what?"

Steven tossed his head back and roared with laughter. He bent down and kissed me lightly on the forehead before wiping a smudge of soot from my nose. "I was just counting my blessings. You look like you have put something together. Fill me in."

I frowned and shook my head. "I think it would be best..."

"No. My family, my trouble. Tell me, even if it means I won't like the answer." He waited while I thought about it. "If it means I can help us save Elizabeth, I want to hear it."

"I have an idea." I pressed my hand against his chest, fisted the fabric, and pulled him down for a kiss. He didn't put up a fight. His mouth claimed mine without hesitation as I slid off the barstool. His arms wrapped me up tightly and he tugged me as close as possible. After a minute, I pushed against his chest. He released me with a frown but didn't say anything. "I think we should have a tea date."

"A tea date?" Steven was still fighting with the passion that had been brought on by my sudden kiss. I had hoped to distract him from his request for information. While the look in his eyes was still glazed, he still seemed determined. "What does that mean?"

"It means that we are going to brew up a wicked pot of tea then sit and chat while I drink it. Do you have a tea pot and thermos?"

"Yes." I watched as he pulled those items from a cabinet and set them on the counter. He then pulled two bottles of water from the fridge and ran his fingers through his hair in frustration.

"Perfect. Tell me, do you always drink bottled water?"

"No. These were left over from that party I had a while back where Vic..." he cleared his throat. "I had bought six cases. We only went through three. Most of the time I drink tap water. Why?"

"I am wondering if there is something happening with our memories because of the water. I was just curious. It is probably nothing. Will you be sleeping over or would you like to try sleeping here tonight?"

"Where do you plan to sleep tonight?" he teased, tugging a stray lock of my hair that had escaped my ponytail. He took a swig of his water. "I have a feeling you are sleeping in your car."

"Why Steven," I blushed and fanned my face. "You have only known me for a little while, but it seems like you know exactly how my mind works."

"That's because I do, my lady."

He winked and I chuckled. "Exactly right, my handsome knight. I plan to stake out Elizabeth's place to see if I can catch sight of this elusive stalker."

"Then I believe the side seat of your car will be comfortable enough for me." He winked again as he headed towards the living room. "It will also give me a chance to use my night camera while I get to interrogate the most beautiful woman in town."

"Not much interrogation going on there..." I mumbled and rolled my eyes as he disappeared into the house. I busied myself with putting a kettle of water on to boil. I stepped outside and grabbed the herbs out of my bag that Daisy had said I would need. Once the kettle whistled, I sprinkled a little of each herb into the pot and allowed it to steep. I was just getting ready to strain it into the thermos when I heard a loud clatter downstairs.

Steven rushed in from the living room with a camera bag slung over his shoulder. We hurried down the stairs, me tripping once again on the last stair, him catching me before I fell flat on my face. His drum set in the far corner had been shoved over. As we watched, his bass drum lifted into the air and flew at his head. We ducked to avoid being smashed in the face.

I watched the new mangled bass drum roll on the floor for a moment when a cymbal launched at us. It buried itself into the stone of the basement wall, missing us by an inch. I grunted as the snare drum hit my shin before rolling away. That one didn't have the same force behind it, but it was enough that my shin was smarting. Steven took a hit from his drumsticks to his bicep.

Which ghost was doing this? I duck walked over to the stone pillar a few feet from us as other items crashed against the walls. The ghost was losing energy with everything it was hurling. After five minutes, the room was now quiet. Peeking out from behind the pillar, I noticed that it was now calm. Steven had also taken refuge behind a pillar as well and was glancing furiously around.

"I don't see the ghost." I murmured.

"I don't either." He shook his head as he stood up and rubbed his tender shoulder. "Well, we knew she was going to be mad after yesterday."

"Yea." I nodded. I was not sure it was the female that was doing this. I followed him up the stairs and back to the kitchen while he finished getting his things. I strained the now overly steeped tea into a thermos and then thought a little more. Could the ghosts be great grandparents to Steven's family? Did they have something to do with this estate and the mystery? Steven returned from upstairs with several bags slung over his shoulder and I gave him a weak smile.

"Shall we my, magnificent mystic?"

"Of course." I laughed as I wrapped my arm around his. "Shall we follow the translucent yellow brick road while we are at it?"

"Hmmm...munchkins and flying monkeys. Who could resist the intrigue?" Steven remarked.

We both chuckled as we ducked out of his house. I did something I had not done in a very long time. I handed my keys to Steven and allowed him to drive us back to town. I did not trust people easily and by giving him my keys, I was placing my car and my life in his hands. I felt no ill will or foul intent. That meant that I was right in all ways possible about Steven.

This man was not a murderer. He was not evil. He was just caught up in the wrong place at the wrong time. Randolph was the person I was figuring to be behind all of this. He seemed to have more negative energy around him. I could also figure George into this but since I couldn't read him, it might be the wrong way to look. No, I was laying my bets on Randolph.

Steven and I stopped and picked up some snacks and sandwiches for our stake out. My mind never settled while we found a good location to watch Elizabeth's house. I drank a cup of tea when we first arrived and hoped that shortly my memories of the Ravens Estate and Steven's family would quickly return. That had to be the reason that Daisy gave me these specific herbs, right?

"A tea date then..." Steven started as he stretched lightly. He stared straight ahead at the house. "Does that mean this is our official first date?"

"First date?" I felt my cheeks heat again as I avoided his quick glance. "Uh, sure. We can call this a first date."

"Finally."

The quick exhalation of breath that he expelled had me giggling for no reason. The sun began to slowly sink below the horizon as he handed me a sandwich and popped open a bag of chips. We ate in silence as I mulled over the situation some more. The pieces still didn't fit together. The tobacco tin of jewels and bonds were worth a fortune. That could mean anyone was the murderer. They only had to know that they were in the house.

The night that the male ghost assaulted me I distinctly remember a scream. That scream didn't come from me. I glanced at Steven out of the corner of my eye with a sly grin. It hadn't been Steven either, unless he was hiding his feminine side from me. The more I thought about that scream, the more I was sure it was the female spirit. Why would the female spirit scream like that?

This whole situation was more than I could handle. I wasn't even sure why I was still trying to figure this out. I wasn't a detective. I wasn't a cop. I wasn't even a very good psychic. I was just a boring woman who loved coffee, hated exercise, and enjoyed reading a good book. None of that made me a good candidate to figure out what was going on.

"Vi?" Steven inquired as he bumped my elbow with his. I shook my head and focused on him.

"I'm sorry, what?"

"Did you see that shadow move?"

I glanced in the direction he had pointed. The bushes along the house did appear to be moving. I frowned as I glanced up at the deepening sky. It was getting more difficult to see as the sun disappeared completely. We were now entering the dark of twilight. None of the tree branches moved and as I rolled down the window on the car, I noted the lack of wind. If those bushes were moving, it wasn't because of nature.

"It appears that we have a prowler..." I murmured softly as we watched the movements. After a moment I giggled. The giggle became a belly laugh.

Steven only watched me, waiting for an explanation.

"It's a cat or dog. This time of night, could even be a raccoon."

We watched a little longer and sure enough two stray cats popped out of the bushes as they hissed and spit at each other. Steven smirked. He diverted his attention from the house to me on occasion as his hand reached over and twined with mine. I didn't mind. It was warm and comforting. I hadn't felt safe for a very long time. It had been since my parents had both passed. I had been strong for the family from that moment on. Never had I felt secure enough to let my guard down. Right now, at this moment, holding Steven's hand and listening to his soft breathing, I felt secure and safe.

"Tell me Violet..." Steven spoke softly as he averted his gaze toward me. "What does a psychic do to unwind at night?"

"It depends on the day." I watched as a raccoon scurried by and investigated the bushes that the cats had popped out of. "Most nights I sit on the couch with a good book. On stressful nights, I sit in a car and watch for prowlers that are intent on murder."

"This isn't a normal night for you then?" he teased as he tugged gently on my hand.

"Not in the least. Despite what others have led you to believe, I am not normally one to stick my nose into other people's situations. I find it stressful to deal with drama." I glanced down at his hand in mine and used my thumb to brush against his. "I have a small stake in this drama though."

"Your murder and your niece's involvement?" he offered with a nod.

"Not just that." I peered up at him through the dark of the car. I swear I could see those brown orbs gazing into my soul. "It seems there is a very stubborn and admirable man that I had to get involved with. The fates wouldn't allow me to get out of it."

"You believe it was these fates that pushed us together then? Not a lucky turn of events?"

"Everything is ruled by the fates." I smiled in the dark, knowing that he wouldn't be able to see. I patted his hand softly as I turned my gaze back to the house. "We may think we are making choices of our own, but I can promise that the fates had already determined those choices to begin with. What is that?"

Steven let go of my hand and reached into the back of the vehicle for his camera bag. He pulled out a camera. After a few moments and some clicking, I heard him snap a picture of something. He turned the screen toward me. We studied it for a moment. I couldn't tell if it was a person or just a tree branch. He must have felt the same as he dropped the camera back into his lap.

We were quiet most of the night. Occasionally I would ask Steven a question about himself. I had expected him to avoid answering or to push the conversation back to me. When he answered, it helped me gain more insight into the man I was infatuated with. He would offer up a few questions about me and I would answer him. By one in the morning, I had enough of starring at Elizabeth's house. If the killer was going to strike, it wasn't going to be tonight.

I hesitated as I started up the car. Steven let out a heavy sigh as he turned his head towards the window. We both cast one last look at the house before I put the car in gear and drove home. Both of us crashed into our separate beds and fell instantly asleep. Sitting in a car was exhausting and frustrating. I had to find the killer and soon.

Chapter Twenty-One

Pounding. Loud shouting. More pounding. I slowly woke and glanced at the clock on the nightstand. It was five-thirty in the morning. Who could be shouting this early in the morning? Also, where was that pounding coming from. I rolled over and sat up on the edge of the bed when I realized that the pounding was someone at the front door. Groaning, I glanced down to see that I was still in my clothes from last night. Shuffling and yawning, I headed quickly to the front door.

"Ms. Blueblade." Detective Johns shouted. He seemed to realize how loud he was and quieted his voice. "Will you come with me to the station please?"

"What?" I frowned, looking at the two police officers behind him. Steven was standing behind me and put a hand on my hip. "Why?"

"Don't make this difficult, Ms. Blueblade. If you will just come with me to the station to answer a few questions." He lifted his gaze to Steven behind me. "You too, Mr. Smalls."

"It is five in the morning, Detective." Steven grumbled as he tugged me lightly to the side. "What is this all about?"

Without thinking of the consequences, I reached out and touched Detective Johns hand. He flinched back lightly, enough that the cops immediately reached for their guns, but not enough to make anyone move towards me. My eyes glazed over as the vision of Elizabeth's dead naked body flooded my mind.

How? How did this happen? We had staked out the house last night and hadn't seen one thing that pointed toward the killer.

"Elizabeth is dead..." I cried softly. Steven wrapped me up in his arms as I shook off the vision. "We were too late."

"Ma'am?" Detective Johns tilted his head slightly to the side and a crease appeared in his forehead as he studied us. "What do you mea..." He shook his head and motioned to his car parked in front of my house. "If you two will join me at the station please."

We stepped out of the house and climbed into his unmarked vehicle. Steven and I sat in back and between bouts of tears, I noticed that Detective Johns kept glancing at us in the rearview mirror. I sniffled lightly and Steven pulled me into his arms. I rested my head against his shoulder as I allowed myself to grieve for the woman. She may have been unpleasant when I met her, but any loss of life was a failure.

Once at the police station, we were both put in the same interrogation room, given a cup of coffee each, then left to wait. I glanced into the two-way mirror and shuddered. Unlike the last time, I didn't have visions of the people who had been in the room before. Instead, I was appalled at my appearance. My hair was a mess of tangles and sticking up in places. Using my fingers, I combed my hair back into some semblance of neatness.

"How did we miss it?" Steven groaned as he slumped in his chair and ran his fingers through his own hair. "Did the killer show up after we left?"

"I don't know." I shook my head, sniffling as I felt the tears flood my eyes again. "Maybe the killer snuck around the back of the house?"

"Mr. Smalls. Ms. Blueblade." Detective Johns stepped into the room with a folder and a cup of his own coffee. He settled into the chair across the table and looked at both of us. He sighed, rubbed his face in a tired motion, then pushed the folder forward. "Let me start by apologizing for this morning."

"We didn't kill Elizabeth." I pleaded.

"I know that Ms. Blueblade." He stood, sighed, and began pacing behind the table. "I find myself in a unique spot that I am not sure how to navigate. I have the captain demanding that I bring you two in. I have the reporters demanding that I tell them all the facts. Then I have you two." He dropped into his chair. "We have had three murders in the last two months. Three. In the last ten years, we only had two murders. Not to mention the fact that you are both tied up in each of them."

"But..." Steven began. Detective Johns raised a hand and grimaced.

"I don't believe in the mystical mumbo jumbo like you two do, but I have a gut instinct that tells me you are not the killer. What I can't figure out is why you two are being implicated. With the first murder, we were sure it was you Mr. Smalls. This one though..." he pushed the folder towards me, and I shivered.

Goose pimples rose on my arms as I shakily reached out a hand and opened the folder. I closed my eyes and gasped. Even though I had seen these images in my head, the stark reality of seeing it on paper made my gut heave. Steven caught my hand in his and I felt his peaceful energy fill me. Opening my eyes again, I looked down at poor Elizabeth.

Her red hair was fanned out on the grass. She was indeed naked but had been covered in a white and red sheet. No, that wasn't right. The sheet was white, but it had blood on it. I slid that photo to the side and found another. The sheet had been opened and then photographed. Written in blood on the white sheet was a message. I closed my eyes again as I steadied my beating heart.

"Are you able to explain this message?" Detective Johns nodded at the picture on the table.

It was there, clear as a day, in full color. The white sheet spelled out my failure. My name had been written with what I assumed was blood. I shook my head and pushed the folder back to the detective. I had seen enough. I wanted to go back home, take a long hot shower, then crawl into bed and never come out. I knew that reaction wouldn't save me, but it would be comforting.

"Ms. Blueblade..."

"Call me Vi. At this point, I have a feeling we are going to know each other extremely well Detective." I watched as he nodded.

"Vi, why would the victim be covered in a sheet with your name written on it?"

"I have no idea."

"We have reports that she came to your coffee shop yesterday."

"Yes. She wanted a reading. Said she was being harassed by a man and that everything else hadn't worked for her. She had hoped that I could give her some insight on how to get rid of him."

"What did you tell her?"

"I..." I slumped and put my head on the table for a moment. Feelings of disgrace filled me. "I told her that the situation would resolve shortly."

"You had no idea that this would happen." Detective Johns softened his features and nodded at the file folder that Steven was now glancing through.

"That is where you are wrong Detective Johns. I saw her death and knew that it would end that way. I didn't want her to spend her last moments on this plane of existence filled with worry and dread. I gave her false hope."

"I know this handwriting..." Steven murmured. He ran his hand through his hair and tugged, tilting his head to the side. "I've seen this somewhere before." It was quiet in the room for a moment as we waited for Steven. With no revelation forthcoming, I turned my attention back to the detective.

"Vi, we were told that two people, matching you two, were seen sitting in a car outside of the victim's house last night."

"We were there." Steven nodded, closed the file, and pushed it back to the detective. "We had hoped to catch the man harassing Elizabeth and to catch the killer. We figured they were the same person. We sat outside the house from six in the evening to about one in the morning. We never saw a single person at the house. I don't think she was even home. I never noticed any lights go on or off during the time we were there."

"What time did you say you got to the house?"

"Around six."

"And you two were together the whole time?"

"Except for having to use the restroom, yes."

"Where did you go to the restroom?"

"There was a gas station five blocks down the street."

I tuned out the interrogation as I thought about Elizabeth. How could I have possibly missed the killer? I don't remember taking my eyes off the house much. Even with the few conversations we had. Was she taken during the day? As I thought about it, I had to agree with Steven's statement. I don't remember the lights coming on at dark or going off. The house had remained dark. Was Elizabeth not home while we watched her house for the killer? Is that why we didn't catch them?

If the killer had taken her, then that meant it had to be during the day. I needed to find out where Elizabeth went after she stopped for her tea and reading at my cafe. Would any of the other shop owners remember her? Had Reggie seen her maybe? If I could trace back the last hours of Elizabeth's life, I might be able to find a clue as to who had murdered her. Suddenly, antsy to get out of this room, I glanced up to find both men watching me.

"I know that look." Steven warned as he glanced over at Detective Johns. "It means she has put some clues together or thought of a plan."

"I am beginning to wonder if I shouldn't deputize you two." Detective Johns sighed and shook his head in frustration. "I will figure out something to throw the captain off arresting you. If you find anything," he glared at me. "And I mean anything that can help me with this investigation, you call me right away. I can't have two civilians getting themselves hurt trying to catch a killer."

"You have my word, Detective." I agreed. "Enough people have been hurt by this monster. It is best if we catch them quick."

"I haven't forgotten what you told me, Vi." His gaze softened as he stood. "We will catch him before it happens."

"Let us hope so." I sighed and stepped out of the interrogation room. "I pray to the Goddess that it is so."

Chapter Twenty-Two

Steven and I returned to my house. Detective Johns had a cop take us home. I could see the nosy neighbors glancing out their windows as we pulled up and were let out of the back of the cruiser. I never really cared what anyone thought about me, but suddenly I felt like a criminal in my own neighborhood. I watched as the particularly grouchy neighbor next door said something and pointed at me through the doorway. Wrapping my arms around my waist, I shrank into myself.

Steven wrapped me up in his arms and murmured encouragement to me softly. We walked slowly up to the porch and inside. Once I closed the door to the outside world, I let out a heavy sigh and trudged up to the bedroom. I grabbed a clean set of comfort clothes and headed to the bathroom. I was being a bad hostess and not giving Steven the opportunity to shower first, but I couldn't help it. I hoped he would forgive me.

Clean, dressed in my tennis shoes, jeans, and a black t-shirt, I stepped out of the bathroom. I headed to the kitchen and made a pot of coffee. I could hear the water kick on and knew that Steven was taking his turn in the shower. I stood there watching the coffee perk and wondered where I should start first. As I pulled out the ingredients to make waffles and bacon, I formulated a plan.

The last place I knew Elizabeth had been was in my shop. I closed my eyes for a moment as I thought back to yester morning. From the little alcove in my cafe, I could see the door.

I watched her step out of the cafe. Which direction did she head? I opened my eyes and poured the batter into the waffle maker. Steven appeared at the kitchen door and studied me for a moment.

"What are you trying to remember?"

"What?" I glanced up at him as he sat a carton of eggs on the counter. He began to crack them in a bowl and whip them up.

"I see those wheels turning and you are chewing on your lip. That means you are trying to remember something. What are you trying to remember? Maybe I can help."

I stood there with my mouth hanging open as I watched him scramble up some eggs then remove the bacon from the oven. He was so comfortable in my home. He had only slept over twice now and yet he seemed to know where everything was. For a moment I felt creeped out. Could I really be so sure that he wasn't the killer? Had he been watching me before all of this had started?

Shaking myself for being an idiot, I pulled the waffle out and poured more batter into it. Steven couldn't be the killer. He had been with me when Miranda had been murdered. There was no way he could have been the killer. I plated up the second waffle. Steven loaded each plate with half the eggs and half the bacon and together we settled at the table with cups of coffee. I returned to his question as we sat there and ate our breakfast.

"Elizabeth was at my cafe first thing yesterday. Then sometime last night or this morning, she was found murdered in the park."

"Yes." He nodded as he enjoyed his waffle. "Delicious. Does your niece get her baking skills from you or is this a witchy thing?"

"Neither. I like food, and Tessa went to culinary school." I twirled a forkful of egg around in my hand as I looked at him. "We sat on her house for almost seven hours and didn't see anything. Not even Elizabeth herself."

"Correct." He took a sip of his coffee and waited.

"If I am right, then the killer took her sometime between her reading and six last night. Which means..."

"That someone might have seen her with him." He tapped his thumb against the coffee mug and smiled. "Your brain is freaky scary sometimes. If we trace back where she was and talk to those who were around, we might get a clue to lead us towards the killer."

"Exactly. I am trying to remember which direction she turned when she left the cafe. I can almost see it, but it gets misty. Like I am not supposed to know."

"What did Detective Johns mean when he said he remembered what you told him and that he would catch him before it happened?"

My head spun from the quick change in conversation. I put my coffee mug on the table and looked at him. I could sense that he was nervous. There was also an underlying hint of fear coming from him. Anyone else wouldn't see that. They would see him sitting calmly in the chair, watching me with those brown eyes, his head slightly tilted to the side. His black hair was getting long enough to fall softly over his forehead as he waited patiently for the answer.

Should I tell him the truth? What difference would it make if I told him I was the next victim? We still had clues to follow. We still had a killer to catch. I didn't like the thought that I would be dead shortly. I didn't like the idea that my nieces would also be caught up in this. Would telling Steven change any of that? I swallowed hard, averted my gaze to the table, and began to idly fiddle with my napkin.

"I am the next victim."

I inhaled a shaky breath and waited. I expected him to explode. I anticipated his seething anger for keeping this a secret. I hoped that he would promise me that it wouldn't happen. What I got was not what I was counting on. He nodded, took another sip of his coffee, then dumped his breakfast in the trash can. He had barely eaten a couple of bites. He turned, crossing his arms over his chest, leaned against the counter and waited.

"I am sorry. I should have told you sooner."

"What difference does it make?" He shrugged off my apology and sighed. "I know now. We have a killer to catch and sitting here getting angry or upset will not catch him faster. Eat up Vi. We have a lot of walking to do today."

Steven disappeared into the house. I felt like what little I had eaten was going to make a reappearance. Dumping my breakfast in the trash, I sighed heavily. How do I fix this? How do I fix all of this? I didn't know how long I had before the killer came after me. I didn't know how long before the girls became involved. All I knew was that we had to backtrack where Elizabeth had been yesterday. Grabbing my keys off the hall table, I noticed that Steven had already grabbed his and his car was gone. My heart sank into my stomach. It looked as if I was going solo today. I had upset him greatly. It would be alright though. Steven always came back, no matter how angry he was with me.

I was halfway down the porch stairs and to my car when I stopped. Where did that come from? How did I know that Steven always came back after he was angry? A memory surfaced.

I knew it was a memory and not a vision because the edges were not fuzzy and misty. I was playing in a large green space with a bunch of other children. As my younger self turned, I could see the Ravens Estate behind me.

I turned back around to find Steven standing behind me, trying to sneak up. I reached out, tapped him on the shoulder, and yelled tag. He got angry and ran away. I shrugged, rushing around to catch another kid. I heard someone holler for us to come over to the tables for lunch. The voice was garbled and hard to distinguish. I threw a fit because I was having fun and didn't want to stop just to eat. Steven came up behind me, slung his arm over my shoulder, and we walked to the tables.

Steven always came back after he was angry. That was how I knew. I had known him when I was a kid. I knew Randolph and George too. How could I have forgotten? I climbed into my car and set off for the cafe. Daisy's herbs were the cure for my memory block. Now all I had to do was figure out how to cure the rest of the town, find a killer, and keep myself from getting murdered. I could do this. It would be a piece of cake. I just had to believe I could.

Chapter Twenty-Three

Steven did indeed come back after being angry. I had arrived at the cafe and had a decent cup of coffee and a muffin while I waited. I brewed a small batch of tea, poured it into a to-go cup, and sat it on the counter. I gave Serena instructions to take it over to Gertie at the library. I needed to see if I could get her to remember more on the history of the town. I was sure that she had clues that we needed.

When Serena returned, I caught them up on what happened last night. They exchanged glances between themselves. I knew they were hiding something. I coughed lightly behind my hand, took a sip of my coffee, and tried to hide my smile. Why they thought they could hide it from me, I didn't know but watching them squirm was fun. Tessa finally dropped dramatically into the chair across from me and spilled everything with one well-placed look from me.

"Aunty Vi, I saw your death last night. That means you are next, right? Serena said she felt like she had been tied up. Then just a moment ago she said it felt like a flood. I saw a bunch of images rushing by so fast that I couldn't catch any of them. It is happening now, isn't it?"

"Ah, my sweet peas." I replied softly. I tucked a strand of hair behind Serena's ear as it had escaped her bun. "I am so sorry all of this has swept you up. I promise I will do everything I can to keep you safe."

"Stop worrying about us." Serena shook her head, and the hair popped back out. "What are we experiencing?"

"You did see my death and yes, I am next." I nodded as I patted Tessa's hand. "Serena, you were tied up. I have a feeling that poor Elizabeth was abducted yesterday before being murdered. I am not sure what the flood is. Tessa, I am pretty sure your images were my memories coming back. It seems that the whole town has had their memories wiped."

"Wiped? Of what?" Serena growled.

"Of who? And why?" Tessa added.

"The Ravens Estate and the Small's family." I gave them both a smile as the chimes above the door tinkled. I glanced up to see Steven. He looked at me, nodded, and made his own cup of coffee before joining us. "I have no idea who or why though. I can't even figure out how."

"How what?" I filled Steven in quickly on my suddenly returning memories. He frowned when I told him about us playing together as children. "That leaves me with how. How do you wipe a whole town's memory?"

"What does the how matter?" Serena questioned. "I mean we just make up more of those memory teas and give them out to everyone for free. The whole town will regain their memory, right?"

"You can be so thick sometimes!" Tessa rolled her eyes and crossed her arms over her chest. "We can give everyone the tea and bring their memories back, yes. What we can't do is expect it to hold. If we don't know how we lost our memories in the first place, we could do the same thing and lose them again. It must be something subtle if everyone has lost their memories."

"What does everyone in this town do?" Steven nodded and tapped his fingers against the table. "We all eat. We all drink. We all breathe."

"It would be difficult to put a memory charm into the air. It wouldn't be powerful enough." I jiggled my leg up and down as I thought. "Food and drink would be easier."

"Aunt Vi, didn't you get a reading from Daisy?" Serena offered. "What did she say?"

"Oh, the usual. You know how Daisy can be." I stilled my legs and looked over at the window. Reggie was walking slowly along the walkway. He glanced inside the window and nodded at me, then moved on. "Wait a moment...what did Daisy tell me?"

I stood from my chair and shifted my weight back and forth. I was the type of person who paced when trying to remember things. In such a tight space, there was no room to pace. Steven reached over and caught my hand. Quiet energy soothed my frayed nerves as I tried to think about what Daisy had said. I settled back into my chair, closed my eyes, and began to mumble.

"Murder, misfortune. No. No. Misfortune, murder, mystery. Love and fortune will pierce. No. Love and fortune come from the veil. No, that isn't it either. One who rarely speaks." I glanced out the window again and saw Reggie standing on the corner. "Reggie rarely speaks. Reggie is also rich but poor." I nodded as the girls and Steven waited. They looked to be holding their breath. "Reggie knows the truth. I need to talk with Reggie."

We all rose from the table at the same time. I looked to Steven who gave me a soft smile as he held his hand out. Together we walked outside towards Reggie. I had made sure to bring a cup of coffee and today's lunch special. Reggie gave us a welcome smile as he accepted the food. I wrapped my arm around Steven, and he tugged me closer.

"Reggie," I started. "Daisy told me you had an answer for me. Do you know what answer she thinks I need?"

"Don't drink the water, liebchen."

"Don't drink the water?" Steven looked down at me. His eyes widened as he thanked Reggie and turned us around. "Don't drink the water!"

"Yes. What did you figure out?"

"Serena!" Steven hollered as we walked back into the cafe. "Did you ever do a search for pictures of caverns with water?"

"Yes."

"Do you have them?"

"Um." She rustled around in her purse and smiled. "Yes, here they are."

Steven began sorting through them quickly, looking at the locations printed under the pictures. He pulled two out of the stack and sat them on the counter. I gasped and covered my mouth. They looked exactly like the vision I had at the police station. This was the room we were in when I was murdered. I checked the location and felt the first hint of relief. It was the town's water supply.

"The town's water supply?" Tessa frowned and tilted her head. "What does the town's water supply have to do with all of this?"

"Don't drink the water." Steven pointed at the picture. "The memory charm is in here somewhere. Every time someone drinks water from the tap, they wipe their own memory. It is self-renewing. That is why I don't seem to have problems remembering the town. I have been drinking bottled water for a few months."

"Then what we have to do is..." I began.

"Put the herbs into the water supply and we defeat the memory charm!" Tessa finished.

"NO!" I shouted and shook my head at the same time Steven said the same thing.

"Yes!" the girls both replied.

"No. You two are not getting more involved in this!"

"Aunty Vi!" Tessa let out a huff. "Think about it. We can fix the town's memory, but we still have a killer to catch. You can't do two things at once."

"Exactly." Serena tossed her hair over her shoulder and crossed her arms over her chest. She glared at me. "Let Tessa and I go and take care of the memory problem while you and Steven work on the murderer. Which do you think is going to be the safer option?"

I couldn't argue with them about that. Tracking down the killer would be the more dangerous option. I also felt as if the memory charm was tied to the murderer. What if the killer caught them pouring those herbs into the water supply? I opened my mouth once more to voice an objection when Steven dropped his arm over my shoulder.

"Let the girls handle the memory charm." His voice was quiet, his gaze fixed far off.

Steven was having some sort of vision. When I glanced down, I noticed that he had popped the lid off his cup, and he had curled his finger into the liquid. He was picking up on his abilities quickly without my help. I nodded and heard the girls squeal with delight as they rushed out to my car. I waited patiently as the vision slowly released him. I caught the cup before it spilled onto the floor.

"You are learning quickly. What did you see? Anything that will help us?"

He shook his head and removed his cup from my hand. The girls returned and started making plans to visit the town water supply after they closed the shop. I settled back at my table in the alcove with Steven next to me. We sipped our coffee's quietly for a moment. Where do we start first? If only I could remember which direction Elizabeth turned when she left my shop yesterday.

"She went left." Steven had his eyes closed as he mentioned this. I closed my eyes and pictured yesterday as well as I could. The image of Elizabeth was still fuzzy once she left the alcove. I sighed and nodded. It is a little eerie that he knew what I was trying to figure out. Then again, we seemed to be in tune. "That means she went past Daisy, Kristofer, the clothing store, and the knick-knack shop."

"Yes. We can stop in at Crystal Cove and see if Kristofer saw her. The clothing store and the knick-knack shop would also be good bets." I nodded and finished off my coffee.

"Why not stop at Daisy's as well?"

"Daisy is not always the most reliable source unless she is doing a reading. She gave me a reading a few weeks ago. I am not sure she would be able to pick up on the subtle changes."

"I haven't had a reading from Daisy. She merely gave me a locator tea that led me right to my lady love." Steven winked and threaded his fingers through mine. "I have to thank her for that too, might as well do both at the same time."

I rolled my eyes but shrugged. The goal was to find where Elizabeth went. If that meant having to listen to Daisy talk about fairies and adventures, then I could do it. Once Steven had finished his coffee, we left the shop and stopped over at Crystal Cove. Kristofer smiled warmly as he watched us walk into the shop holding hands. He spied the snowflake obsidian around Steven's neck and frowned.

"Kristofer," I began. "Did you notice a lovely young woman yesterday walking down the sidewalk? She had red hair. It was probably around eight."

"Violet," Kristofer crossed his arms over his chest and shook his head. "You are not a detective child. You need more than just a little snowflake obsidian to protect you from what is happening."

"I know. Did you see her?"

"I did happen to notice her head down the street. I can't say I know where she was going."

"Was there anyone with her? Did it appear as if anyone was following her?"

"I didn't notice. It was unusually quiet at that time of the morning. You know how we are in these small towns. We don't like to get up much before nine around here."

"I know. Thanks Kristofer. I appreciate it."

"Strike one." Steven murmured as we stepped out of Crystal Cove.

We turned in the direction of the knick-knack shop and repeated our questions. The owner was a young woman with a blonde pixie cut. Her large green eyes looked up at Steven with admiration. I swallowed down the surge of jealously I felt as he smiled at her and asked our questions in a purr. She told us she hadn't noticed her. She usually opened the shop at around nine and had been running a little behind yesterday. Letting out a heavy sigh, we set our sights on the clothing shop.

Refabulous was a second-hand clothing store. The owner had a hard time getting the shop up and running a few years ago. Most of the town didn't want a second-hand clothing store. They felt that it would decrease the aesthetic of the shopping plaza. Thankfully there were enough of us small shop owners who were able to veto that and get her the permits and items she needed to open. I glanced around and noticed a few customers going through items near the back of the children's section, but I didn't see the owner.

"Violet!" I turned to find Penelope near the back entrance. She was buried in a pile of boxes. I watched as she climbed over them to get to me. "Girl, I haven't seen you for at least two months. I thought you had finally retired."

"You wish, Pen." I chuckled, let go of Steven's hand, and wrapped her up in a tight hug.

Penelope was sporting a new hairdo from the last time I had seen her. Where she used to wear her hair long and styled in fancy hairdo's, she had cut it down to a lopsided bob. It framed her face nicely, setting off the freckles along her button nose and apple cheeks. I loved that her brown eyes were framed with winged eyeliner. Penelope was slim, stylish, and extremely caring.

"If I closed my shop, then I would have to be here bugging you every day. You know I can't stand to be idle." We both chuckled at that as her gaze finally strayed to Steven. "Penelope, I'd like you to meet Steven. He has moved back to town and bought the old Beerman shop down the street."

"That doesn't appear to be all." Pen's face broke out into a large happy smile. "Rumor has it that this hunk of a man hasn't spent more than a day away from you, Vi! Could it be possible that someone has finally picked up on how fantastic you are?"

"She is not fantastic." Steven shook hands with Penelope then tugged me into a side hug. "She is out of this world."

They shared a smile and a wink before Pen turned her gaze back to me. "What brings you down to my shop? Are the girls bickering too much today?"

"No, but it is still early." We shared a knowing look as I rubbed tiredly at my face. "I don't know if you heard, but another woman was killed last night."

"I did. Detective Johns stopped by all the shops this morning to warn us and ask questions. He said she had last been seen leaving your cafe." Pen placed a warm hand on my shoulder. "I am sorry you are caught up in this Vi."

"Thank you, Pen. Did you happen to see her yesterday?"

"I did. She stopped in here a little after eight. She went through some of the racks of women's clothing. When she didn't find anything, she started to leave. She stopped at the rack by the door. Oddly enough, she purchased a handbag."

"What is so interesting about a purse?" Steven inquired. He glanced at me, and I shrugged. I wasn't one of those women who kept up on fashion and handbags.

"If it had been a purse, that would have been a different matter. A purse is a small bag that you put small items into. She seemed more that type of woman. A handbag is usually bigger and allows you to carry bigger items. She did not seem the type to need something that large. It wasn't her color either."

"Did you see her come into the store? Or which direction she went when she left?"

"I didn't see her come in, but when she left, she headed towards the library."

"Did it seem if anyone was following her?"

"I didn't see anyone but her that morning." Pen noticed that her customers were moving towards the register, so she pulled me in for a hug and a kiss on the cheek. "Don't be a stranger, girl. Let me know if you need anything else."

"I will, Pen. Thanks for the help. Can you send over a new sleeping bag and a heavy winter coat? Put it on my tab and I'll have Serena or Tessa bring over the cash tomorrow."

"Of course. I'll make sure I send it over to the shop after I handle these customers. This one is a keeper, Vi. Don't screw it up."

Chapter Twenty-Four

"You heard her, right?" Steven teased me as we stepped out of the shop. "I am a keeper."

"She is only saying that because of your looks." I rolled my eyes at him. "The library is this way." We walked in the direction of the library. I kept my eyes open for any other storefront that would have been open yesterday morning.

"Are you getting that bag and coat for Reggie?"

"Yes. I noticed last week that his was getting worn. Winters can be extremely cold around here and while we are almost done with winter and into spring, there are still a few colder nights to go."

"Why not just ask Reggie to stay with you at your house or get him a shelter?"

"He has refused too many times to count."

I stopped in front of the bookstore. Elizabeth had not seemed the type to read, but the shop opened at seven. There was a good chance that someone inside could have seen her. We stepped inside to the wonderful smell of books and coffee. My eyes darted from side to side as we walked towards the middle row of shelves. I could see the head of a person. I approached the sales associate and gave him a bright smile.

"Excuse me, did you happen to work the open shift yesterday?"

"Yes," was the surly reply. He gave me a brief once over and then returned to stocking a row of books.

"Did you happen to notice a lovely young woman yesterday around eight in the morning? She would have been by herself. I think she was heading towards the library."

"Yeah, what of it?"

"Was she heading that direction?"

"Look," he sneered as he turned. "Your boy toy here is a cheater. I watched him with her. He swallowed her tongue for about five minutes right there against the window as if no one could see them. They walked off after I pounded on the window."

"You saw him?" I gasped as I pointed at Steven.

"Yep. He had a major case of Roman Hands, if you know what I mean. They swapped spit then headed off that way." He pointed towards the library and then dismissed me by turning his back and walking away.

"I wasn't even here." Steven protested quietly as we watched the associates back for a moment. He stopped at another box on the floor and began pulling those books and shelving them. "How could he have seen me?"

"It wasn't you." I started towards the door of the bookstore, but Steven caught me.

"You know it wasn't me, right?"

"Steven, you were with me. I know it wasn't you. It was George."

"George." He got a furrow between his brows as it suddenly dawned on him. "He was pulling another of those impersonations." He nodded and then a look of fright. "That means he is the killer."

"Not necessarily."

We stepped out of the shop and studied the street. The only other thing here was a small diner and the library. I hurried our steps to the diner. If my instincts were right, Elizabeth and George came in here. I settled at a small booth in the front window and took in the scene. Steven slid in across from me.

The diner was fashioned after a truck stop. The whole of the shop was no bigger than a rail car. There were small two-seater booths along the windows. The booths were covered in a pistachio green vinyl. The tables were buttercup yellow laminate. The diner had an eye for details as the menus were posted on small jukebox replicas on the edge of the table against the windows.

There were barstools set up along the other side. They were lined along the counter that was situated in front of the window to the grill. There were two waitresses and from first glance one short order cook behind the window. The woman who approached us was wearing an old-fashioned cinched waist dress with a white apron around her waist. She pulled out a plain pad of paper and a pen.

"Need a minute or are you ready to order?" The name on the tag said her name was Krystal. She clicked her pen a couple of times as she looked at Steven.

"Two coffees." Steven put on his most charming smile. "Tell me, did you happen to see a beautiful woman in here yesterday with red hair? It had to be sometime around eight thirty or maybe nine?"

"Oh honey!" Krystal placed her hand on his shoulder and shook her head in sadness. "You need to lay off the wild grapes if you can't remember who you had breakfast with yesterday." She turned and gave me a shocked look. "No offense. Hot stuff here seems to have a different woman every time he comes in."

"No offense taken." My stomach flipped at this news. Steven and I shared a heavy look.

"I know he was in here yesterday with a woman with red hair, but how many have you seen him with?"

"Oh, there was the woman with black hair. Poor thing ended up murdered. Then there was a blonde. She had the prettiest blue eyes. The red head yesterday, and now you sweetie." Krystal poured our coffees. In the middle of pouring my cup, her hand began to shake, and she darted her gaze to Steven again. "Um, did you want something to eat?"

"No, thanks. It isn't what you think," I called to her as she rushed behind the counter.

"She just put the pieces together like we did, huh?" Steven frowned.

"Seems likely. Cheese and crackers! I think it is probably smart that we leave or call Detective Johns before she calls the cops on us." I pulled money out of my pocket and dropped it on the table.

"I think we are too late."

Steven hustled out of the diner behind me. We made it to the library and inside before I heard sirens. I watched from one of the small front windows as the cops ambled into the diner. They probably thought the call was a prank. I heard a soft chuckle behind me and turned to find Gertie watching us. She beckoned us closer.

"I wondered how long it would take you two to get together." She shook her head as she slowly climbed onto the stool behind the counter. "You two were always causing problems in here."

"You remember?" I breathed a sigh of thanks. "Gertie, the whole town has forgotten about the Ravens Estate and the Small's family."

"Nonsense child." Gertie rolled her eyes. "Oh, thank you for the tea. That was a delicious combination. You need to put that on your menu permanently."

"You are welcome, but I am telling you the truth Gertie. I can't find information anywhere on the Ravens Estate. I was told that you did your dissertation on the town history. I thought you might have some information to help me."

"But you have," she motioned to Steven and frowned.

"Trust us." Steven gave her a look of frustration. "Everyone has lost their memory. Ask anyone else if they have heard of the Ravens Estate."

"The estate sits in the middle of the town. Everyone drives past it."

Gertie gawked at us for a moment, then slid off the stool slowly. She hastened towards the stacks. We exchanged another worried glance. When Gertie returned, she was walking more sedately, her brow furrowed, her hands wringing in front of her. She opened the door behind the counter and motioned for us to join her. I settled into the chair in front of the desk with Steven in the other.

"I didn't believe you. The two of you were always pulling pranks on us when you were younger. I figured this was another lark. I remember the time you put baby powder in..."

"Gertie," I prodded as I placed my hand on hers. "The tea I sent you this morning was to bring your memories back. Do you have any information for us?"

"Yes." She snapped back to the present. She opened a drawer on her desk and pulled out a large scrapbook. She dropped it down in front of me and Steven with a sigh. "This is the history of the Ravens Estate and the Small's family. Although, back then, it was Arthur Raven and his wife Heloise."

Steven opened the scrapbook and we both stiffened. We were intimately familiar with the couple in the picture. The woman was the phantom that we first saw at Steven's home. She was the one that had been tied to a stake and burned to death. The man was the phantasm that assaulted me the night I stayed at his place. I snuck a quick peak at Steven and then back at the picture. The family resemblance was uncanny.

I looked at the pictures and the documents as Steven flipped through the book. Arthur had died first. He had been found sleeping with a married man's wife. The husband had found out and shot him. Arthur had survived the shooting but had died from an infection. The wound didn't heal properly and three weeks later it killed him. Heloise was a force to be reckoned with though.

From the research, it appears that Heloise hated her husband. She knew about his philandering ways. She also knew that he was making a fortune off the poor. He would build cheap shoddy homes for the poor. He charged a fortune to build them. He paid his workers the bare minimum and made them work in unhealthy conditions.

There was a drawing of the sapphire necklace. It was an engagement present from Arthur to his wife. According to the history, she wore it every day to show her commitment to him. Apparently when they had married, Arthur was just starting out on his nefarious deeds. Heloise attempted to change him for the sake of their daughter growing in her womb. It didn't work. He increased his fortunes off the death and misery of his workers and the poor people in this town.

Heloise had enough and turned her back to him. There was no such thing as divorce back in those days, so she started amassing her own wealth. She had clairvoyance. She started telling fortunes in secret for her friends. Her business eventually grew, and she held seances. These were always covered by calling them bridge parties with the ladies in town.

Once Arthur passed, she was free to give her readings without fear of being caught. She didn't charge money for her guidance. It was when she started making ointments and salves that she started bringing in cash. It was enough to keep the house paid up and fixed, to care for her and her daughter, and to make a tidy little nest egg.

Our little town was no Salem, but from the history, one townsman took an instant dislike to her. He called what she did witchcraft and incited the town to take action. He preached day in and day out that it was devil's work and she and her daughter should be burned for their crimes. The town ignored him until one day Heloise gave a reading to the mayor and told him that his reckless ways would soon bankrupt the town.

The mayor began to spread rumors of witchcraft and pointed the finger at the Raven family. By this time, Heloise's child was just turning of age. Her beautiful Adelaide also had the sight. She cast a protection spell over the sapphire necklace that Arthur had given her. Giving that to Adelaide, she made her promise to wear it and never take it off. That simple little necklace saved her daughter from being burned at the stake the night the town came for her.

I shuddered and sat back in the chair. It was the first and only time our town committed this heinous act. After they burned Heloise, the mayor was caught in his deeds. The town ran him out of town and life went back to being peaceful. Adelaide had used her mother's small fortune to purchase the Ravens Estate back from the town. After that it was passed down to the oldest male child.

"Well, at least I now know where I get my visions from." Steven eased back from the desk.

"If the town has had their memory wiped of this history, there has to be a reason." Gertie nodded. "I supposed you two already have a plan?"

"Yes." I glanced at my cell phone as it rang. It was Detective Johns. "The girls should be handling that right about now. I am sorry for cutting this off so abruptly Gertie. Thank you very much for your help." I stepped out of her office and answered the phone. "Detective Johns?" I waited a moment as he explained why he was calling. "Yes, that was us. We will be there shortly."

"Back to police station then?" Steven frowned as he stepped out behind me.

"Yes. The waitress called us in as suspects in the murder investigation."

Chapter Twenty-Five

"Serena, what in the hell?" Tessa demanded as she got an eyeful of her sister's outfit. She slapped herself on the forehead and sighed. "We are going to the town water supply. In a cave. This is the outfit you chose?"

"What?" Serena peeked at her outfit and smiled. She was wearing a pair of black strappy heels, a knee-high black skirt, and a fashionably tattered black t-shirt buckled around her waist. "This is the only black items I own. Besides, it isn't like you have on the proper outfit."

"There is no reason we have to be in black."

"I thought we had to be stealthy, which is why we are doing this now. After the sun has set for the day."

"With all that pale white skin showing, you are not stealthy."

"I could just let you do this and go home."

"Yep." Tessa watched as Serena flipped her hair over her shoulder and rolled her eyes. "Then you would whine because you were hungry and there is no food. Let's just get this over with. Did you at least remember to bring the lights?"

"Oh." Serena dug around in her purse and frowned. "I thought I put them in here. I guess not. Do you have the herbs? Do you think there is enough? I mean the town water supply is massive. Should we have gotten more from Daisy?"

"I don't think Daisy would sell Aunt Vi short on the herbs she thought she needed. I think Daisy has a direct connection to an ultimate being. Do you think a god or goddess would send their protectors into battle without the proper number of weapons?"

"Tessa, you are just as daffy as Daisy." Serena rolled her eyes again but pulled out her phone and turned on the flashlight. "Let's get this done so we can go home and have dinner. I am starving."

Tessa sighed heavily and rubbed her face. Grabbing her own phone, she opened the car door and grabbed the bag of herbs. They walked the short distance down a sidewalk to a set of concrete stairs. The stairs led down to a door of a small shack. The shack was only big enough for two people standing side by side. Serena reached out and grasped the huge padlock.

Tessa frowned. She didn't think about the door being locked. It made sense. You wouldn't want just anyone to mess with the town water supply. She watched as her sister pulled two hair pins out of her hair. When the padlock opened after a moment, she shook her head. She wasn't sure if she should be happy that her sister knew how to pick a lock or upset. She chose happy and followed her into the room.

The light from their phones showed an electrical box on the wall. Serena flipped the lever and lights popped on in front of them. The lights illuminated both sides of a staircase leading down. As quietly as they could with Serena's strappy heels, they descended into the large room that held the water supply. There was a ledge that ran from one side to the other, but otherwise, it was rock cavern walls and water to the other side. Tessa guessed it was at least a hundred or two hundred feet across. The lights ran along the length of the room. How they got them strung up along the cavern walls, she wasn't sure. Serena grabbed some of the bags of herbs and began to open them.

"Hold on."

"Why? There's the water supply. These are the herbs. Let's get them dumped in here and we can go have dinner."

"Wait." Tessa scrunched her face up in concentration. "If everyone keeps wiping their memory, that means there is something in the water doing it, right? Look around along the ledge, see if there is something tied up. We must remove it first and then we can dump the herbs in."

"Ohhh..." Serena giggled and nodded. "Right-o. You take that side and I'll take this side."

Tessa began watching the ledge as she paced down the length of her side. She didn't see any strings or bags. She reached the far wall and traveled back. She worked extra slow to make sure she didn't miss a single thing. As she met up with Serena, they looked at each other puzzled. There was nothing. Tessa looked across the water at the far wall, hoping to catch sight of anything that looked out of place.

"Tessa," Serena began. "Maybe the killer comes back and pours the herbs or charms or whatever into the water to keep it fresh. That means we wouldn't find anything, right?"

"How right you are, brat!" A gruff male voice remarked behind them.

Tessa turned and came face to face with a man holding a gun pointed at them. Serena screamed and dropped her herbs. She immediately thrust her hands into the air and dropped her head to look at the concrete beneath her feet. The man pointed at the bag of herbs in her hand, and she dropped them. Tessa allowed her hand to hover near her pocket where she had put a pocketknife earlier. She had a feeling it might come in handy.

"Hands up! I know you have a knife. You two play along like good little kids and this will all be over soon. I promise."

Chapter Twenty-Six

"Why do we have a report of you two in a diner harassing a waitress?" Detective Johns demanded as he stood behind his desk with his arms crossed over his chest.

"Hold on." Steven held his hands up. "We were following Elizabeth's last steps and decided she had gone to the diner for breakfast. We were only asking if she had seen her."

Detective Johns turned his gaze to me, and I copied Steven's hand up gesture. "Honest answer. We stopped in there to see if she had been there. That is all."

"I get the feeling that you two know something more."

"Do you want us to tell you what we know here in front of everyone?" I offered. "Or do you want us to tell you somewhere more private?"

"Does this involve any of the other stuff?" I shrugged and waited for him to make a decision. He settled into the chair behind his desk. Steven grabbed another chair, and we both sat.

"Here is what we know. I think my cousin George is the one killing these women."

"George?"

"He still doesn't have his memories." I reminded Steven as he grew frustrated. "He doesn't remember you, Randolph, or George."

"Right, almost forgot." Steven ran his fingers through his hair in frustration. "George Smalls. He is a bartender not far from here."

"You think he is the suspect?"

I put my hand on Steven's knee. He was getting very frustrated and was visibly upset. The moment my hand touched his knee, he calmed. I explained the similarity between George and Steven. I also explained how the waitress had told us he was with a woman with black hair, blonde hair, and red at the diner. The fact that he had been seen with all three of the murder victims was enough evidence to have him brought in for questioning. At least I thought it would be. The look on Detective Johns face didn't match up with my thoughts.

"Why would I drag in someone who lives in another town to question about our murders? This doesn't match up. I have Steven here. Just because his cousin looks like him, it doesn't make sense if he doesn't live here."

"Yes, but Steven wasn't seen with the blonde. He doesn't even know her."

"But he did know Victoria and Elizabeth. Are you sure he is being honest when he told you he didn't know Miranda?"

"Detective Johns," I shook my head and tried to put as much feeling as I could into my words. "I can promise you that it wasn't Steven who murdered those women. He was with me the night Miranda was murdered and then again when Elizabeth was murdered. How could it possibly be him?"

"You said his cousin looks exactly like him. Maybe they switched out and George was with you those nights while Steven went and murdered them."

"I said they have a likeness. If you are taking a quick peek, you would be hard press to tell the difference. If you are talking with them, you would know." I lowered my voice and leaned closer. "When I touch Steven I get feelings, visions, woo-woo stuff. George doesn't put off any of that. He is a void to me. I would know because of my witchy powers."

"I need evidence to bring him in."

"Correct me if I am wrong, Detective Johns, but you dragged Steven in for the first murder on the word that someone had seen the two together."

"No." This time he held up his hands. "I brought Steven in for questioning on the first one because the rumor was, they were in a relationship. In my line of work, it is always the..."

"It is always the husband or boyfriend," Steven growled.

"In this instance you were wrong. What if I told you that George was Victoria's boyfriend?"

"That gives me a basis to question him." He nodded. "Is that all you two have?"

"For now."

"Good. I will let the officers know the call was a prank and we will leave it at that. I will see if I can find this George Smalls and get him in here for questioning. You two need to tread very carefully from this point forward." Detective Johns gave me a quick glare. "I don't need the next murder happening too quickly. You make sure you stick to her side like glue."

He tossed that last bit at Steven as we rose and left the police station. I gratefully allowed Steven to drive us to my house. We settled into the routine of cooking and eating dinner. I was too on edge to settle down after we ate. I had the strangest feeling that something was wrong. I paced between the living room and dining room.

We had good reason to believe that George was the killer. Why then, did I feel like something wasn't right? On my fifth circuit through the lower level of the house, Steven caught my arm and tugged me over to the couch. He had been reading one of my books on the metaphysical. He tucked a strand of my hair behind my ear and looked deep into my eyes.

"What has you on edge?"

"I don't know. Something doesn't feel right."

"Take a deep breath." I rolled my eyes at him but did as he asked. "Close your eyes." He threaded his fingers through mine. "Think about the events and piece it together slowly with what you know. Relax and let a vision come to you."

This was a basic technique taught in every metaphysical book I have ever read. They were basic techniques for a reason. Instead of arguing with him, I centered myself, cleared my mind of everything, and focused instead on deep and steady breathing. I had been meditating for years. It only took me a minute to reach a relaxed state.

With our hands entwined, I felt the thrum of Steven's energy. I could feel his passion, his anger, his fear, and his love. Pushing those out of the way, I focused on the three women who had been murdered. My mind flashed with an image of the girls tied up in the town water supply. I caught a glimpse of a hand holding a gun. I saw myself lying dead on the concrete with a pool of blood around me.

No new images came to me. I sat there breathing deeply and holding Steven's hand. When no new images came to the surface, I opened my eyes and pulled my hands out of his. He tugged me into his side, and we leaned against the back of the couch. I got comfortable and snuggled down against him. He let out a happy sigh as he held me close.

"Let's try a different approach, shall we?" he asked as he pulled a blanket off the back of the couch and covered us. "You feel like the house is tied into all of this. Why are the ghosts haunting me? Why do they only appear after someone has been in my house?"

"Hmmm." I listened to the steady beat of his heart and whoosh of his breath as I thought about this. "I don't think the woman, er, sorry, Heloise is haunting you. I think she is protecting you."

"Protecting me from what?"

"I think she is trying to protect you from Arthur. She tried to fix him while he was alive, but it didn't work. I think he is still greedy. Those bonds and jewels you found were hers, purchased from the donations people gave her for her readings and seances. I think he wants them for himself."

"He is dead."

"Yep, but he doesn't care. He was a greedy womanizer while alive. We know the womanizer part is true." I shivered as I remembered his grimy ghostly hands on me. "I heard a scream that day when he disappeared and it wasn't me. I think it was Heloise pushing him away."

"Arthur was the one attacking me every time someone came into the house?"

"That is what I think." I pinched him and heard him chuckle. "This is all pure guessing on my part mister."

"Who do we think entered my house then?"

"I am not sure. Does it matter? They entered, they searched, they pissed him off, and then bang, he attacks you."

"Fair enough." He began rubbing his hands up and down my shoulder as he thought some more about it. "If George was the one searching the house, that means he knew about the riches and wanted them. He was dating Victoria. He cared for her. Why would he murder her?"

"That I don't know. It doesn't make sense."

"OK, then let's flip lenses for a moment." He rested his cheek on her head and sighed. "Randolph would be the next in line to inherit the estate. Maybe he didn't like the fact that I am the oldest and inherited the house. Maybe he knew about the treasure that was hidden and wants it all for himself. Getting me arrested for the murder would have only put the house into foreclosure."

I nodded in agreement and yawned behind my hand.

"Not to mention the murder of the three women. Victoria I could see to get me framed for murder. Why Miranda and Elizabeth? What would he gain from two other murders?"

"I don't know." I replied groggily. "Sleep now...think in the morning." I slipped off to sleep with a soft chuckle from Steven ringing in my ears.

Chapter Twenty-Seven

When I woke the next morning, I was snuggled deep against Steven's chest on the couch. At some point in the night, we had shifted from sitting to lying on the couch. My front was pressed solidly against his. I felt warm and comfortable with my head pillowed against his shoulder. The steady sound of his breathing and his heartbeat was soothing. I placed my hand against his chest and felt the beat of his heart as I listened to it. For this moment, it was like the world had stopped and everything was right once again.

There was a loud pounding on my front door that startled Steven awake. We untangled ourselves and rolled off the couch. I peeked out the door and found George standing there. I couldn't remember giving him my address. The night I went to see Gertie, Steven had also told me that he had gotten my address from George. My gut clenched in fear. Steven caught sight of his cousin in the window and stepped in front of me to open the door.

"What do you want George?" he snapped angrily.

"Have you heard from Randolph?" There was a soft rustle outside that I assumed was George shifting uncomfortably back and forth. "I tried his cell and his house phone, but he isn't answering."

"I don't know where he is. What do you care?"

"I need a lawyer." There was more soft shuffling. "I just got released from the police station. They think I had something to do with these murders."

"Did you?" I challenged as I stepped out from behind Steven.

"I didn't, I..." he let out a soft groan and shook his head, tossing his hands in the air. "I would never have hurt them. Steven, I know that you hate me for stealing your girlfriend and doing all those stupid things when we were younger, but I am telling the truth."

"Why should I believe you? All you ever did when we were teenagers, was run around pretending to be me. How do I know you are not doing this just to pin everything on me?

"Will you let me come in and explain it?"

"This is not my home. You'll have to ask Vi." Steven glanced at me.

"I know how you are connected to Victoria. Want to explain how you are connected to Miranda and Elizabeth?"

I stepped back from the door and headed to the kitchen, allowing George to come inside. While I fixed a pot of coffee, Steven and George settled at the table. While Steven was not on friendly terms with his cousin, and I had my own feelings about him, I could not waste the chance to find out more. I put a plate of muffins on the table with some butter and then settled down with a fresh hot cup. Steven put a muffin on a plate and scooted it closer to me before he took a long swig of his hot magic brew.

"I loved Victoria. We had planned on moving in together. Miranda was a friend. She liked to hang out at the bar during closing time. I think she had feelings for me, but I pretended she didn't. She was funny and smart. I had no idea that being friends with me would get her killed. We met for breakfast a few days after I found out about Victoria. She was there to console me." George inhaled deeply, taking a sip of his coffee before resuming.

"A week went by, and I didn't see or hear from her. She hadn't come to the club for a while. I went to her house to see if she was sick. She wasn't home. It looked as if she hadn't been home for a while. There were dishes in her sink, and her clothes were on the floor in her room. She wasn't messy like that. She always kept a clean house. I didn't think anything of it at the time. Then I saw the papers that said she had been killed. I was devastated.

Elizabeth was her best friend. I called her and she asked me to meet her outside of the bookstore. I didn't think anything of it. We meet and then went into the diner to have lunch. We chatted for a bit, sharing memories and good times we had with Miranda. It was getting close to time for me to drive over for my shift at the Lunar Disco, so we parted. She asked if we could meet again and I agreed.

Then the other day, I met with Elizabeth again for a late breakfast. We met outside of the bookstore. She grabbed me and pushed me against the window. I didn't stop her. For a moment I felt like I was kissing Victoria again. Then I remembered that Victoria was dead and that Elizabeth wasn't her. I pulled away from her. She looked angry but followed me to the diner. We ate and chatted for a bit. I told her I needed to get back home and that I wouldn't be back for a while. She seemed irate. That was the last time I saw her before...before..."

Steven cleared his throat and nodded in understanding. "It sounds like you were in all the wrong places at all the wrong times."

"Exactly. Why is this murderer killing all the women I know?"

"That is the same question we are trying to answer." I looked deep into his eyes and sighed. "I am not going to lie to you George. We had a good reason to suspect you as the killer. With this new information, we might have been looking in the wrong place though."

"Randolph told me it was all going to be over soon." George blew out a deep breath and slumped into his coffee. "Now when I need him the most, I can't find him at all."

"He went home a month ago." Steven frowned as he poured a second cup of coffee and took a bite of the muffin.

"No, he was here two nights ago. Said he had business to take care of before he could go home."

"What?" Steven gulped. "After Victoria passed, he told me he didn't have time for this hokey crap. He was going home and letting me deal with the fallout."

"He didn't go home. He was still here a few days ago."

I exchanged a glance with Steven as we both processed that information. My gut instincts had told me that these murders and the hauntings at Steven's place were connected. At the time I had thought that it was either George or Randolph that was murdering the women. Now, with the new information that George had provided, that left Randolph as the killer. I gulped down the last of my coffee and considered any loose pieces I might have missed.

"George, how did you know where I lived?"

"Randolph told me."

"All signs are pointing to Randolph?" Steven questioned as he tapped a rhythm on the table. His anger towards George seemed to have thawed some as he mulled over the new information.

"So far, yes." I swallowed hard. "Remember the night we went to visit Gertie?"

"Yes." He smiled at the memory. "I'd like to see a reappearance of that black dress, but it was an uneventful night. Why?"

"I asked you how you knew where I lived. You told me that George told you."

Steven blushed and averted his gaze. I waited. George seemed shocked by that answer and was watching him as well. "I lied. I had asked Serena one day. I swear I wasn't stalking you or anything."

I took a moment to weigh this answer. My heart wanted to trust him, but my head wasn't so sure. At the same time, I had wanted to trust Randolph as well. It was so hard to tell who was being truthful and who wasn't. "OK. Now the question I have is how does Randolph know where I live?"

Steven and George looked at each other for a moment, then shrugged and shook their heads. All signs were pointing to Randolph. I rose from the table without another word and headed upstairs to shower and change. While I showered, I thought about all the pieces of this very convoluted puzzle.

Last night before I fell asleep, Steven had asked why Randolph would kill those women. I knew that he killed Victoria to frame Steven for the murder. That one was easy to figure out. Miranda and Elizabeth were the puzzle. I had to fit these pieces into the puzzle with Randolph now as the frame. They didn't seem to fit. We all left the house and headed over to the cafe to start the day and hear how the girls did with the memory potion.

When Steven pulled up to the parking lot, my gut clenched again in fear. George disappeared, saying he was going to head over to the hotel to see if he could catch Randolph. I watched him head off in the direction of the hotel when I glanced back at the cafe. There were no lights on. Frowning, I started down the walkway with Steven behind me. The shop was locked and closed.

"Where are the girls?" Steven murmured as we glanced up and down the sidewalk.

"I don't know."

Reggie began howling about a curse as he pointed towards the cafe. I stepped back and looked the building over from top to bottom. I saw no signs painted on the doors or windows. The sidewalk was cleaned of the graffiti from the last tagging. I looked from him to the building and back again. He was shouting at the top of his lungs now. His arm was shaking as he pointed at the building.

Steven tried to calm him down as I walked around the cafe to the back alley. There was no graffiti back here either. The alley was quiet and empty at this time of the morning. I walked to the back entrance. The door was still padlocked. I slipped a small set of keys out of my pocket and opened the cafe. Once inside, I noticed that the ovens were still cold, and the coffee pots were empty. Everything looked as it would if the girls had not opened the shop. I unlocked the front door and joined Steven in trying to calm down Reggie.

"Reggie, the girls are running a little late this morning." I remarked calmly. "Why don't you come inside and rest for a moment while I get some coffee on?"

Reggie shook his head and wrenched his arm out of Steven's grip. He took off behind the cafe shouting about a curse and hex. We watched as he rounded the corner and disappeared before heading back into the cafe. I didn't bother turning the sign over to proclaim that we were open. If the girls were not here, there was no one to run the cafe. I settled down on the couch and Steven settled next to me. We listened to the silence for a few minutes.

"Have the girls ever been late before?" he inquired softly.

"Once or twice each, but never together." I shrugged lightly. "There is a first time for everything, right?"

The look Steven gave me said it all. We sent the girls out last night to take care of the memory problem. Somewhere between the cafe and the town water supply they were either abducted or killed. A tear slid down my cheek at the thought of them being dead. I wiped it away in frustration. If the girls were dead, I would have seen that in my vision. I was confident that they had just been taken. I had a chance to get them back alive.

I stood, locked the front door, and headed to the back door. Steven joined me as I replaced the padlock. I had to find the girls and get them back. I climbed behind the wheel and waited for Steven. I turned the car in the direction of the street and paused. I glanced at the cafe and then toward the water supply.

"What clicked now?" he encouraged, as he caught my now familiar look.

"Reggie was yelling and screaming about a curse and pointing at the cafe."

"Yes."

"What if he wasn't pointing at the cafe?" I pointed at where the town water supply was located. "What if he was trying to warn us of a curse but not at the cafe? What if he meant the town water supply? What if this whole time he had been trying to tell us what was wrong?"

Steven glanced back at the cafe and then closed his eyes. He lined up the image in his head like I had just done. He braced his hand against the dashboard and grimaced. "Floor it Vi."

Chapter Twenty-Eight

I t only took fifteen minutes for me to drive to the town's water supply. We walked down the concrete stairs to the metal door. The lock was open, and the door was ajar. I stepped cautiously into the opening and glanced around. The room was dark. From the first rays of the sun peeking through the door, I spied the electrical box on the wall. Steven caught sight of it at the same time, and he flipped the lever.

Light spilled over another set of stairs leading down into the cavern. We moved quietly down the stairs until they ended in the wide-open space of the cistern. I glanced left and right but didn't see the girls. How could I have been so wrong? My vision showed them here in this room. They were tied up.

Closing my eyes, I allowed my intuition to guide me. Walking towards the left, I positioned myself right where the vision showed the killer had been standing. Steven was off to my right near the edge of the platform. The girls would have been to my left, bound and gagged against the cavern walls. I opened my eyes and looked down at the cavern wall. The girls were not there. Frowning, I turned and felt my heart skip a beat.

George was creeping up behind Steven with a gun. He lifted his hand and slammed it against the back of Steven's head. The cracking sound the gun made as it hit his skull made my breakfast rise into my throat. I swallowed it down as I stared down the barrel of the gun. George sneered at me.

"This whole time you thought you were smarter than us." George spat. Steven moaned which earned him a savage kick to the stomach. "We really showed you, didn't we?"

"We?" I whispered. I heard a soft grating sound and whirled to find a portion of the rock wall slide back and in. Randolph materialized. He was also armed with a gun. I began to wonder if it was smart for us to come rushing over here without any weapons.

I peered into the hidden room that Randolph had come through. The girls were tied up inside against the wall. I was elated to find that they were unharmed, but angry that they were still in danger. I swallowed as my mind raced through all the information, still trying to piece it together.

"Randolph?" I acknowledged him with a tight-lipped sneer.

"Bitch," he grinned as he stepped out of the room. Watching both men as they moved into position in front of me, I noticed they were both left-handed. What were the odds of that? Which of these two did I need to be more afraid of?

"I don't understand." I furrowed my brow "How? Why?"

"George masterminded it all." Randolph supplied. He looked as if he was completely bored with this whole plot. "He promised that if we could take out Steven that we could share the wealth of the Ravens Estate."

"Shut up Randolph." George growled. "She is stalling for time. Shoot her already and toss her into the water."

"What are we going to do with him?" Randolph motioned with his gun to Steven.

"Well, getting him arrested for the murders is out of the question. That dumb detective believed every word they fed him. Shoot him too and shove him in."

"I can't..." Randolph stalled.

"Wait," I interjected. I peeked into the hidden alcove and noticed that the girls were gone. Not wanting to bring attention to their escape, I tried stalling even more. I needed to buy them time to get to the police. "Help me understand. How are you two going to share the wealth of the Ravens Estate? How do you share a house? Steven said the money was in a trust to repair and fix the estate."

"You are not as smart as people say you are." George rolled his eyes. "There is money hidden on that property. We have been searching for it since Steven moved in. That whore ancestor of ours hid it well."

"There is money?" I tried hard to act like I didn't know about the hidden money. I knew exactly what they were talking about. Even in this stressful situation I was doing a good job of acting. Holding my hands out, I pleaded. "I have been through that house from top to bottom with Steven."

"Money, jewels, bonds, I don't care really. The family history said that our great, great, great grandfather had wealth and that his wife did too. There must be something hidden worth a fortune. You two were too stupid to find it." Randolph tugged on his ear as he sighed. "The problem was getting Steven out of the picture so we could search. Hell, we can even sell off the estate in several chunks and make a nice fortune."

Stalling was the name of the game at this point. I needed to give Serena and Tessa time to get to Detective Johns. I watched the two men and furrowed my brow again. "The estate passes down to the oldest male heir. If you get rid of Steven, the estate will go into foreclosure and then you would inherit, Randolph. That inheritance will come with having to pay the money owed.

Is it worth it to pay that much in the hopes of finding a fortune? What if there isn't a fortune?"

"What?" Randolph turned away from me. His hand with the gun dropped to his side as he yelled at George. "You didn't tell me that there would be fees involved in my inheritance."

"Shut up!" George averted his gaze, and I used that time to step back a few steps towards the hidden room. Maybe I could escape as well. I would have to come back for Steven and hope they didn't kill him. "A little money won't kill you. It will all be worth it in the end."

"Who would have to pay those fees, George? Me. I would have to. With the divorce, child support, spousal support, and now the hotel charges for the both of us, I have no money left. I can't afford to pay any fees."

Randolph appeared to be sweating now. He ran his free hand through his hair and puffed out his red cheeks. At the angle I was standing, I knew exactly who he reminded me of. Randolph was the spitting image of his dead relative, Arthur. I shuddered as I remembered the ghostly feel of him pinning me to the bed.

"It doesn't matter. We will find the money. Now shoot them and let's get on with it."

"I can't shoot them." Randolph stuffed his gun in his trouser pocket. "I am a doctor. I took an oath to do no harm. The agreement was that I would help you frame Steven and search the house. You would do all the dirty work."

"I have had to do the dirty work and come up with the plan. The least you can do is help a little. Why should I be the one with all the blood on my hands." George had turned his attention away from me and was flinging his hands wildly in the air towards Randolph. "You act like you are innocent in all of this. You wanted the money more than I did. You agreed to this plot."

"Don't move, Aunt Vi." Tessa whispered softly. I felt a hand touch mine and then cold metal. "Serena went to get help." I nodded ever so slightly so as not to draw attention to myself. My heart felt lighter. "I'm going to see if I can use the hidden tunnel to circle around behind them. Keep their attention on you." I nodded ever so slightly to let Tessa know that I heard her.

"What are you doing?" George screamed as his attention focused on me again. I had taken another step towards the hidden room which had caught his attention. At his shout, I froze.

I didn't move as Randolph rushed his bulky body to the hidden room. The gruff curses he erupted with told me that Tessa had escaped again. Snarling, Randolph kicked me in the calf as he grabbed the back of my neck and hauled me closer to them. I was dumped like a sack of potatoes at George's feet. I landed directly on Steven and gasped as Tessa's knife dug deep into my palm.

I saw Steven open his eyes for a moment when I fell on him. He was awake. I had feared he was badly hurt. I felt his hand twitch toward me to help steady me. Even in this situation, this man was trying to help me. I felt my heart squeeze at the love that I knew I felt for him. I rocked my head back and glared at Randolph. He only chuckled and crossed his arms over his chest.

"The girls are gone."

"It doesn't matter. Who would believe them anyways? It is their word against yours." George smiled maniacally.

"Mine!?" Randolph exclaimed. "Why mine?"

"You are an esteemed heart surgeon. Who would ever believe that you plotted and murdered those women just for a crumbling estate?"

"I didn't murder anyone." Randolph argued.

"Are you sure?"

George smiled as a gun exploded. The reverberation thrummed in my head as I watched Randolph crumple to the ground. Steven jerked up, pushing me to the side. He tried to stand but fell back. I caught him before he smacked his head. George noticed the commotion and turned with a heavy sigh and a shake of his head.

"If you want something done right," he began.

I sat, looking up the barrel of the gun once more. He pulled the hammer back and sneered at me as his finger squeeze the trigger. I closed my eyes and swallowed as I imagined the hot metal tearing through my flesh. The pain of bleeding out. I waited for the moment of death. For the blissful peace of doing all I could to solve this mystery. I waited and continued to wait as my heart pounded in my chest.

It felt like an eternity of waiting. Hours of wondering when the moment of death would claim me. I finally opened my eyes and let out a breath I didn't realize I was holding and looked up. Reggie had snuck into the cavern and was wrestling George for the weapon.

I sent out a quick prayer to the Goddess for her intervention. Standing slowly, I watched as Reggie backed George further away from us and towards the entrance. I inhaled a steadying breath, raised the hand with Tessa's knife, aimed, and threw.

Slick from blood, wobbly from my frightened energy, and weakly thrown, the knife skimmed through the air and lodged halfway into George's shoulder. I had never thrown a knife in my life. At that moment I was thankful that the Goddess was guiding me or helping in some way.

George screamed as the knife struck him and punched Reggie hard in the stomach. I watched as our savior dropped to a crouch and gagged. Siren sounds filled the cavern, echoing eerily around the chamber. Our heroes in blue had shown up. That meant that Serena had made it back into town and found Detective Johns. George turned, screamed at me, then shot off down the other side of the cavern. He pressed against the wall and another door opened.

Who knew the town water supply had two hidden tunnels in it? I rushed to Reggie to check on him. He mumbled his thanks but shoved me back towards Steven. Dropping down next to him, I felt the back of his skull. There was a large knot on his head behind his left ear. When I pulled my hand out, it was covered in blood.

The cistern became full of cops as they swarmed us with their guns out and shouted commands to freeze. Detective Johns inspected the scene and radioed for the paramedics to come in. A pained groan filled the silence that ensued, and I watched as Randolph grabbed his side and tried to sit up. Three cops surrounded him with their guns drawn.

"Is Reggie alright?" Steven murmured.

"He is fine."

"The girls?"

"They escaped through the hidden tunnel. George got away."

"I am so sorry, Violet." He clutched at my hand and looked up at me with sincerity. "I had no idea..."

"I know, Steven." I smiled and patted him on the hand. "Let's get you over to the paramedic to be checked out. Think you can stand?"

"For you, Violet," Steven professed as he stood slowly. With my help, we walked toward the stairwell. "I would dance down the moon."

Chapter Twenty-Nine

Steven, Reggie, and Randolph were both swept away in ambulances to the hospital. Detective Johns asked me to meet him at the police station in thirty minutes. I nodded as I made a slow exit. It was only ten in the morning, but I was exhausted. I was also furious that I allowed George to get away. Climbing behind the wheel of my car, I sat quietly for a moment.

Tessa might still be in those tunnels looking for a way around. I glanced around the lot at all the police vehicles. I didn't see the girl's car anywhere. That didn't mean anything though. I had not seen it when I arrived in the first place. I took a deep breath and let it out. I would guess by now Tessa had come out when Serena arrived and they both went home. I put that worry behind me for a moment as I took another deep breath.

My vision had shown that I was going to die down there. I had survived. Did that mean I had averted the course of the vision? Did that mean that I would be back in the cistern again one day to face my inevitable death? The Goddess would surely show me in time. I put the car in reverse and backed out of the crowded parking lot.

I drove over to the police station and worked on a calming meditation while I waited for Detective Johns. The desk sergeant was kind enough to bring me a cup of coffee. It was slightly cold and stronger than paint, but I appreciated every drop of it. It was closer to an hour than thirty minutes, but I eventually spied the detective's unmarked sedan as it pulled into the lot. I joined him and walked to the door where he led me inside and we settled at his desk. It took me two hours to impart all the information on what happened.

Once he released me, I drove immediately to my house. The girls lived next door, and I walked the short distance across the yards to pound on their door. I chewed on my lip while I waited for someone to answer. Serena answered. She examined me for only a second before she wailed and wrapped me up in her arms. I held her tight and rocked her back and forth while murmuring soothing words to calm her. Sniffling she pulled away and we walked inside.

Tessa appeared in the hallway and grinned from ear to ear as I assessed her for any damage. They both looked unharmed, and I sent another small prayer to the Goddess for that favor. I settled on the couch and filled them in on the details of what had happened after they had escaped. Serena curled up on the couch and covered herself in a blanket while she listened. Tessa had more nervous energy than she knew what to do with, so she headed into the kitchen and began mixing up a batch of banana bread.

"We are still in danger then?" Tessa called from the kitchen.

"I don't know." I leaned back in the chair and closed my eyes. "I have never been able to change a vision. Did I change this one? Or will it still come to pass?"

The girls were quiet for a moment while they thought about it. It was Serena who ventured a guess. "Why would the Goddess give us the sight if not to give us a chance to change it? I think we were successful. We averted your death."

"The visions might be more prophetic." Tessa supplied. "But I must agree with Serena on this. I think we averted it. You said that some things were the same as the vision and some were different."

"Yes. No matter how we see the gift though, George is still loose. You two promise that you stick with each other like glue until the police round him up."

"We will, Aunty Vi." Serena sniffled once more and snuggled closer in her blanket. "I wish I could stop crying. I don't even know why I am crying."

"My baby girl," I sympathized. I moved to the couch and hugged her tight. "It's your empathy, darling. Tessa and I are pushing our tears away right now so we can be strong. You are crying our tears."

"Well stop it you two!" she grumbled as she blew her nose once more. "I am tired of crying."

"I am going to go to my house and soak in the tub. I will cry over there. Does that sound good?"

"Go now please." Serena begged as she sniffled again.

"Aunt Vi, keep your phone close. You might be next door but that doesn't mean we will hear you if something happens," Tessa warned as she came into the living room wiping tears off her own cheeks.

"I will, I promise."

I trudged over to my house and drew a steaming hot bath. I tossed in some lavender and jasmine to help soothe my frayed nerves. While I soaked, I allowed the tears to flow so that Serena could finally relax. While I had a little experience with empathy, I knew it was hell for them to have to experience everyone else's moods. I needed to go check on Steven at the hospital.

I dressed quickly and then drove to the hospital on the other side of town. I checked in with the nurses to see how Reggie was doing. The head nurse blushed as she promised he was in fine health. I inquired as to how long he would be there. I was told it would only be overnight, and he was free to leave tomorrow. I made a mental note to make sure he had a full breakfast tomorrow for what he did for us. Thanking her I was directed to Steven's room.

The lights had been dimmed, and the curtain was pulled over the window to allow him to sleep. I heard the steady beeping of the heart monitor. Stepping inside, I settled into the chair next to his bed. A nurse came in to check his vitals and I asked her how he was. She promised it appeared worse than it was. He had a bruised rib and a mild concussion, but they were going to watch him overnight.

I snickered at that. Hospitals were always watching someone overnight just to be cautious. I threaded my fingers with Steven's and eased down into the chair to close my eyes. It was amazing how we escaped this whole ordeal with a concussion and some bruises. I thought about checking on Randolph since he was related to Steven, but then I decided he didn't deserve my concern. If it wasn't for him and George, we wouldn't be here at this moment.

"Hey you..." I felt a tug on my hand and watched as Steven opened his eyes. "Would you know someone who can investigate a haunting in my hospital room?" he teased. I smiled as he tugged harder on my arm. "Snuggle with me, Vi."

I crawled into the hospital bed with him and snuggled against his uninjured side. He closed his eyes after resting his face against my head. Breathing in his scent and listening to the steady beep from the machine lulled us both off into slumber.

The stress of the whole day had left us both in need of a nap. I felt as if I had just closed my eyes when someone woke me.

"Miss!" a woman hissed. Groggily I peeled open one eye and spied a nurse standing next to the hospital bed. "Miss, you can't be in bed with him."

Of course I couldn't. Heaven forbid Steven be comforted in the hospital after a traumatic event. I rolled my eyes but slid softly over the side of the bed. I watched the sun rise through the hospital window. For the first time since I could remember, I didn't feel the warmth and the comfort of the sun as it rose above the horizon. I felt a cold pit of fear open in my gut at the thought. Was the solace of my sun salutation forever ruined?

I texted the girls to make sure they were safe. My heart beat a little slower when the response came back immediately. They were fine and opening the cafe to a long line of customers this morning. Tessa excitedly shared a picture of the line. It was backed up down the street to Steven's shop. I replied with hearts and confetti emojis.

The towns people had been boycotting the Mystic Brew Cafe since all of this had started. It appeared that they didn't want to patronize a cafe that served a murderer. This was an unspoken apology from the town. They had all heard what happened last night and were showing their support once more. I let out a pent-up breath. A quick peek over at Steven showed that he was still sleeping. I tip toed out of the room and went in search of Reggie.

The room Reggie had been issued was empty. When I inquired at the nurse's station, they explained that Reggie ate dinner, then sometime in the middle of the night he had checked himself out. I smiled and then nodded. That sounded exactly like Reggie. I made a split-second decision and asked if the nurse could point me in the direction of Randolph's room. Even though the man was an accessory to murder, I couldn't help but make sure that he was ok.

When I entered Randolph's room, it was much like Steven's had been. The lights had been dimmed, and the shades had been pulled over the window to keep most of the light out. Randolph was pale. He had lost a bit of blood between being shot and waking up here in the hospital. The nurse was taking his vitals when I stepped into the room. She gave me a sympathetic pat on the arm before ducking out of the room.

"Randolph..." I murmured softly as he turned his gaze away from me.

"Imposter..." he sniffed.

"Randolph," I began. I wasn't even sure what I wanted to say. What does one say to a man who had a hand in so many murders? A man who assisted with kidnapping your family? A man who had been told to kill you? "Why?"

"Why?" Randolph spun his gaze to me as if I had shocked him. Anger bubbled up inside him until his face was beet red. "Why?" he demanded yet again. He flung his hands in the air. "Why did I do this? Why was I stupid to allow George to talk me into this? Why didn't I just stay away?"

"Just why?" I allowed tears to slip down my cheeks as I took another step closer to his bed. "Why would you help George harm those women? Why would you try to pin this on Steven? Just, why?"

"Steven has always been the favorite child. Mom and Dad always loved him best. He could never do any wrong in their eyes. He picked the crummiest, the sluttiest women, and still they loved him like he was a rock star. I had it all. The career, the wife, the children. That was, until my wife divorced me and took the children with her. I made one wrong decision during a surgery, and my career was toast."

Randolph looked at me with pleading eyes, but I couldn't and wouldn't respond. I merely waited for an answer. His red face dissipated back to the pasty white complexion he had when I entered the room. He let out a deep puff of air before he continued.

"I was out of money. My damn ex-wife and children were bleeding me dry with alimony and child support payments. I had no new funds coming in. I am living in a tiny one-bedroom apartment that costs a fortune. When Steven told me about the inheritance, I thought it should have been mine. I should have the mansion. I should have the money. I could sell it and make a profit. I could finally get back what I had lost."

"You did all of this for money?" I couldn't keep the astonishment from my face. "Money? You helped George kill those women for money?"

"I didn't kill them. That was all George. All I did was get them to a location he told me about."

"It is the same thing, Randolph. If you hadn't lured them there, he wouldn't have been able to kill them."

"Sure, he would have. It would have just taken a little longer. George can be very persuasive when he wants to be. Did Steven ever tell you about the time that George pretended to be him and stole his girlfriend?"

"Yes." I let out a snort and shook my head. "I wish you luck, Randolph. May the path that you have forged, serve you well."

I strode out of his room without another look back. The thought that someone had been callous enough to assist with murder for the sake of money shocked me to my core. I took a detour through the hospital corridors to the cafeteria for a cup of coffee and a muffin. I needed the time to process what I had learned. I wasn't sure if I could understand this depraved way of thinking. All life was sacred, even that of a murderer and an accomplice.

"There you are beautiful." Steven sat gingerly in the chair across from me in the cafeteria. "The doctors gave me a clean bill of health. When you didn't return to the room, I wondered where you had disappeared to."

"I needed a moment to think and gather my thoughts." I had purchased two coffees and pushed the second one towards him. I had half my muffin left and offered it to him.

"I see." He nodded as he popped a bit of the muffin in his mouth. He chewed thoughtful while staring at the table. "Did this thinking have anything to do with me?"

"What?" Suddenly I understood why Steven looked a little upset. "No. Good Goddess Steven, it wasn't anything to do with you. I needed to think about Randolph and George. What George's plan might be. Where he might go. How they could possible do all this over money." I reached out and patted his hand with a smile. "Trust me, it had nothing to do with you."

"Does that mean, you for sure, don't think I am a killer now?"

"I haven't thought that for a while now."

"Right." Steven chuckled and winked. "You mean like the other day it didn't cross your mind at all?"

"Well," I swallowed a large mouthful of my coffee before I ducked my head and nodded. "Ok, for a moment I did have a brief thought that you were just putting the moves on me to distract me from all the murders. I swear," I held my hand up and put my other over my heart. "I swear on the Goddess that from now on, I will never think that you are the murderer."

"Good." Steven smiled broadly and leaned over the table to place a kiss on my forehead. "How about we go and have a second date. Let's forget all this nasty business and be two normal humans getting to know each other better?"

"That sounds fantastic."

"Not going to fight me on this, princess?" he teased as I rose from the table and threaded my fingers with his.

"Not this time. I think I have run out of excuses not to go out with you."

"A whole day to pamper my lady." Steven pulled me under his arm and chuckled. "I have been waiting for this moment for a long time."

"Not as long as me, my dear. I can promise you that."

Chapter Thirty

Steven and I headed over to my place first. I showered quickly and changed into comfortable clothes. It might be a date, but I was going to be prepared for anything. I took a moment to look at myself in the mirror. My brown eyes were framed with purple smudges underneath. My shoulder length brown hair was tired and worn out. My complexion was a little pale and drawn. What could Steven possibly see in me?

Shaking my head and pulling my hair into a loose bun at the nape of my neck, I put on a little lip gloss and stepped from the bathroom. The look Steven gave me when I stepped downstairs made my insides feel all gooey and warm. I gave him a bright smile as we stepped outside and headed over to his place. I made sure to text the girls what we were doing. It was Serena who replied with the confetti and hearts this time.

Steven insisted on stepping inside his house first. When nothing was thrown at him, he opened the door wide, and he ushered me inside with a sweep of his arms and a bow. I couldn't suppress the giggle that escaped me as I brushed by him into the kitchen.

I loved this house as much as I loved my place. It was large and expansive with plenty of charm. I loved the wood frames and paneling. I loved the wooden floors and the marble island in the middle. It felt like home to me. With a sniffle, I watched as Tiger appeared in front of us. Her back end wagged frantically as she bounced up and down for a second. She dropped her forepaws and barked silently before rolling onto her back and presenting her belly.

"Looks like Tiger is happy to see you." Steven chuckled as he tugged me into the living room. "Come my fair lady. Let us partake of the moving pictures and..." he paused for a moment as he thought really hard. "Ok, I can't think of the old way of saying snuggle on the couch."

"I don't think they said things like that back then," I snickered as he settled onto the couch, and I snuggled up against him. "I think they had a little more class than that."

"A little more class? Does that mean we can't snog for a bit?"

"Why Steven," I fanned my face in the best imitation I could of an old-fashioned woman with the vapors. "I do believe you are an impertinent rake. However, do you think my nieces will approve of you?"

"I will endeavor to make sure that I turn on the charm."

We both giggled as he flipped the television on and picked a movie. It was a good old-fashioned show about a con artist that worked for a woman that had once been rich. She was now poor, and they were running cons to keep her in the comfort that she was used to. It was a great pick me up and kept me intrigued as we sat cuddled up on the couch. We were just nearing the end of the show when Tiger appeared in my lap. She was barking her little head off and trying to tug on my shirt. Frowning, I cupped her with my hands.

"What is it little one?" I asked.

"She looks upset."

"Come on Tiger. What is it girl?"

We both followed Tiger over to the fireplace where she continued to bark and scratch at the firebox. Steven sank down to his knees to check out the tiles. We couldn't find anything that appeared out of place. I watched as Steven crawled into the fireplace much like I had a few days before. He pulled out the tin that we had found and showed it to Tiger. She continued to bark and scratch at the fireplace.

Steven frowned and set the tin to the side as he ducked back into the tight space. He felt around a bit and then jerked hard. I heard him smack his head against the stones and watched as he crumpled into a pile. My heart began to beat frantically as I tugged him out of the fireplace. Once he was free, the apparition of Arthur appeared in the firebox. He appeared outraged. I was on my knees at this point but fell back against my feet.

"YOU DARE!" the apparition bellowed. The house felt as if it shook. "STAY AWAY FROM MY RICHES!"

"Heloise!" I shouted.

I prayed that my suspicions were true. Arthur began to zoom around the room. He would pick up items randomly from the tables and throw them around. At some point I knew his energy would drain and he wouldn't be able to sustain his tirade, but I didn't want there to be any more damage to Steven or me while we waited. It took only a moment before Heloise appeared in the room.

She gave me a soft maternal smile before she focused on Arthur. I watched in fascination as she caught him in a bear hug. The man struggled against her grip. Death seemed to have given her plenty of strength to fend him off. She held him tightly as she pulled him back toward me.

"Now child, you must banish him," came the soft feminine voice of Heloise.

"I don't know how to."

"Yes, you do."

Heloise smiled as images of what I must do inundated my mind. Steven groggily came to. He jolted upright and struggled backwards in a crab like fashion until he was against the wall. He looked from Heloise and Arthur, then to me. I grasped the pendant that I wore every day and closed my eyes. Here was hoping that what I saw would truly work.

"In the presence of the Goddess, I banish thee, Arthur. In the presence of the Goddess, I banish thee, Arthur." Steven caught my hand in his and repeated what I said. "In the presence of the Goddess, I banish thee, Arthur. By the power of three, it shall be!"

There was a loud pop. It was like the sound of a balloon popping, only much louder. I covered my ears but didn't dare take my eyes off the specters in front of me. Arthur's ethereal form imploded into a tiny speck of black. I could hear his scream of frustration as he disappeared. Swallowing hard, I looked up at Heloise who was suddenly much brighter and more solid looking than before. She held her hands together in front of her mouth as she looked at Steven and me.

"Thank you both. Arthur had been draining me for years. I tried to stop him as much as I could. I wish I could do more for you. Know that I will watch over and protect you forever." She paused as Tiger rushed into the space and jumped up and down in front of her. "Oh, my precious little one. You two rescued her as well. That is good. I had feared what Arthur had done to her. Take care, my babes."

Steven and I gawked at the space as the two turned into pinpoints of purple light and disappeared up the chimney. We sat there for a good ten minutes, staring at the fireplace in astonishment. When I finally turned my gaze to him, he merely shrugged. Yep, that was sort of how I was feeling. I wasn't sure if there were any words to describe what I was feeling or what I had witnessed. I climbed to my feet, and we settled into the couch once more.

"You know, Violet," Steven offered quietly. "I don't think a day with you will ever be normal."

"Did you want it to be?" I questioned with a tremble in my voice.

Steven was silent for a long time. I began to feel a ball of ice form in my stomach. My hands shook lightly as I folded them and placed them in my lap. This was it. This was the moment I had feared the whole time Steven had pestered me for a date. He was realizing that I was not the woman he had hoped for. I sat waiting for him to answer. I couldn't bring myself to look at him. He reached out a warm hand and gently turned my face to look at him.

"No, Vi." He kissed the tip of my nose and looked deep into my eyes. "I can't imagine myself living a normal life when I could experience the abnormal with you every minute of every day. You brought excitement and adventure into my life, and I love you for it."

"Truly?"

"Yes, Violet. This whole horrible fiasco may have brought me to your cafe, but I think deep down that I was meant to meet you. You are the fire that I have been missing. The sunrise to my dreary world."

"Where have you been my whole life, Steven?" I demanded in a squeaky voice. I was on the edge of tears at this point.

"I was waiting for you to be ready."

For the second time in my life, I did something I would never do. I pulled Steven closer and kissed him. Our lips meshed as if they were one. Our breathing became erratic, and I felt heat blossom in my gut. His hands trailed down my shoulders to my arms and then to my waist. He lifted me as if I weighed nothing and settled me on his lap. Tongues parried and kisses became exhales of delight as we explored the sensations we were feeling.

I pulled back and rested my forehead against his, trying to get needed oxygen into my lungs. We still had a killer to catch. George was still on the run. While he was free, the girls and I were still not safe. I placed a kiss on his nose and stood. Grasping his hand, I pulled him to his feet and led him upstairs to the bedroom. Those were worries for tomorrow though. Tonight, I was going to enjoy my second date night.

Chapter Thirty-One

"Ah, there is my sunshine. Good morning my love!" Steven murmured softly in my ear the next morning. He wrapped his warm strong arms around my waist and tugged me closer.

"Stop," I snickered as I wiggled to get out of his grip. I had been pretending to sleep for at least an hour as I thought about what I had done.

"Why? Last night was..."

"A mistake?" I nodded as I finally broke free. I had scooted only to the edge of the bed when I was grabbed by the hips and tugged back. He pinned me down and frowned at me. "Steven, it is alright. You don't have to..."

"Violet Sage Blueblade!"

"How..." I inhaled deeply and stopped struggling as I looked up at him. "How do you know my middle name?"

"Your nieces are long-winded and knowledgeable in all things Aunty. I must confess I spent a few days grilling them on everything." He gave me a sly grin as he made himself comfortable while still pinning me down. "That is quite the name."

"Hippie parents. No need to explain more. If you will..."

"My lovely and beautiful Violet. You are going nowhere until you comprehend that we are not a mistake. This, I hope, will be a regular occurrence in our relationship."

"After everything that has happened?"

"Violet." Steven let out an exasperated sigh as he rolled onto his side of the bed. Instead of crawling out from under the covers and getting dress, I turned onto my side to study him. He had tossed an arm over his eyes and was shaking his head back and forth. "I don't know how many ways I can say it, love. I love you. I want to spend the rest of my life with you. I want to see what strange and unusual things you can unearth. I want you and only you. Why can't you see that we are perfect together?"

"I don't believe in perfect."

"Then we are two halves of a whole. Do you believe in that? Soul mates? You compliment me. Once I get the hang of my gifts, then we can be an amazing ghost fighting, murderer catching, puzzle solving team. Or maybe it is me you are running away from. After all, there seem to be many criminals in my family."

The silence hung heavy for a minute as I contemplated all that he said in that short tirade. He eventually peeked out from under his arm, his eyes begging me for an answer. I opened my mouth for a quick response. That was how I always handled rejection. A quick response, a rapid retreat, then lick my wounds in private. This wasn't a rejection, but I was acting as if it was. I closed my mouth and chose my words carefully. When I spoke, I felt the words resonating inside my heart.

"I have spent my whole life being rejected because of how I look. My first reaction is and always will be to assume that I am not what a man is looking for. As with all bad habits, it will take me a long time to learn to accept that you want me. I hope that your love will come with understanding and patience. I do believe in soul mates. I never thought I would find my soul mate, but I agree that we do complement each other."

I pulled his arm off his head and threaded my fingers with his as I kissed him lightly on the lips. "I don't care about the criminals in your family, Steven. No family is perfect as there is no such thing as perfection. Do you accept my explanation and forgive me?"

"Hmmm." He tugged me back down for a more passionate kiss. "I forgive and accept you as you are Violet Sage Blueblade. Know that I plan to remind you every time you naysay yourself or our relationship. If you accept that, then I guess we need to get up and get ready for the day. George is still on the loose."

"Right to the heart of the matter," I frowned as we both crawled out of the bed.

"Do we have a plan?"

"Shouldn't we leave this to the police to handle? They are better equipped to deal with a murderer."

"Where is the fun in that? Think of all the danger we can thwart. The excitement of trying to find George. The..."

"I get your point." I giggled as I tossed a pair of pants at him from his dresser. "Do you want me to make breakfast, or shall we head over to the cafe? The girls have told me that business is picking up again."

"Mmmm, coffee and a scone. Yes please."

I rolled my eyes as we dressed and headed out of the house. We stopped dead in our tracks once we stepped outside. From the side entrance we could see part of the front stoop and the whole front lawn. There were several cars parked on the side of the street and five groups of people were milling around gazing at the property. Gertie was gazing in our direction at the overgrown garden that Steven had yet to fix. She hustled over to us faster than I thought a woman her age should move.

"In all my years, I never thought I could forget a place steeped in such history as this one. I can't believe how good it looks. You are doing an amazing job of fixing it up. Would you be upset if I wandered through the garden?" Gerti gushed. She placed her hand over her heart and looked at Steven with a plea in her gaze.

"I would be delighted if you did but please be careful. Some of the paths have broken stones. Don't hurt yourself." Steven replied as we climbed into the car, and I broke out into a fit of laughter.

"It appears the girls were successful in getting those herbs into the water supply. There is one thing we don't have to worry about now."

"I am not sure I like the idea of the whole town coming around to lollygag around my house. Although I can't deny Gertie. She looked so enthusiastic."

"The novelty of your place will wear off once again. Remember, the whole town was made to forget everything about you, your family, what happened, and even more about this massive estate that has been the center of town. They will calm down."

We made our way slowly through the parked cars and traffic into the cafe. The girls were enjoying a nice boom of business as we walked through the door. Serena handed me two china cups of coffee and then shooed both Steven and I into the alcove. We settled at the table and were chatting about how Gertie had appeared more youthful as she had wandered through the garden when there was a light knock outside the alcove. I glanced up to find one of my regulars wringing their hands.

"Gladys, come in." I motioned her forward as Tessa brought us both a scone. She winked, slid a newspaper to me, and then quietly stepped out of the room. "What can I do for you?"

"I was hoping, that is, I thought maybe." She cleared her throat and settled at the table. One quick glance at Steven before she focused back on me. "The paper said you helped catch that murderer. I was wondering if you could help me with a small matter."

"I didn't..."

"What Vi means," Steven interrupted with a patient smile and a quick pat on my knee. "She was in the right place at the wrong time. She didn't catch him she was only there when it happened. That doesn't mean that she can't assist you. What matter do you need help with?"

"Well, I, uh, you see..."

"Aunty Vi..." Tessa poked her head through the beaded curtain. "Detective Johns is here. He would like a moment with you when you are done with your reading."

"Thank you, Tessa." I pulled out my tarot deck and shuffled them a time or two before tossing out a few cards. "Are you trying to find something Gladys?"

"Yes!" she let out a relieved sigh as she leaned forward to look over the cards. "I had an old book, first edition, worth a lot of money. It has been handed down in our family. I have searched all through the house and I can't seem to locate it. I brought a picture."

I tried to hide my nerves as she dug around inside her purse looking for the picture. I needed to find the right way to turn her down. I was not a private investigator. I had no idea where to even start on something like this. Steven threaded his fingers with mine as she finally produced the picture. It was an old-fashioned photograph in black and white. I nodded at her and started to speak when Steven spoke up for me.

"Do you mind if we hold onto this for a few days?"

"Yes, of course!" Gladys looked relieved as Steven took the photograph. "I knew that you would be the right person to talk to, Vi. The paper wouldn't have said that you could do all those things if you didn't. You know where to find me when you locate that book. I, um, don't make much money, but I promise to pay you something when you find it."

"I can't..." I started, but once again Steven interrupted.

"We will investigate this and get back to you. Please know that we may not be able to find this item, but we will do some research and let you know."

"Thank you so much." She stood, turned to leave, then turned back. She reached out and took his hand. "I am so sorry I believed what they said about you. Please forgive me."

"I would have done the same thing in your place ma'am. Don't think about it another moment."

"We will look into it?" I demanded with a raised brow as Gladys disappeared beyond the beaded curtain. "I am not a private investigator, a cop, or anyone who can do anything but read auras, tarot, and make a delicious cup of coffee. Why are you giving out false hope?"

"I did no such thing." Steven winked. "I told her we would investigate and let her know. That was the quickest way to get to Detective Johns. Unless you want me to go get Gladys once more. We can tell her that we cannot under any circumstances, attempt to help her."

"I..." I frowned as I thought about what he said. He was right. He didn't give her false hope. It didn't mean that I liked this idea, though. Swallowing hard, I nodded and rose from the chair. "Detective Johns," I ushered him into the alcove and watched as he hesitated at the beaded curtain. "How can I help you today, Detective? Has there been another murder?"

"No." He gave me a reassuring smile before settling into the chair across from us. "Our force searched high and low for George, and we have been unable to locate him. I am going to put a detail on you two. Have you heard from him?"

"The man that wanted to kill me?" I snorted and shook my head. "I have not. I don't think he would be stupid enough to contact me for anything at this point."

"Have you," Detective Johns cleared his throat and paused as he thought for a moment. "Have you had a vision of your death lately?"

"No."

"If you do, would you let me know?" He pulled out a card from his pocket and sat it on the table in front of me. "That's my cell, text me day or night. If you get a vision of your death again, that means that George is still around. I will keep the force on high alert for him, but he may have already fled the county."

I nodded in understanding as he rose and left. For a moment Steven and I both stared at the card in front of me. I wasn't sure if I was thrilled with the idea that Detective Johns was starting to believe in the whole woo-woo of my gift or if it scared the crap out of me. I was leaning more towards scared. While I knew that George was still a threat to me and the girls, I hadn't thought that he would still commit murder.

Chapter Thirty-Two

"Are you sure you don't want to try and find George first?" Steven offered as he scooped up the business card and tucked it into his pocket. "It would beat hanging around and waiting for him to do something first."

"I don't know."

I pulled the newspaper from the side of the table and began to read the front-page article. My mouth dropped open as I read. It appeared that the journalist was taking liberties with the facts of the case. We had been dubbed as the Witchy Blueblades. The Witchy Blueblades that run the Mystic Brew Cafe were instrumental in bringing one of the criminals in for the murders. The journalist also surmised that whatever had the town forgetting about Steven's family and the Ravens Estate was also fixed by us. At least that part was true. Although I made a note that Daisy had been more instrumental in that than we had been.

Steven read through the article after I passed it over to him. We both sat in silence while we ate our scones and drank our coffee. It was getting close to lunch at this point and the cafe emptied of the morning rush. Serena and Tessa could be heard arguing over something, so I stepped out to find them standing behind the counter. Both had their hands on their hips and were leaning towards the other as they argued.

"What in the world?" I snapped.

"They came up with the dumbest thing to call us," Serena whined.

"It is not like it isn't true. We are witches and we are Blueblades." Tessa snarked.

"That isn't the point. They could have come up with a better name. I mean the Witchy Blueblades? They could have given us something more interesting."

"Girls." I held my hands up.

"Serena does have a point." Steven offered as he leaned against a wall and shot us all a grin as he listened in. "I mean, that is sort of on the nose. For a journalist, you would think they would have gone out of the way to get something more eloquent."

"Not you too." I groaned. I let out a frustrated sigh. "Regardless of what the journalist wrote or called us we were not instrumental in bringing Randolph in. We happened to be in the right place at the wrong time. Now we need to focus on George."

"Are you coming around to my way of thinking?" Steven gasped and put a hand on his chest in shock. "About time."

"Aunty Vi didn't want to go hunting for George, huh?" Tessa quipped with a grin.

"Bet she told you that we needed to leave it up to the police." Serena agreed, rolling her eyes. "Come on Aunt Vi, we are made for this. We should be out there actively looking for George before he does something else."

"While I feel it is still best left to the police," I answered slowly. "I see the wisdom in uniting our gifts to try and ferret out where he has gone to ground." I had to wait until the girls were done whooping before I continued. "Does anyone have an idea on how to start?"

"Detective Johns asked if you had any more visions of your death." Steven started as we all settled in the conversation area.

Steven and I settled onto the couch while the girls took the easy chairs. "Your visions used to happen when you touched me. Have you had any new visions?"

"No. I didn't lie to the detective. I haven't had a vision of my death since we were caught with George and Randolph in the town's water supply."

"Aunty," Tessa began as she fiddled with a washcloth that had been threaded through her apron strings at her waist. "What would it take to force a vision? Most of the time our visions happen on their own, but is there a way to force one?"

"I suppose we could try. We would need some basil, bay, sage, thyme and mint. Each of us would need some moon charged salt which I think I have at home. A piece of labradorite or obsidian would be helpful." I thought for a moment of all the things I have at home. "Yes, I know I have an obsidian mirror we could use."

"I have all the herbs growing in the backyard at home!" Serena beamed as she twirled her hair around her finger. Will this, uh, increase my empathy?"

"No baby girl." I smiled softly at her as Steven just watched the conversation with an incredulous face. "This is to enhance psychic power and divination."

"Oh. Thank the goddess!" Serena gasped out.

"It sounds like we have a plan?" Steven hedged.

"What is this look for?" I teased as I leaned into his chest.

"I know that I have accepted that I have gifts and that all of this is real. I just," he cleared his throat and wrapped his arm around my shoulders before he rubbed his face. "Listening to you rattle off all those things made it sound like witches putting together a potion."

"Essentially, we are." I giggled as I rested my head against his shoulder and watched a few customers come in. "Potions in old times were essential a list of ingredients that made something. It could have been a meat pie, a sweet tart, or a tea. We are going to make a tea. The tea is going to help us enhance our ability to see. It isn't as eerie and evil as television makes it out to be."

"Then shall we divine the direction my malevolent cousin has disappeared tonight?"

"I think I could convince the girls if you are willing to host. They would love to get a sneak peek into your mansion. I am sure Tessa is dying to get a glimpse of the ghosts as well."

The look Steven gave me had me laughing. I explained to the girls the plan and they nodded their agreement as we headed over to my place. I packed an overnight bag with items that we would need. I added the pieces of selenite and magnets in case we needed them. I had banished Arthur, but that didn't mean I had completely cleansed the mansion of any other negative energy.

Back at Steven's place, he immediately dipped into my overnight bag, grabbed my clothes, then headed upstairs. Curious, I followed him. He opened a drawer on his dresser and casually put away my personal items. He had already cleared out a drawer in his bureau. My face and chest warmed until I felt as if I was sweating. This man was a gift that I didn't deserve. Swallowing down the feelings, I went back downstairs to work on dinner.

As I cut up vegetables and made a loaf of bread, I tried not to think about George. How could a person murder someone just for money? It made no sense. He had professed with a straight face that he had loved Victoria. What also made no sense was how he could come from a magical family and not have an aura. I shuddered as I remembered that first day when he touched me and I couldn't get a read on him. He had to be a nullifier.

A nullifier was a person who had no magical abilities and was used in ancient times to prevent others from using their magical abilities. They were extremely popular in hunting down witches. I had never met a nullifier in real life. I had only read about them in the history of witches. He would not have been able to put that memory charm in the town's water supply then. That meant Randolph had done that part.

I sighed as I scooped the cut vegies into a container and popped them into the refrigerator. I turned to pull out the chicken to marinate it when I noticed that Tiger was sitting primly in the middle of the floor between me and the counter. I smiled, bent down and patted her head, then grab items from the cabinet. My hand touched the container of salt, and I knocked it to the floor as a vision hit me.

"Vi?" Steven caught my arms as I fumbled to catch the container.

"No! No!" I gasped as I wrapped my hands around Steven's biceps. As the foggy vision cleared, I felt the trail of tears down my cheeks. Steven maneuvered me to the stools next to the island. He got me settled, filled a cup with water, and sat next to me. I inhaled deeply.

"A vision?" he inquired.

"Yes. I couldn't make it all out."

"It had to be bad. It made you cry." He hesitated before he offered. "I don't think you even cried at the visions of your death."

"We must be on the right path. I didn't see, so much as feel."
I gulped down some water and shuddered. "I felt the cold sharp
blade of a knife as it pierced through my chest. It wasn't my chest
though. I don't know how to explain it."

"I think that explains it well enough." Steven frowned as
he brushed my hair off my forehead. "Should we cancel the
divination party?"

"No. I didn't see anything. The tea we are going to brew
should help shed light."

There was the soft chime of the doorbell and Steven pressed
a kiss to my forehead before heading off to let the girls in. I could
hear the excited chatter as they wandered around the house
getting the tour. I eventually shoved myself off the stool and
cleaned up the salt. I returned to making the preparations for
dinner. When the girls finally popped their head into the
kitchen, I had steadied my nerves.

"I forgot to mention this morning..." I offered to the girls as
they immediately began pulling things out to help. "Congrats on
getting those herbs into the water supply with everything that
happened. Which of you two did that?"

"I did." Serena remarked. She tilted her head down and
blushed lightly. That was unlike my outgoing girl. "I snuck in just
after they took everyone to the hospital. When I got free, I ran
through the tunnels and found a small hidden room. I waited
until I was sure it was clear before sneaking back in."

"A small room?"

"Well, more like an alcove. It was just an indentation in the
wall that was deep enough to hide in the shadows."

I nodded in understanding. I tossed all the ingredients into
a casserole dish and popped it into the oven. We passed the time

chatting as dinner cooked. I had Tessa work on steeping up a batch of tea as we settled down to eat. The conversation didn't touch on George at that point. We had enough stress, and we needed this moment to enjoy life. We would worry about the hunt after we ate.

Chapter Thirty-Three

"I couldn't eat another bite." Steven groaned as he patted his belly.

He was sprawled in the wingback chair in front of the fireplace in the living room. The girls had claimed the couch and were sprawled in much the same manner. I smiled, pleased with how everyone felt about my cooking. We all had a cup of the special steeped tea after the meal. It was now a waiting game for the herbs to kick in.

"Aunt Violet!" Serena whispered harshly. "Wh-who is that?"

I glanced behind me at the fireplace and watched as Heloise and Tiger made their appearance. They floated gracefully from a light purple light near the fireplace to a more solid and vibrant blue as they settled onto an empty stool near the coffee table. I nodded at Heloise as she motioned to the obsidian mirror.

"Heloise, these are my nieces, Serena and Tessa." I motioned to the girls. "I trust that you are here to help guide us?"

"I am here to help guide Steven." Her eyes brimmed with love as she looked at Steven. He hesitated only a moment before dragging his chair closer to the table. "Our gift is slightly different from others. We divine our visions from water or from mirrors. The obsidian mirror, perfect. Pick up the mirror, my dear."

I watched as the girl's sat with their mouths open watching this scene unfold. It was wonderful to know that my instincts on Heloise were correct. Heloise meant no ill harm to Steven and only wanted to help him. She gave him instruction on how to gaze into the mirror until he saw his reflection, clear his mind, and then focus inward on that inner peace and calm.

Steven tried for a while to produce a vision. When nothing happened, I recommended that he relax and breath for a moment. I closed my mind and opened it to any vision that was willing to come. Tessa did the same. We sat for several moments, hoping for something to come to us. When nothing happened, we finally gave up.

Heloise sighed and patted Tiger on the head as she gave a hopeful smile. I rose from the chair and Steven joined me as we disappeared into the kitchen to dish up a scoop of ice cream for the girls. I sat one in front of Tessa and was retreating to my chair when I heard the crash of china on the floor, the clatter of a spoon against the bowl, and Steven gasping in shock. When I turned, I couldn't believe my eyes.

George stood behind Steven, the blade of a kitchen knife was stabbed through his chest, blood seeped from the wound as he stumbled forward, hit the coffee table, and landed face down against the rug. The girls both shouted in unison as George turned to me. He was holding a gun. That gun was aimed directly at me. My gaze darted around the room. Heloise and Tiger had disappeared, and the girls were huddled together in a tight ball on the couch as far away from George as possible.

"And now for you, you fucking meddling bitch!" George growled.

George took one step closer to me, squeezed the trigger, and then a shrill shriek filled the air. He cringed, put his hands up to cover his ears, and turned. Heloise had transformed from the genteel old-fashioned woman I had seen into a raving banshee.

She clawed and shrieked at him, forcing him back and back until he was against the fireplace.

I knew that Heloise wouldn't be able to hold him for long. Arthur had spent years draining her of the energy she had. I scrambled for a cell phone. Mine was in the kitchen in my go bag. Steven's phone was still sitting on the coffee table. I grabbed it and turned it on. There was no lock, and I found that he had programmed in Detective Johns cell. It seemed like forever for him to answer.

"George just stabbed Steven in the chest." I hurried to explain when the call connected. I didn't even wait for him to answer. "I need an ambulance and the police. We have George cornered for now. Hurry!"

I tossed the phone onto the couch and dropped to my knees. I had a little knowledge of first aid. It had helped with how accident prone I had been as a child. A penetrating chest wound was beyond my limited knowledge, though. I eased him onto his side. The blade was sticking out of Steven's chest by a good inch.

"Serena!" I snapped, breaking her out of her terror. "I need clean towels, now."

Heloise was beginning to fade, and I watched as Tessa grabbed the poker from the fireplace. She whacked George hard in the knee while Heloise gave one last effort to claw at him. I watched as he sank to the floor and crawled into the firebox. He had dropped the gun in favor of holding his knee and howling in pain. Tessa grabbed it and held it in his face.

It seemed as if hours had passed before we heard the sirens of the police. The officers that streamed through the door relieved Tessa of her burden while I focused on applying even pressure to both sides of the wound in Steven's chest. I wasn't sure how long it was when I heard the paramedics as they rushed into the room.

They had to pry my hands off his chest and shove me to the side. I was in shock at this point and not sure what I was doing. I sat in a pile on the floor, Steven's blood on my hands, small tremors surging through my body. It wasn't until someone gently wiped the blood away with a warm wet dishcloth that I began to come to. Detective Johns was gentle as he pressed a cold soda into my hands.

"Take a sip." He encouraged. "Strangely enough, sugar helps with the shock."

"I-I-I d-d-don't..."

"Trust me." Detective Johns motioned for me to take a sip. He waited patiently as I did. "I know you want to get to Steven as quickly as possible. Are you feeling well enough to drive?"

"Yes, I can, uh," I struggled to find words and my feet at the same time. "The girls?"

"They are fine. I have my officers with them right now." He caught my arm and assisted me to a standing position. "I am going to take you to the hospital to be with Steven. We can discuss what happened here on the ride over."

"The girls," I objected.

"I will have the officers bring the girls over once they get settled."

Detective Johns steered me out of the house and into his unmarked car. I was quiet and still shaking as he drove to the hospital. The man kindly enough turned his heater on and waited until my shaking subsided before turning it down and asking me questions about what happened. I found that the whole situation spewed from my mouth with no filter. I didn't even notice until he parked the car and helped me out. The pallid look of his skin made me snicker, then chuckle, then laugh.

"I'm sorry!" I pleaded.

"No need to apologize. Trauma like you experienced causes people to react differently."

"It is just the look on your face. Oh, cheese and crackers!" I covered my face with my hands when I realized what had him so pale. "I should have censored that."

"I appreciate that you didn't. I am not sure how I am going to edit it for my report, but I will figure something out."

Detective Johns was a gentleman and walked me into the hospital and up to the information desk before he left me to go find his officers. I was instructed to a waiting room on the third floor. The person sitting at the desk told me that he was still in surgery with no more information than that. I aimlessly wandered the waiting room, not sure what I should be doing.

I had not completely realized how much I loved that man until this moment. The thought of him not making it through this surgery had me dropping into an uncomfortable chair to sob. It took forever for the tears to stop flowing and even longer for the girls to show up. When they did, we fell into a crying hugging mass of bodies. A nurse in scrubs entered the waiting room and headed in our direction.

"Ms. Blueblade?" she inclined her head.

"Yes."

"Normally we don't give out information on a patient's status unless they are family, but Detective Johns politely asked that we keep you informed." I watched as a blush formed on her cheeks. "Steven is still in surgery, but the knife missed his heart and lung. His rib deflected the blade effectively. There was a slight nick in his major artery. Thankfully, you kept the knife in him until the paramedics arrived. That alone was enough to plug the nick until we could rush him in for surgery. It will be a few more hours until he is out, but the doctor is confident he will make a full recovery."

"Thank you so much!"

"Aunty Vi, do you want something? I can go get us some coffee." Tessa offered as we all three collapsed into the chairs.

"No thank you baby girl. I think I will just find a water fountain."

"I'll go get us some waters." Serena remarked as she jumped up from the chair and out of the waiting room.

"That was some next level crazy shit!" Tessa remarked as she twisted to stretch her back.

"Tessa!" I hissed.

"What?"

"Watch your language, child."

"Right. I forgot. There might be children here to overhear." She rolled her eyes.

"No, because it isn't appropriate." I giggled. "Ok, it was some next level shit." The look of shock on Tessa's face was so worth the curse.

"Did you know that ghosts could do that?"

"I didn't. I am learning a whole lot more than I knew to begin with." I sighed and scooted down in my chair until my head rested on the back. I memorized the pattern in the ceiling tile. I counted the ticks of the second hand on the wall clock. I watched the fake plant sitting under an air vent as it swished back and forth. I found that focusing on the mundane things helped soothe my nerves and relax my jitters.

"Here you go Aunty Vi." Serena handed me a bottle of water. I gulped it down in appreciation. "Can we talk about how useless my gift has been?" she whined. That caused Tessa and I to laugh.

"Your gift isn't useless." I promised. "It will come in handy soon. Why don't you girls go home and get some rest. It is all over now."

"Are you sure?"

"Positive. I am going to stay here until I know for sure that Steven is out of surgery and then I will do the same."

"You didn't drive here, Aunt Vi." Tessa answered. "We can all stay until you are ready to leave."

I didn't argue with the girls. I simply didn't have the energy. It took longer than a couple of hours to hear that Steven was out of surgery. They told us he would spend the next day or so in intensive care, but they were still confident that he would make a full recovery. With that good news, we headed home to get some rest.

Chapter Thirty-Four

S teven's recovery took a several weeks. I spent all my free time at the hospital checking on him. Reggie had stopped back into the cafe a few days later. I smiled brightly at him as I made him a coffee and got him something to eat. He had patted me softly on the arm and gave me a warm hug. I pulled out the new sleeping bag and coat for him. The smile he gave me was payment enough. Knowing what he had done to help me through all of this, I couldn't help but feel I would never do enough for him. I told him exactly that.

"My liebchen, you have done more for me than anyone I know. I was only looking out for you. You just promise me that you look out for your happiness, and we will call it even."

"I promise." I wiped a stray tear off my cheek as he stood to leave. He grabbed the coat and sleeping bag with a smile, waved, then stepped out the door.

The shop had settled back into a steady pace. We had a few more visitors than normal. They came with questions of fame and fortune, money and love. I gave more fortunes in the last few days than I had ever given. It seemed strange to find that Steven was not by my side. My morning sun salutation had been temporarily put on hold while I waited for Steven to be released.

The girls and I had gone over to the Ravens Estate a few days after George had been captured. We spent time cleaning the living room from top to bottom. I then did a ritual cleansing to banish the negative energy that George had brought into the house. When I was done with that, I did a light walk through of the house to see if I could feel any other energy spots that needed a cleanse. Happily, the only energy I could find was Heloise and Tiger. They were still hanging out in the fireplace in the living room. They needed to replenish their energy.

It had been almost three whole weeks when I finally got the approval to bring Steven home. I drove to the hospital to pick him up, loaded him into the car, and took him home. Heloise checked in on him when I finally got him settled into the bed. Tiger curled up next to him on the covers.

"How is he?" Heloise inquired as she appeared.

"Uh, oh. He is doing well. He is on bed rest for a few more weeks."

"I am happy that he found you." Heloise turned her fond gaze on me. I blushed as I eased down onto the corner of the bed. "I don't know how much longer I will be able to appear. Holding those monsters took a lot out of me."

"I understand."

"Train him well."

"I will do my best."

With another fond smile at both me and Steven, she disappeared as quickly as she appeared. Tiger remained, letting out a little huff before backing up against Steven even more. I sat there watching him. George had been locked away. Detective Johns had promised that they had a solid case against him. The Mystic Brew Cafe was gaining even more business after the journalist wrote another article proclaiming our involvement in this new arrest. Steven was making a complete recovery. What could be better than this?

"Hey there beautiful..." Steven murmured as he caught my hand and tugged. I crawled into the bed next to him and allowed him to wrap his arm around me. "What do you say we take a nap and then when we get up, we can talk about that missing book."

"You just got out of the hospital from almost dying." I complained. "I think we are done with the investigating. We should stick to tarot readings, selling photos, and making coffee and scones."

Steven chuckled, then groaned, hugging me tighter as he fought against the stab of pain in his chest. "Right now, let's just settle for a nap. I'll argue with you when we wake up about the rest of it."

"Whatever you say."

"No argument," he furrowed his brow as he looked down at me without moving. "That isn't like you. What happened to the woman I fell in love with?"

"She realized she shouldn't argue with her partner." I leaned up and placed a kiss on his cheek. "Sleep now. Argue later."

"As you command, my love."

Don't miss out!

Visit the website below and you can sign up to receive emails whenever Brandi A. Mendenhall publishes a new book. There's no charge and no obligation.

https://books2read.com/r/B-A-RFEU-VCYIG

BOOKS 2 READ

Connecting independent readers to independent writers.

Also by Brandi A. Mendenhall

Mystic Brew Cafe
Coffee, Murder, and a Scone: A Mystic Brew Cafe Novel

The Caster Chronicles
Forbidden Runes

About the Author

Brandi lives in a small town in Kansas with her brother. When not at work, she spends her time reading, writing, quilting, crocheting, and working on her property. She leads a simple quiet life.